CW01270594

FOLK TALES OF THE BRITISH ISLES

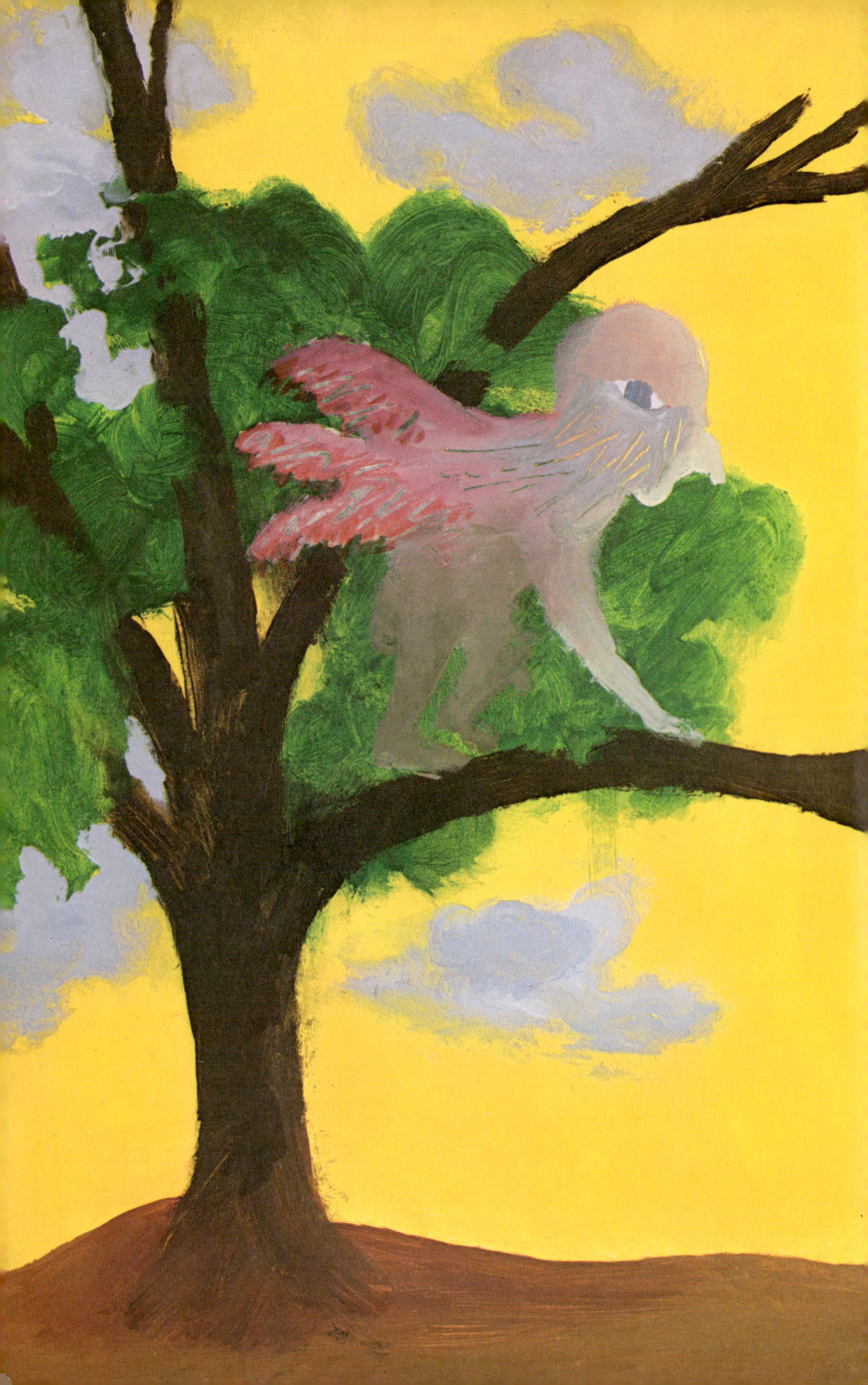

Folk Tales of the British Isles

Edited by
MICHAEL FOSS

Illustrated by
KEN KIFF

M

Published 1977 by Macmillan London Limited
London and Basingstoke
Associated Companies in Delhi, Dublin,
Hong Kong, Johannesburg, Lagos, Melbourne,
New York, Singapore & Tokyo
© Book Club Associates 1977

DESIGNED BY CRAIG DODD

All Rights Reserved.
No part of this publication may be reproduced,
stored in a retrieval system, or transmitted in
any form or by any means, electronic, mechanical,
photocopying, recording or otherwise, without
the prior permission of the Copyright owner.

ISBN O 333 23436 7

CONTENTS

Introduction 7

GIANTS, DEVILS AND OTHER BEASTIES

The Giant of Grabbist *(English)* 10
The Red Etin *(Scottish)* 12
Chips and the Devil *(English)* 16
Tom Tit Tot *(English)* 21
Nicht Nought Nothing *(Scottish)* 24
The Sprightly Tailor *(Scottish)* 28

THE POSSESSED

The Cakes of Oatmeal and Blood *(Irish)* 32
The Hunted Soul *(English)* 36
Wild Alasdair of Roy Bridge *(Scottish)* 38
'Kintail Again' *(Scottish)* 41
Brewery of Eggshells *(Welsh)* 44
Teig O'Kane and the Corpse *(Irish)* 45

LITTLE PEOPLE OF THE OTHERWORLD

The Little People *(Irish)* 54
Goblin Combe *(English)* 59
The Three Cows *(English)* 59
Peerifool *(Scottish)* 60

REWARDS AND PUNISHMENT

Tattercoats *(English)* 64
Three Heads of the Well *(Scottish)* 67
That's Enough to go on with *(English)* 70
The Fairy Wife *(Irish)* 72
Orange and Lemon *(Gypsy)* 75
The Old Man at the White House *(English)* 78
The Fairy Follower *(Welsh)* 80
Silken Janet or Mucketty Meg *(English)* 82

Continued overleaf

HUMOUR

The Man who had No Story *(Irish)* 86
Rat's Castle *(English)* 88
Whuppity Stoorie *(Scottish)* 90
Summat Queer on Batch *(English)* 93
The Old Woman who lived in a Vinegar Bottle *(English)* 93
Sir Gammers Van *(English)* 97

FORCES OF NATURE

The Apple Tree Man *(English)* 100
The Soul as a Butterfly *(Irish)* 101
The Dead Moon *(English)* 103
The Speckled Bull *(Irish)* 107
The Man Who went Fishing on Sunday *(English)* 118
Spirit of the Dog *(Irish)* 121
The Queen of the Planets *(Irish)* 123
The Shepherd of Myddvai *(Welsh)* 127
The Green Ladies of One Tree Hill *(English)* 131

HEROES AND WARRIORS

Assipattle *(Scottish)* 134
Finn in Search of his Youth *(Irish)* 140
The Everlasting Fight *(Irish)* 142
Young Conall of Howth *(Irish)* 150
The Vows of Cronicert *(Irish)* 162
Conall the Yellow-Hand *(Irish)* 168

Acknowledgements 176

INTRODUCTION

We stand on the margin of a mysterious lake, the near waters of which lap the feet of the present though the far shores are hidden by a dark antiquity. The lake is fed by the streams of folk-memory into which we cast lines and retrieve pieces of our past. To the student of folk-lore these pieces are profoundly interesting, as evidence of man in nature, of the mythology and religion he devised under nature, and of the social and moral organisation he developed to maintain his precarious place, subject to forces that seemed both implacable and inscrutable.

But to the ordinary reader these pieces—these folk-tales—are even more interesting as the oldest and purest examples of the story-teller's art, an art produced for the most important reason of all, to help a community puzzle out the maze of being, to comfort and reassure a people so often overwhelmed by the fear of the unknown. A successful folk-tale is thus something more than a pleasurable bit of fiction, tasted and soon forgotten. It is, at its best, a small illumination concerning the nature of things, setting man in a frame with beasts and plants, world and weather, and with the magic, deeply-felt other-world of the supernatural.

Because the tellers of these tales were unsophisticated people with strong emotions, the incidents represented are often wild, grotesque or fantastic, and the characters rough or merciless. But the vigour of the imagination gives the good folk-tale its peculiar strength, and the certain judgment of right and wrong, brutally executed, gives it a solid foundation that invites belief. The people of the folk-tale, we may say after G. K. Chesterton, 'are innocent and love justice; while most of us are wicked and naturally prefer mercy'.

The ancient writer Plutarch guessed that the souls of enlightened men return to be the schoolmasters of the living. It may be that folk-tales, which are in one sense nothing more than the voice of former times, re-iterate the truths of the inner world, which the present age shrinks from in its material, scientific delirium. But doubt and apprehension are not banished; they are as hard to placate as the demons of sky and underworld. In the enchanted world created by the imagination of the folk-tale, which so gladly embraces fantasy, mystery and magic, there is comfort to be found amid all that we do not know of man and nature.

Many collections of folk-tales repeat the familiar French and German stories of Perrault and the Brothers Grimm, often softened and made sentimental to suit a supposed juvenile taste. Here are new, unvarnished joys from nearer home, many unfamiliar but some only unfamiliar versions of well-known stories; for after all, every folk-tale rises from that same mysterious lake where, hidden from sight, they live and breed at will.

The stories gathered together in this volume have been taken from the tales and oral traditions of the British Isles, though the material available from Celtic Ireland far outweighs that from other parts and is far richer in variety and imagination. The Irish collector Sean O'Sullivan has claimed that the rural parish of Carna in West Galway has more unrecorded folk-tales than all continental Europe together. The archives of the Irish Folklore Commission bulge with some two million pages of stories taken verbatim from native story-tellers. This prodigious wealth of Irish lore, a unique body of legend and hero-tales, makes it difficult, in a volume such as this, to balance the claims of other nations within the British Isles. However, each people does contribute a characteristic voice, from the bleak sea-dramas descending from the Norsemen of Shetland to the jovial antics of the giants of Anglo-Saxon Somerset, as down-to-earth and bucolic as farmers at a West Country fair.

GIANTS, DEVILS AND OTHER BEASTIES

THE GIANT OF GRABBIST

We haven't got many giants about in Somerset, I hear, but we have one down at Dunster. Ah! Come up from Cornwall, he did, and he didn't like staying in Devon, 'cos his cousins there were a bit rough like. He come up to Exmoor, nice peaceful friendly place it is. But the folk on Exmoor they didn't like the size of him; bit scared they were. But then they found out he didn't harm anyone. They got quite fond of him. And then farmers' wives they began to put their heads together. 'What did the poor great fellow feed on?'

Well, I think they were ready to cook a dinner for him, but they found they needn't. You see, he was fond of fish. He did wade out down channel right out to sea, and all the fishing boats had to do was to follow him. Oh! they come into Minehead harbour loaded, they did. He'd go and wade out there, and water would come up to his armpits, and he'd scoop up great shoals o' fish, and 'twas a wonderful time for the fishing boats.

Well now, one time old Elijah Crowcombe in the leaky old *Dorcas Jane* was loaded right up and she was a-wallowing in the waves when a storm comes up. Well, they thought they were a-going down, when through the storm the giant comes astriding, and he picks up *Dorcas Jane*, and afore they could say Thank you, he puts her down quiet and safelike in Watchet harbour.

Well now, the giant he was very happy on Exmoor, and then the Old Nick came back 'cos he didn't like seeing the little thatched churches going up all over the way. So when the folk of Hawkridge thought they'd build themselves a church, and the giant would help them, Old Nicky didn't like it. Ah! so when giant was coming by Spire Cross, with a load of great stones, Old Nicky tripped him, and stones went all abroad.

Well, giant didn't say anything, he didn't lose his temper as Old Nicky hoped he would, and cause a storm. No, he just patiently bent, and he picked them up one after another, and he put them up on Hawkridge for the church. And a great broken one he tossed into the very wood where the Old Boy was a-sitting chuckling, and that made him go off in a hurry. And the rest of the stones, that weren't no good for church, he laid them across the river Barle, and made Tarr Steps.

Well, the giant he made up his mind that there wasn't room for him and Old Nicky up on moor, and Old Nicky he just about made up his mind the same. So two o' them got together Porlock way, and they said they'd have a competition like. They'd each throw a big stone from Bossington Beacon over to Porlock Common, that be four miles, and whoever lost would have to leave the place for good and all.

Well, Old Nick had first throw, and his stone it flew out over the four miles and it landed up on Porlock Common. And then Old Nick he trips up the giant, and his stone fell only three feet away. But giant he didn't go away. No, he just trips Old Nick himself and sat right down on him, and just smoked a pipe quiet like while Old Nick squirmed

The giant picked up the boat and put it safely down in Watchet harbour.

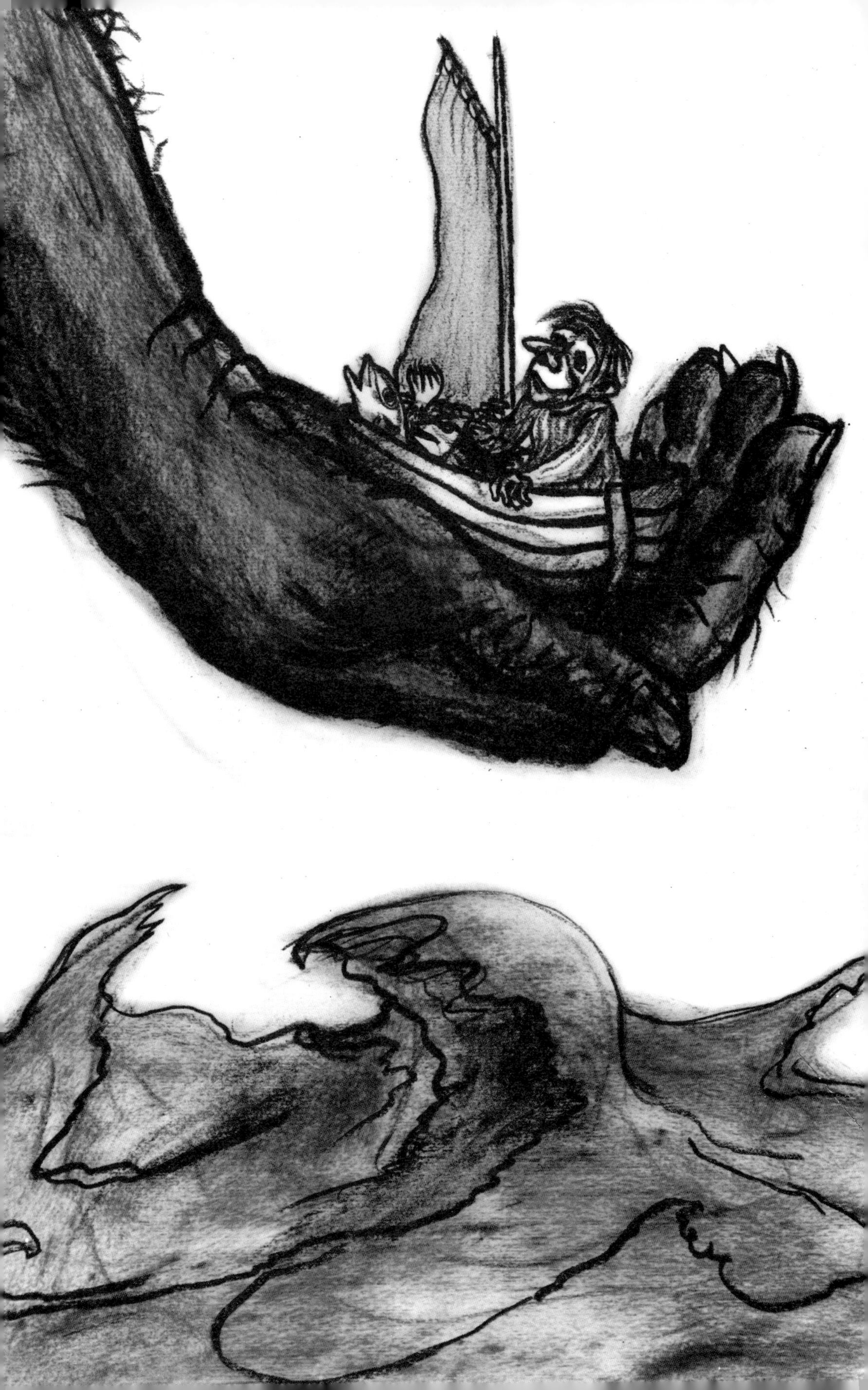

underneath. When he finished his pipe he picked up Old Nick by his tail, and he said, 'That wasn't a fair throw. We'll throw from Quantock later on. Meantime, you go cool your head.' And he tossed Old Nick right out down channel, out over Porlock Bay.

After a while our old giant and Old Nick did meet up by West Quantock, and they were to throw their stones, and this time the giant was ready for Old Nicky, and afore he could do anything, giant picked up his stone and throwed right over to Battlegore, six mile away. 'Your turn now', he says.

Old Nicky was dancing with rage, and I think he was so cross about it, that his stone fell down, and the giant's was the furthest off. 'Now', says the giant, "tis your promise to go away from here, and never come back any more. But as no one can trust you, I'll make sure.' And he picked up Old Nicky by his tail, and he waded out down the Severn Channel, till he was right out to sea, 'twas up to his armpits. And then he gave him a good swing three times round his head, and let go. Well, I reckon the Old 'Un landed about the West Indies.

He's back of course, but he don't show himself in Somerset, 'case the giant be about.

THE RED ETIN

There were ance twa widows that lived on a small bit o' ground, which they rented from a farmer. One of them had twa sons, and the other had one; and by and by it was time for the wife that had twa sons to send them away to seek their fortune. So she told her eldest son one day to take a can and bring her water from the well, that she might bake a cake for him; and however much or however little water he might bring, the cake would be great or sma' accordingly; and that cake was to be a' that she could gie him when he went on his travels.

The lad gaed away wi' the can to the well, and filled it wi' water, and then came away hame again; but the can being broken, the most part o' the water had run out before he got back. So his cake was very sma'; yet sma' as it was, his mother asked if he was willing to take the half of it with her blessing, telling him that, if he chose rather to have the whole, he would only get it wi' her curse. The young man, thinking he might hae to travel a far way, and not knowing when or how he might get other provisions, said he would like to hae the whole cake, come of his mother's curse what might; so she gave him the whole cake, and her curse alang wi't. Then he took his brither aside, and gave him a knife to keep till he should come back, desiring him to look at it every morning, and as lang as it continued to be clear, then he might be sure that the owner of it was well; but if it grew dim and rusty, then for certain some ill had befallen him.

So the young man set out to seek his fortune. And he gaed a' that day, and a' the next day; and on the third day, in the afternoon, he came up to where a shepherd was sitting with a flock o' sheep. And he gaed up to the shepherd and asked him who the sheep belanged to; and the man answered:

> The Red Etin of Ireland
>   Ance lived in Bellygan,
> And stole King Malcolm's daughter,
>   The king of fair Scotland.
> He beats her, he binds her,
>   He lays her on a band;
> And every day he dings her
>   With a bright silver wand.
> Like Julian the Roman,
>   He's one that fears no man.
> It's said there's one predestinate
>   To be his mortal foe;
> But that man is yet unborn,
>   And lang may it be so.

The young man then went on his journey; and he had not gone far, when he espied an old man with white locks herding a flock of swine. This old man also told him to beware o' the next beasts that he should meet, for they were of a very different kind from any he had yet seen.

So the young man went on, and by and by he saw a multitude of very dreadfu' beasts, each one o' them wi' twa heads, and on every head four horns. And he was sore frightened, and ran away from them as fast as he could; and glad was he when he came to a castle that stood on a hillock, wi' the door standing wide to the world. And he gaed into the castle for shelter, and there he saw an auld wife sitting beside the kitchen fire. He asked the wife if he might stay there for the night, as he was tired wi' a lang journey; and the wife said he might, but it was not a good place for him to be in, as it belanged to the Red Etin, who was a very terrible beast, wi' three heads, that spared no living man he could get hold of. The young man would have gone away, but he was afraid of the beasts on the outside of the castle; so he beseeched the old woman to conceal him as well as she could, and not tell the Etin that he was there. He thought, if he could put over the night, he might get away in the morning, without meeting wi' the beasts, and so escape. But he had not been long in his hidy-hole, before the awful Etin came in crying:

> Snouk but and snouk ben,
> I find the smell of an earthly man;
> Be he living, or be he dead,
> His heart this night shall kitchen my bread.

The monster soon found the poor young man, and pulled him from his hole. And when he had got him out, he told him that, if he could answer him three questions, his life should be spared. The first was, Whether Ireland or Scotland was first inhabited? The second was, Whether man was made for woman, or woman for man? The third was, Whether men or brutes were made first? The lad not being able to answer one of these questions, the Red Etin took a hammer and knocked him on the head, and turned him into a pillar of stone.

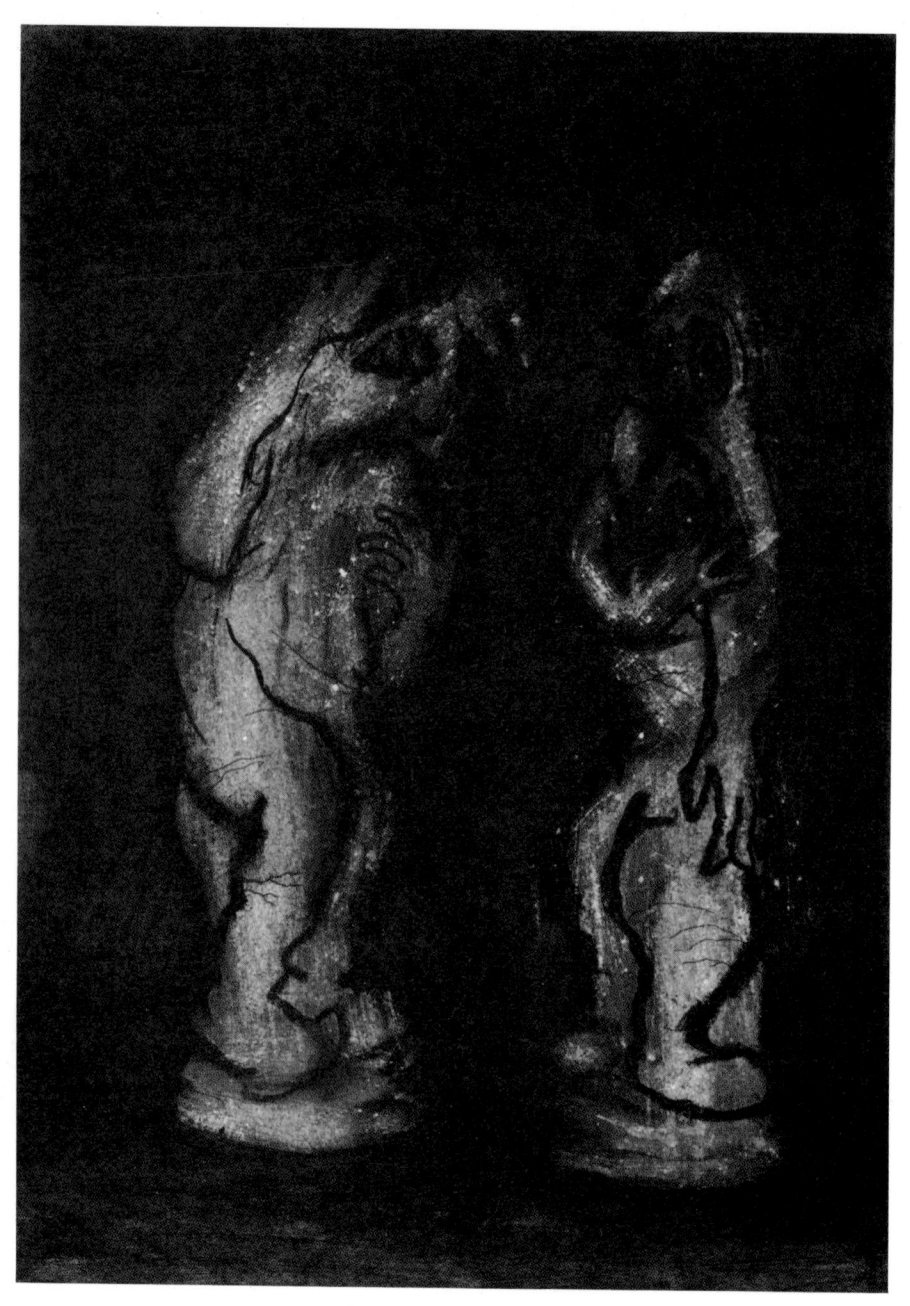

On the morning after this happened, the younger brither took out the knife to look at it, and he was grieved to find it a' brown wi' rust. He told his mother that the time was now come for him to go away upon his travels also; so she requested him to take the can to the well for water, that she might bake a cake for him. The can being broken, he brought hame as little water as the other had done, and the cake

The Red Etin turne them into pillars of stone.

was as little. She asked whether he would have the hale cake wi' her curse, or the half wi' her blessing; and, like his brither, he thought it best to have the whole cake, come o' the curse what might. So he gaed away; and he came to Etin who dealt with him as his brither.

The other widow and her son heard of a' that had happened frae a fairy, and the young man determined that he would also go upon his travels, and see if he could do anything to relieve his twa friends. So his mother gave him a can to go to the well and bring home water, that she might bake him a cake for his journey. And he gaed, and as he was bringing hame the water, a raven o'er his head cried to him to look, and he would see that the water was running out. And he was a young man of sense, and seeing the water running out, he took some clay and patched up the holes, so that he brought home enough of water to bake a large cake. When his mother put it to him to take the half cake wi' her blessing, he took it in preference to having the whole wi' her curse, and yet the half was bigger than the other's whole. got a'thegither.

So he gaed away on his journey; and after he had travelled a far way, he met wi' an auld woman, that asked him if he would give her a bit of his bannock. And he said he would gladly do that, and so he gave her a piece of the bannock; and for that she gied him a magical wand, that she said might yet be of service to him, if he took care to use it rightly. Then the auld woman, who was a fairy, told him a great deal that would happen to him, and what he ought to do in a' circumstances; and after that she vanished in an instant out o' his sight. He gaed on a great way farther, and then he came up to the old man herding sheep; and when he asked whose these were, the answer was:

> The Red Etin of Ireland
>   Ance lived in Bellygan,
> And stole King Malcolm's daughter,
>   The king of fair Scotland.
> He beats her, he binds her,
>   He lays her on a band;
> And every day he dings her
>   With a bright silver wand.
> Like Julian the Roman,
> He's one that fears no man.
>
> But now I fear his end is near,
>   And destiny at hand;
> And you're to be, I plainly see,
>   The heir of all his land.

When he came to the place where the monstrous beasts were standing, he did not stop nor run away, but went boldly through amongst them. One came up roaring with open mouth to devour him, when he struck it with his wand, and laid it in an instant dead at his feet. He soon came to the Etin's castle, where he knocked, and was admitted. The auld woman that sat by the fire warned him of the terrible Etin, and what had been the fate of the twa brithers; but he was not to be daunted. The monster soon came in, saying:

>Snouk but and snouk ben,
>I find the smell of an earthly man;
>Be he living, or be he dead,
>His heart shall be kitchen to my bread.

He quickly espied the young man, and bade him come forth on the floor. And then he put the three questions to him; but the young man had been told everything by the good fairy, so he was able to answer all the questions. When the Etin found this, he knew that his power was gone. The young man then took up an axe and hewed aff the monster's three heads. He next asked the old woman to shew him where the king's daughter lay; and the old woman took him up stairs, and opened a great many doors, and out of every door came a beautiful lady who had been imprisoned there by the Etin; and one o' the ladies was the king's daughter. She also took him down into a low room, and there stood two stone pillars that he had only to touch wi' his wand, when his twa friends and neighbours started into life. And the whole o' the prisoners were overjoyed at their deliverance, which they all acknowledged to be owing to the prudent young man. Next day they a' set out for the king's court, and a gallant company they made. And the king married his daughter to the young man that had delivered her, and gave a noble's daughter to each one o' the other young men; and so they a' lived happily a' the rest o' their days.

CHIPS AND THE DEVIL

There was once a shipwright, and he wrought in a Government Yard, and his name was Chips. And his father's name before him was Chips, and *his* father's name before *him* was Chips, and they were all Chipses. And Chips the father had sold himself to the Devil for an iron pot and a bushel of tenpenny nails and half a ton of copper and a rat that could speak; and Chips the grandfather had sold himself to the Devil for an iron pot and a bushel of tenpenny nails and half a ton of copper and a rat that could speak; and Chips the great-grandfather had disposed of himself in the same direction on the same terms; and the bargain had run in the family for a long long time. So, one day, when young Chips was at work in the Dock Slip all alone, down in the dark hold of an old Seventy-four that was haled up for repairs, the Devil presented himself, and remarked:

>A lemon has pips,
>And a Yard has ships,
>And *I'll* have Chips!

Chips looked up when he heard the words, and there he saw the Devil with saucer eyes that squinted on a terrible great scale, and that struck out sparks of blue fire continually. And, whenever he winked his eyes, showers of blue sparks came out, and his eyelashes made a clattering like flints and steels striking lights. And hanging over one of his arms by the handle was an iron pot, and under that arm was a bushel of tenpenny nails, and under his other arm was half a ton of copper, and sitting on one of his shoulders was a rat that could speak. So, the Devil said again:

> A lemon has pips,
> And a Yard has ships,
> And *I'll* have Chips!

So, Chips answered never a word, but went on with his work. 'What are you doing, Chips?' said the rat that could speak. 'I am putting in new planks where you and your gang have eaten old away', said Chips. 'But we'll eat them too', said the rat that could speak, 'and we'll let in the water and drown the crew, and we'll eat them too.' Chips, being only a shipwright, and not a Man-of-war's man, said, 'You are welcome to it.' But he couldn't keep his eyes off the half a ton of copper, or the bushel of tenpenny nails; for nails and copper are a shipwright's sweethearts, and shipwrights will run away with them whenever they can. So, the Devil said, 'I see what you are looking at, Chips. You had better strike the bargain. You know the terms. Your father before you was well acquainted with them, and so were your grandfather and great-grandfather before him.' Says Chips, 'I like the copper and I like the nails, and I don't mind the pot, but I don't like the rat.' Says the Devil fiercely, 'You can't have the metal without him—and *he's* a curiosity. I'm going.' Chips, afraid of losing the half a ton of copper and the bushel of nails, then said, 'Give us hold!' So, he got the copper and the nails, and the pot and the rat that could speak, and the Devil vanished. Chips sold the copper, and he sold the nails, and he would have sold the pot; but, whenever he offered it for sale, the rat was in it, and the dealers dropped it, and would have nothing to say to the bargain. So, Chips resolved to kill the rat, and, being at work in the Yard one day with a great kettle of hot pitch on one side of him, and the iron pot with the rat in it on the other, he turned the scalding pitch into the pot, and filled it full. Then, he kept his eye on it till it cooled and hardened, and then he let it stand for twenty days, and then he heated the pitch again, and turned it back into the kettle, and then he sank the pot in water for twenty days more, and then he got the smelters to put it in the furnace for twenty days more, and then they gave it him out, red-hot, and looking like red-hot glass instead of iron—yet there was the rat in it just the same as ever! And the moment it caught his eye, it said with a jeer:

> A lemon has pips,
> And a Yard has ships,
> And *I'll* have Chips.

Chips now felt certain in his own mind that the rat would stick to him;

the rat, answering his thought, said, 'I will—like pitch!'

Now, as the rat leaped out of the pot when it had spoken, and made off, Chips began to hope that it wouldn't keep its word. But, a terrible thing happened next day. For, when dinner-time came, and the Dock-bell rang to stop work, he put his rule into the long pocket at the side of his trousers, and there he found a rat—not that rat but another rat. And in his hat he found another; and in his pocket-handkerchief, another; and in the sleeves of his coat, when he pulled

Sitting on the Devil's shoulder was a rat who could speak.

18

it on to go to dinner, two more. And from that time, he found himself so frightfully intimate with all the rats in the Yard, that they climbed up his legs when he was at work, and sat on his tools while he used them. And they could all speak to one another, and he understood what they said. And they got into his lodging, and into his bed, and into his teapot, and into his beer, and into his boots. And he was going to be married to a corn-chandler's daughter; and when he gave her a workbox he had himself made for her, a rat jumped out of it; and when he put his arm round her waist, a rat clung about her; so the marriage was broken off, though the banns were already twice put up—which the parish clerk well remembers, for, as he handed the book to the clergyman for the second time of asking, a large fat rat ran over the leaf.

At last, he was voted mad, and lost his work in the Yard, and could get no other work. But, King George wanted men, so before very long he got pressed for a sailor. And so he was taken off in a boat one evening to his ship, lying at Spithead, ready to sail. And so the first thing he made out in her as he got near her, was the figure-head of the old Seventy-four, where he had seen the Devil. She was called the Argonaut, and they rowed right under the bowsprit where the figure-head of the Argonaut, with a sheepskin in his hand, and a blue gown on, was looking out to sea; and sitting staring on his forehead was the rat who could speak, and his exact words were these: 'Chips ahoy! Old boy! We've pretty well eat them too, and we'll drown the crew, and will eat them too.'

The ship was bound for the Indies. The ship set sail that very night, and she sailed, and sailed, and sailed. Chip's feelings were dreadful. Nothing ever equalled his terrors. No wonder. At last one day he asked leave to speak to the Admiral. The Admiral giv' leave. Chips went down on his knees in the Great State Cabin. 'Your Honour, unless Your Honour, without a moment's loss of time, makes sail for the nearest shore, this is a doomed ship, and her name is the Coffin.' 'Young man, your words are a madman's words.' 'Your Honour, no: they are nibbling us away.' 'They?' 'Your Honour, them dreadful rats. Dust and hollowness where solid oak ought to be. Rats nibbling a grave for every man on board. Oh! Does Your Honour love your Lady and your pretty children?' 'Yes, my man, to be sure.' 'Then, for God's sake, make for the nearest shore, for at this present moment the rats are all stopping in their work, and are all looking towards you with bare teeth, and are all saying to one another that you shall never, never, never, never, see your Lady and your children more.' 'My poor fellow, you are a case for the doctor. Sentry, take care of this man!'

So, he was bled and he was blistered, and he was this and that, for six whole days and nights. So, then he again asked leave to speak to the Admiral. The Admiral giv' leave. He went down on his knees in the Great State Cabin. 'Now, Admiral, you must die! You took no warning; you must die! The rats are never wrong in their

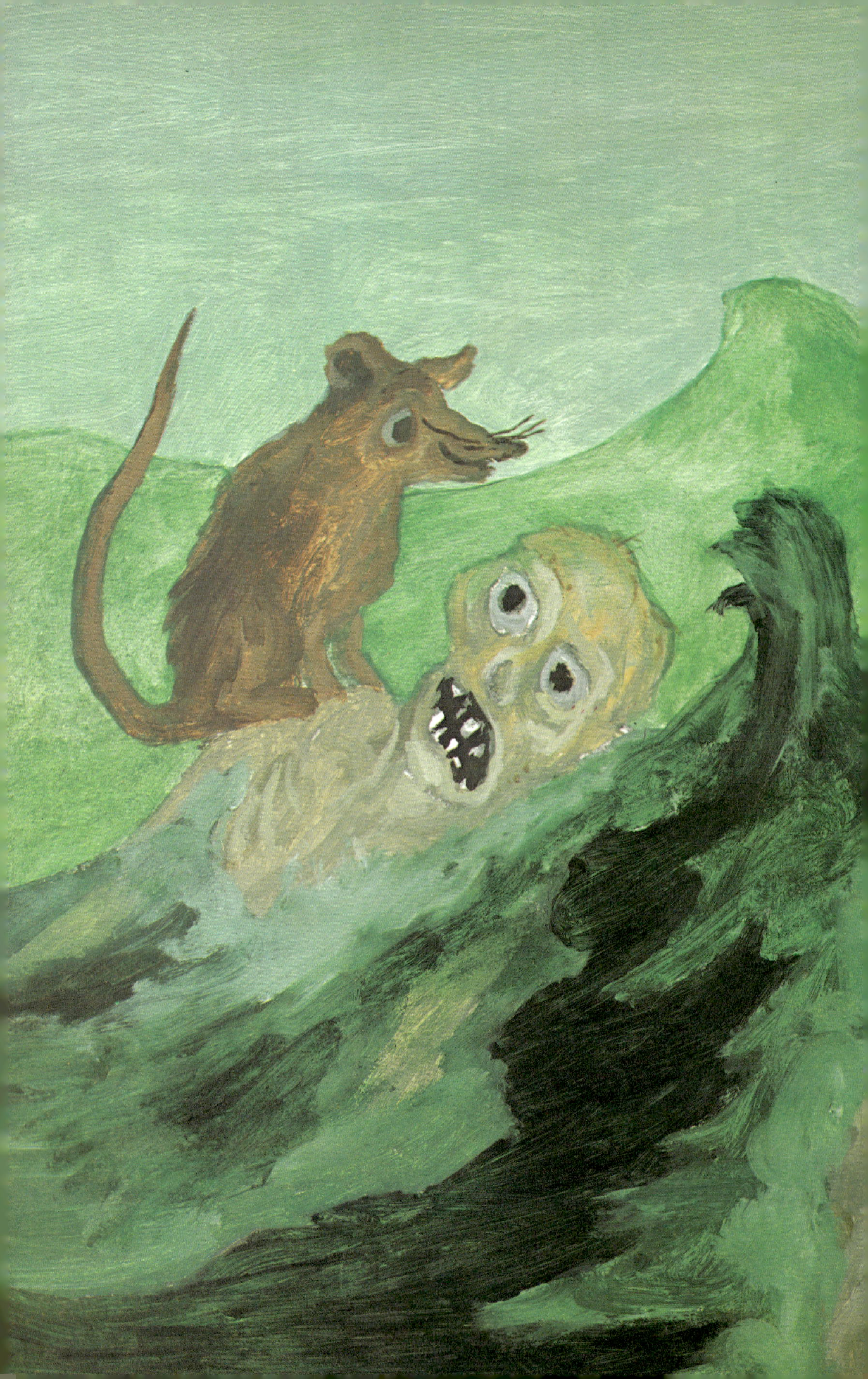

calculations, and they make out that they'll be through, at twelve to-night. So, you must die!—With me and all the rest!' And so at twelve o'clock there was a great leak reported in the ship, and a torrent of water rushed in and nothing could stop it, and they all went down, every living soul.

And what the rats—being water-rats—left of Chips, at last floated to shore, and sitting on him was an immense rat, laughing, that dived when the corpse touched the beach, and never came up.

TOM TIT TOT

Well, once upon a time, there was a woman and she baked five pies. And when they come out of the oven, they were that overbaked, the crust were too hard to eat. So she says to her daughter—

'Darter,' she says, 'put you them there pies on the shelf an' leave 'em there a little, an' they'll come agin,'—she meant, you know, the crust would get soft.

But the gal, she says to herself, 'Well, if they'll come agin, I'll ate 'em now.' And she set to work and ate 'em all, first and last.

Well, come supper time, the woman she said, 'Go you and git one o' them there pies. I daresay they've come agin now.'

The gal she went an' she looked, and there weren't nothing but the dishes. So back she come and says she, 'No, they ain't come agin.'

'Not none of 'em?' says the mother.

'Not none of 'em,' says she.

'Well, come agin or not come agin,' says the woman, 'I'll ha' one for supper.'

'But you can't, if they ain't come,' says the gal.

'But I can,' says she. 'Go you and bring the best of 'em.'

'Best or worst,' says the gal, 'I've ate 'em all, and you can't ha' one till that's come agin.'

Well, the woman she were wholly cross, and she took her spinning to the door, to spin, and as she span she sang—

> My darter ha' ate five, five pies today—
> My darter ha' ate five, five pies today.

The king he were a-coming down the street an' he heard her sing but what she sang he couldn't hear, so he stopped and said—

'What were that you was a-singun of, darter?'

The woman she were ashamed to let him hear what her daughter had been a'doing, so she sang instead of that—

> My darter ha' spun five, five skeins today—
> My darter ha' spun five, five skeins today.

'Stars o' mine!' says the king, 'I never heard tell o' anyone as could do that.'

Then he said, 'Look you here, I want a wife, an' I'll marry your darter. But look you here,' says he, 'eleven months out o' the year, she shall have all the vittles she likes to eat, and all the gowns she likes to git, and all the company she likes to have; but the last month o' the year she'll ha' to spin five skeins every day, an' if she don't I shall kill her.'

'All right,' says the woman; for she thought that was a grand marriage that was. And as for them five skeins, when it come to it, there'd be plenty o' ways o' getting out of it and likeliest he'd ha' forgot about it.

Well, so they was married. An' for eleven months the gal had all the vittles she liked to ate, and all the gowns she liked to git, and all the company she liked to have.

But when the time was getting over, she began to think about them there skeins, an' to wonder if he had 'em in mind. But not one word did he say about 'em, and she wholly thought he'd forgot about 'em.

However, the last day o' the last month, he takes her to a room she'd never set eyes on afore. There weren't nothing in it but a spinning wheel and a stool. An' says he, 'Now, me dear, here you'll be shut in tomorrow, with some vittles and some flax, and if you hain't spun five skeins by the night, your hide'll go off.'

An' awa he went about his business.

Well, she were that frightened. She'd always been such a gutless girl, that she didn't so much as know how to spin, an' what were she to do tomorrow with no one to come nigh her to help her. She sat down on a stool in the kitchen, and lork! how she did cry!

However, all on a sudden, she heard a sort of a knocking low down on the door. She upped and opened it, an' what should she see but a small, little black thing with a long tail. That looked up at her right curious, an' said:

'What are you a-crying for?'

'Wha's that to you?' says she.

'Never you mind,' that said, 'but tell me what you're a-crying for.'

'That don't do me no good if I do,' says she.

'You don't know that,' that said, an' twirled his tail round.

'Well,' says she, 'that won't do no harm, if that don't do no good,' and she upped and told about the pies an' the skeins an' everything.

'This is what I'll do,' says the little black thing. 'I'll come to your winder every mornin', an' take the flax an' bring it spun at night.'

'Wha's your pay?' says she.

He looked out o' the corners o' his eyes, an' said: 'I'll give you three guesses every night to guess my name, an' if you hain't guessed it afore the month's up, you shall be mine.'

Well, she thought she'd be sure to guess his name afore the month was up. 'All right,' says she, 'I agree.'

'All right,' that says, and lork! how he twirled his tail.

Well, the next day her husband he took her into the room, an' there was the flax an' the day's vittles.

22

'Now, there's the flax,' says he, 'an' if that ain't spun up this night, off go your hide.' An' then he went out an' locked the door.

He'd hardly gone, when there was a knocking agin the winder. She upped and opened it, and there, sure enough, were the little old thing a-setting on the ledge.

'Where's the flax?' says he.

'Here it be,' says she. And she gave it to him.

Well, come the evening, a knocking come agin to the winder. She upped an' opened it, and there were the little old thing, with five skeins of flax on his arm.

'Here it be,' says he, an' he gave it to her. 'Now, what's my name?' says he.

'What, is that Bill?' says she.

'No, it ain't,' says he. An' he twirled his tail.

'Is that Ned?' says she.

'No, it ain't,' says he. An' he twirled his tail.

'Well, is that Mark?' says she.

'No, it ain't,' says he. An' he twirled his tail harder, an' awa' he flew.

Well, when her husband he come in, there was the five skeins ready for him. 'I see as I sharn't have to kill you tonight, me dear,' says he. 'You'll have your vittles, and your flax in the mornin',' says he, an' away he goes.

Well, every day the flax an' the vittles, they was brought, an' every day that there little black imp used to come mornings an' evenings.

An' all the day the girl she set a-trying to think of names to say to it when it come at night. But she never hit on the right one. An' as that got to-wards the end o' the month, the imp began to look so maliceful, an' he twirled his tail faster, each time she gave a guess.

At last it come to the last day but one. The imp come at night along o' the five skeins, an' he said,

'What, hain't you got my name yet?'

'Is that Nicodemus?' says she.

'No, t'ain't,' he says.

'A-well, is that Methusalem?' says she.

'No, t'ain't that neither,' he says.

Then he looks at her with his eyes like a coal o' fire, an' he says, 'Woman, there's only tomorrer night, an' then you'll be mine.' An awa' he flew.

Well, she felt that horrid. However, she heard the king a-coming along the passage.

In he came, an' when he sees the five skeins, he says, says he, 'Well, me dear,' says he, 'I don't see but what you'll ha' your skeins ready tomorrer night as well, an' as I reckon I sharn't ha' to kill you, I'll ha' supper in here tonight.'

Well, he hadn't eat but a mouthful or so, when he begins to laugh.

'What is it?' says she.

'A-why,' says he, 'I was out a-huntin' today, an' I got away to a place in the wood I'd never seen afore. An' there was an old chalk pit.

An' I heard a sort of a humming, kind of. So I got off my horse, an' I went right quiet to the pit, an' I looked down. Well, what should there be but the funniest little black thing you ever set eyes on. An' what was he a-doing, but he had a little spinnin' wheel, an' he were a-spinnin' wonderful fast. An' as he span, he sang,

> Nimmy nimmy not,
> My name's Tom Tit Tot.

Well, when the girl heard this, she fared as if she could a-jumped out of her skin for joy, but she didn't say a word.

Next day, that there little thing looked so maliceful when he come for the flax. An' when night came, she heard that a-knocking agin the winder panes. She opened the winder, an' he come right in on the ledge. He were grinning from ear to ear, an' oo! his tail were twirlin'.

'What's my name?' he says, as he gave her the skeins.

'Is that Solomon?' she says, pretendin' to be afeard.

'No, t'ain't,' he says, an' he come further into the room.

'Well, is that Zebedee?' says she again.

'No, t'ain't,' says the imp. An' then he laughed an' twirled his tail till you cou'n't hardly see it.

'Take time, woman,' he says, 'next guess an' you're mine.' An' he stretched out his black hands at her.

Well, she backed a step or two, an' she looked at him, an' then she laughed out, an' says she, a-pointin' of her finger at him,

> Nimmy nimmy not,
> Yar name's Tom Tit Tot.

Well, when he heard her, he shrieked awful, an' awa' he flew, into the dark, an' she never saw him no more.

NICHT NOUGHT NOTHING

There once lived a king and a queen. They were long married, and had no bairns; but at last the queen had a bairn, when the king was away in far countries. The queen would not christen the bairn till the king came back, and she said: 'We will just call him *Nicht Nought Nothing* until his father comes home.'

But it was long before he came home, and the boy had grown a nice little laddie. At length the king was on his way back; but he had a big river to cross, and there was a spate, and he could not get over the water. But a giant came up to him and said, 'If you will give me Nicht Nought Nothing, I will carry you over the water on my back.' The king had never heard that his son was called Nicht Nought Nothing, and so he promised him. When the king got home again, he was very pleased to see his queen again, and his young son. She told him she had not given the child any name but Nicht Nought Nothing until he should come home himself. The poor king was in a terrible case. He

What should she see b[ut] a small, black thing with a long tail.

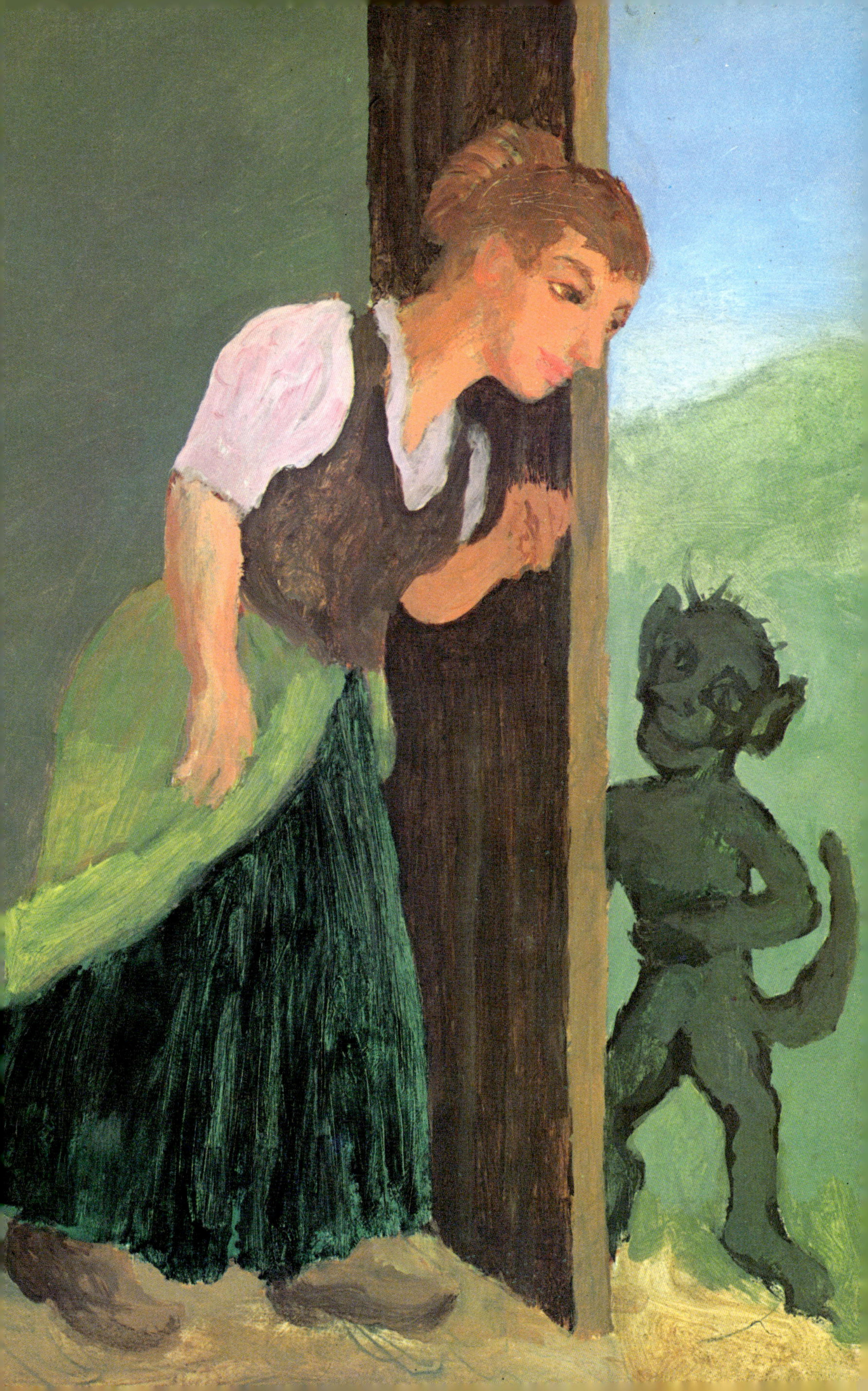

said: 'What have I done? I promised to give the giant who carried me over the river on his back Nicht Nought Nothing.'

The king and the queen were sad and sorry, but they said: 'When the giant comes, we will give him the hen-wife's bairn; he will never know the difference.' The next day the giant came to claim the king's promise, and he sent for the hen-wife's bairn; and the giant went away with the bairn on his back.

He travelled till he came to a big stone, and there he sat down to rest. He said: 'Hidge, Hodge, on my back, what time of day is it?' The poor little bairn said, 'It is the time that my mother, the hen-wife, takes up the eggs for the queen's breakfast.' The giant was very angry, and dashed the bairn on the stone and killed it. They tried the same with the gardener's son, but it did no better. Then the giant went back to the king's house, and said he would destroy them all if they did not give him Nicht Nought Nothing this time. They had to do it; and when they came to the big stone, the giant said, 'What time o' day is it?' and Nicht Nought Nothing said: 'It is the time that my father, the King, will be sitting down to supper.' The giant said: 'I've got the right one now'; and took Nicht Nought Nothing to his own house, and brought him up till he was a man.

The giant had a bonny dochter, and she and the lad grew very fond of each other. The giant said one day to Nicht Nought Nothing, 'I've work for you to-morrow. There is a stable seven miles long, and seven miles broad, and it has not been cleaned for seven years, and you must clean it to-morrow, or I'll have you for my supper.' The giant's dochter went out next morning with the lad's breakfast, and found him in a terrible state, for aye as he cleaned out a bit, it aye fell in again. The giant's dochter said she would help him, and she cried a' the beasts o' the field, and a' the fowls o' the air, and in a minute they carried awa' everything that was in the stable, and made it a' clean before the giant came home. He said, 'Shame for the wit that helped you; but I have a worse job for you to-morrow.' Then he told Nicht Nought Nothing that there was a loch seven miles long, and seven miles deep, and seven miles broad, and he must drain it the next day, or else he would have him for his supper.

Nicht Nought Nothing began early next morning, and tried to ladle the water with his pail, but the loch was never getting any less; and he did not ken what to do; but the giant's dochter called on all the fish in the sea to come and drink the water, and they soon drank it dry. When the giant saw the work done, he was in a rage, and said: 'I've a worse job for you to-morrow; there's a tree, seven miles high, and no branch on it, till you get to the top, and there is a nest, and you must bring down the eggs without breaking one, or else I will have you for my supper.' At first the giant's dochter did not know how to help Nicht Nought Nothing, but she cut off first her fingers, and then her toes, and made steps of them, and he clomb the tree, and got all the eggs safe, till he came to the bottom, and then one was broken. The giant's dochter advised him to run away, and she would follow

She called all the b[easts] of the field and all [the] birds of the air.

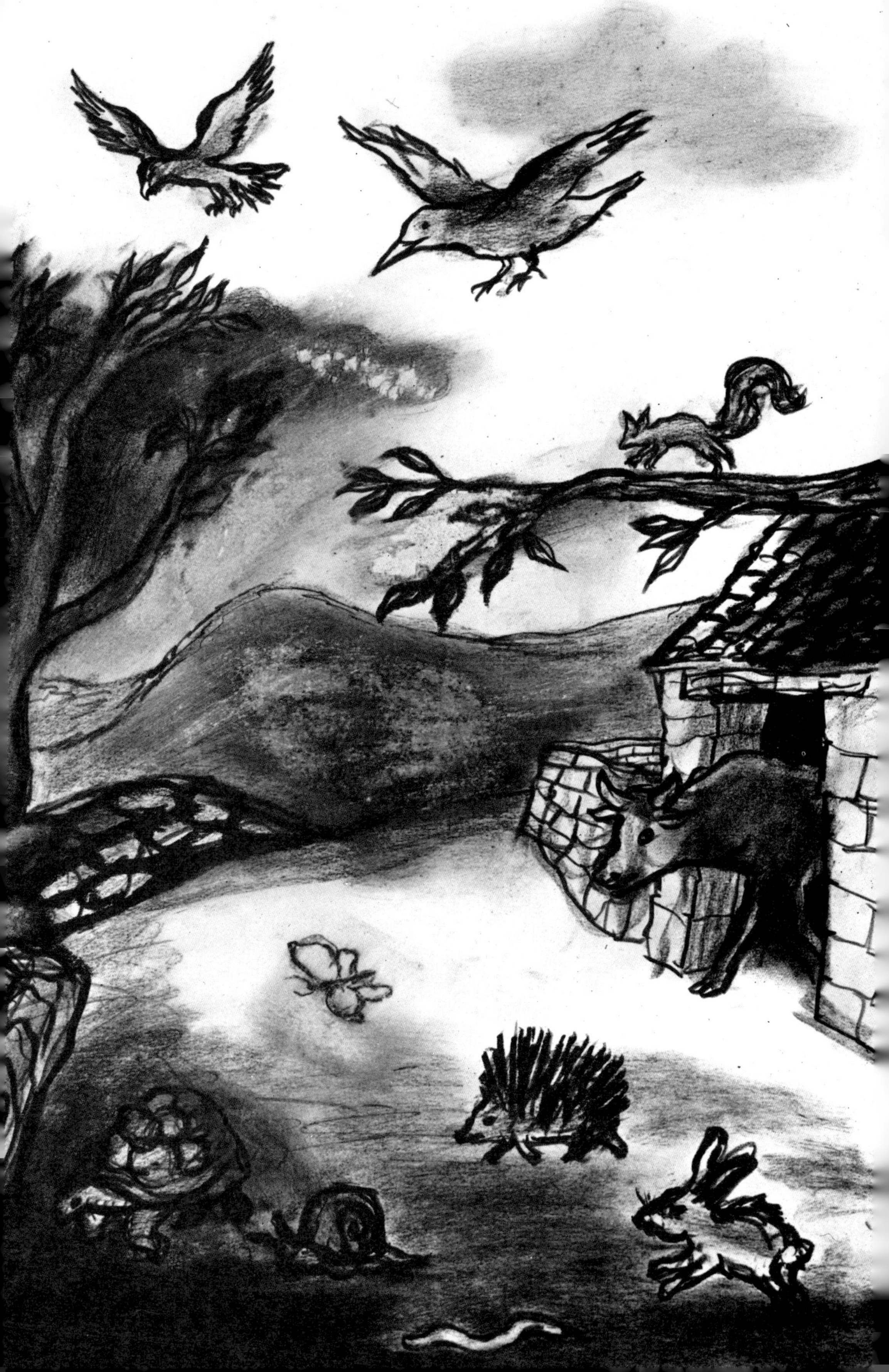

him. So he travelled until he came to a king's palace, and the king and queen took him in, and were very kind to him. The giant's dochter left her father's house, and he pursued her, and was drowned. Then she came to the king's palace where Nicht Nought Nothing was. And she went up a tree to watch for him. The gardener's dochter, going down to draw water in the well, saw the shadow of the lady in the water, and thought it was herself, and said: 'If I'm so bonny, if I'm so brave, do you send me to draw water?' The gardener's wife went, and said the same thing. Then the gardener went himself, and brought the lady from the tree, and had her in. And he told her that a stranger was to marry the king's dochter, and showed her the man, and it was Nicht Nought Nothing, asleep in a chair. And she saw him, and cried to him: 'Waken, waken, and speak to me!' But he would not waken, and syne she cried:

> I cleared the stable, I laved the loch, and I clomb the tree,
> And all for the love of thee,
> And thou wilt not waken and speak to me.

The king and queen heard this, and came to the bonny young lady, and she said: 'I canna get Nicht Nought Nothing to speak to me, for all that I can do.'

Then were they greatly astonished, when she spoke of Nicht Nought Nothing, and asked where he was, and she said, 'He sits there in the chair.'

Then they ran to him and kissed him, and called him their own dear son, and he wakened, and told them all that the giant's dochter had done for him, and of all her kindness. Then they took her in their arms, and kissed her, and said she should be their dochter, for their son should marry her. And they lived happy all their days.

THE SPRIGHTLY TAILOR

A sprightly tailor was employed by the great Macdonald, in his castle at Saddell, in order to make the laird a pair of trews, used in olden time. And trews being the vest and breeches united in one piece, and ornamented with fringes, were very comfortable, and suitable to be worn in walking or dancing. And Macdonald had said to the tailor, that if he would make the trews by night in the church, he would get a handsome reward. For it was thought that the old ruined church was haunted, and that fearsome things were to be seen there at night.

The tailor was well aware of this; but he was a sprightly man, and when the laird dared him to make the trews by night in the church, the tailor was not to be daunted, but took it in hand to gain the prize. So, when night came, away he went up the glen, about half a mile distance from the castle, till he came to the old church. Then he chose him a nice gravestone for a seat and he lighted his candle, and put on his thimble, and set to work at the trews; plying his needle nimbly, and thinking about the hire that the laird would have to give him.

For some time he got on pretty well, until he felt the floor all of a

He saw a great hea out of the floor.

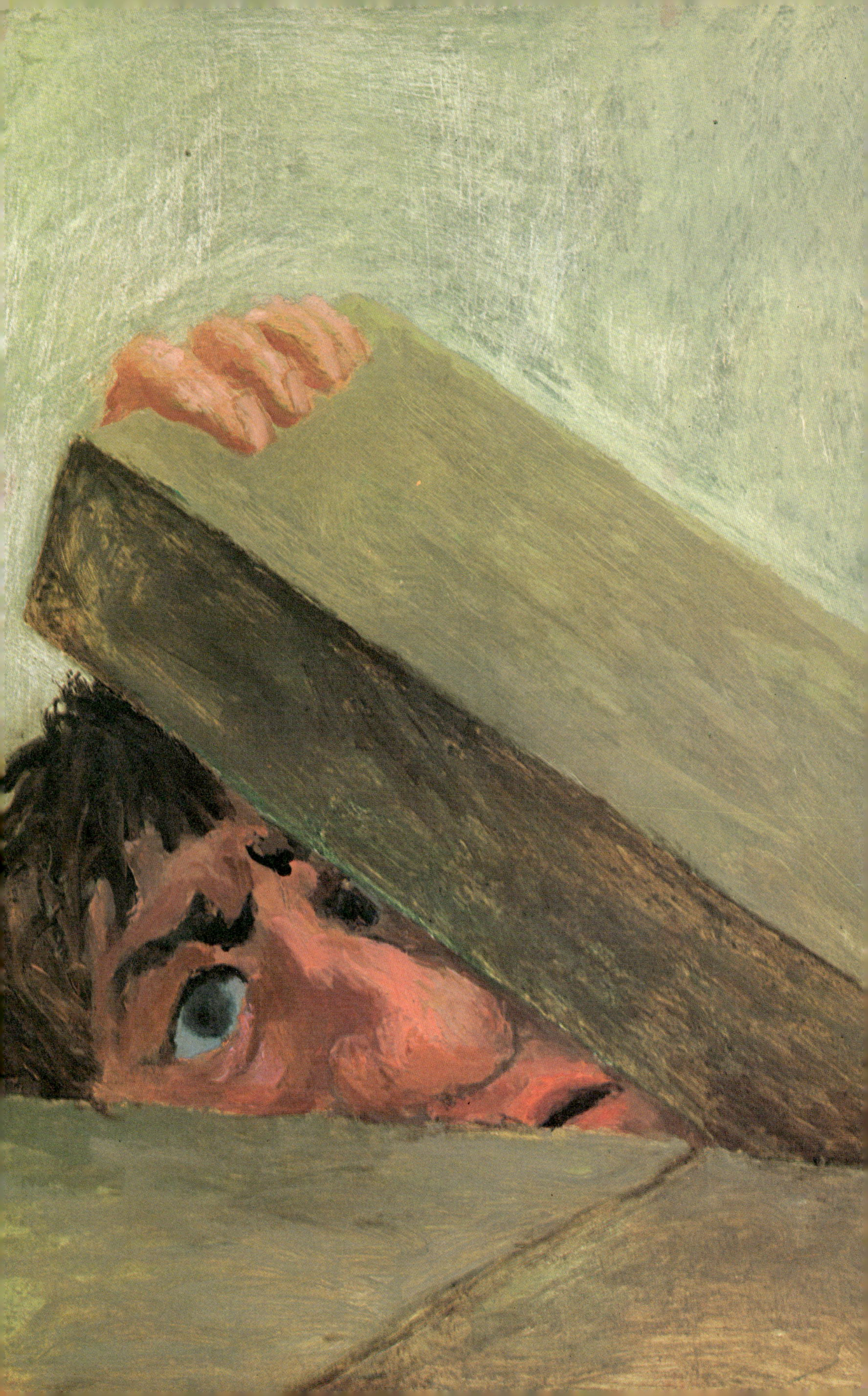

tremble under his feet; and looking about him, but keeping his fingers at work, he saw the appearance of a great human head rising up through the stone pavement of the church. And when the head had risen above the surface, there came from it a great, great voice. And the voice said: 'Do you see this great head of mine?'

'I see that, but I'll sew this!' replied the sprightly tailor; and he stitched away at the trews.

Then the head rose higher up through the pavement, until its neck appeared. And when its neck was shown, the thundering voice came again and said: 'Do you see this great neck of mine?'

'I see that, but I'll sew this!' said the sprightly tailor; and he stitched away at his trews.

Then the head and neck rose higher still, until the great shoulders and chest were shown above the ground. And again the mighty voice thundered: 'Do you see this great chest of mine?'

And again the sprightly tailor replied: 'I see that, but I'll sew this!' and stitched away at his trews.

And still it kept rising through the pavement, until it shook a great pair of arms in the tailor's face, and said: 'Do you see these great arms of mine?'

'I see those, but I'll sew this!' answered the tailor; and he stitched hard at his trews, for he knew that he had no time to lose.

The sprightly tailor was taking the long stitches, when he saw it gradually rising and rising through the floor, until it lifted out a great leg, and stamping with it upon the pavement, said in a roaring voice: 'Do you see this great leg of mine?'

'Aye, aye: I see that, but I'll sew this!' cried the tailor; and his fingers flew with the needle, and he took such long stitches, that he was just come to the end of the trews, when it was taking up its other leg. But before it could pull it out of the pavement, the sprightly tailor had finished his task; and, blowing out his candle, and springing from off his gravestone, he buckled up, and ran out of the church with the trews under his arm. Then the fearsome thing gave a loud roar, and stamped with both his feet upon the pavement, and out of the church he went after the sprightly tailor.

Down the glen they ran, faster than the stream when the flood rides it; but the tailor had got the start and a nimble pair of legs, and he did not choose to lose the laird's reward. And though the thing roared to him to stop, yet the sprightly tailor was not the man to be beholden to a monster. So he held his trews tight, and let no darkness grow under his feet, until he had reached Saddell Castle. He had no sooner got inside the gate, and shut it, than the apparition came up to it; and, enraged at losing his prize, struck the wall above the gate, and left there the mark of his five great fingers. Ye may see them plainly to this day, if ye'll only peer close enough.

But the sprightly tailor gained his reward: for Macdonald paid him handsomely for the trews, and never discovered that a few of the stitches were somewhat long.

THE POSSESSED

THE CAKES OF OATMEAL AND BLOOD

There was an upstart of a fellow one time, who was always arranging a mariage between himself and some girl, but in the end he never married any of them. He couldn't make up his mind which wife would be best for him. There happened to be a funeral one day, and after coming home, a little tipsy, he was invited to a dance in a neighbour's house. He went to the dance; there were lots of young men and women there, and some of his own relatives as well. They asked him had he any thought of getting married.

'I have, and every thought,' said he, 'but I don't know what kind of wife would be best for me.'

''Twould be better for you to marry me,' said one girl.

'Don't, but marry me!' said a second girl.

'I'd be a better wife than either of the two of them,' said a third girl.

'Well,' said he, 'I had a nice blackthorn stick with me, when I was in the graveyard today, and I left it stuck into the ground near the grave of the old woman we buried. I'll marry whichever of the three of ye will go there and bring me home my stick!'

'You may go to the Devil!' said two of the girls. 'We wouldn't go into the graveyard for all the sticks in the wood, not to mention your little, blackthorn one!'

'I'll go there,' said the third girl, 'if you keep your promise to marry me, if I bring you the stick.'

'I promise to marry you,' said he.

She set off for the graveyard, without any fear. She went into it and was searching around for the stick, when a voice spoke from one of the graves.

'Open this grave!' called the voice.

'I won't,' answered the girl.

'You'll have to open it!' said the voice.

She had to open the grave. There was a man in the coffin inside.

'Take me out of this coffin!' he ordered.

'I couldn't,' said she.

'You can very well,' said the man.

She had to take him out of the coffin.

'Now take me on your back!' said he.

'Where will I take you to?' she asked.

'I'll direct you,' said he.

She had to take him on her back and took him to the house of one of the neighbours, near her own. He told her not to go any further. She carried him into the kitchen. The family were all asleep. The man stirred up the fire.

'See can you get something for me to eat!' said the man.

'Yerra, where could I get anything for you to eat?' she asked. 'I have as little knowledge as yourself of the way about this house!'

'Go on! There's oatmeal in the room. Bring it here!' said he.

She found the room, and the oatmeal was there.

'Hold that candle f[or me] now,' said he.

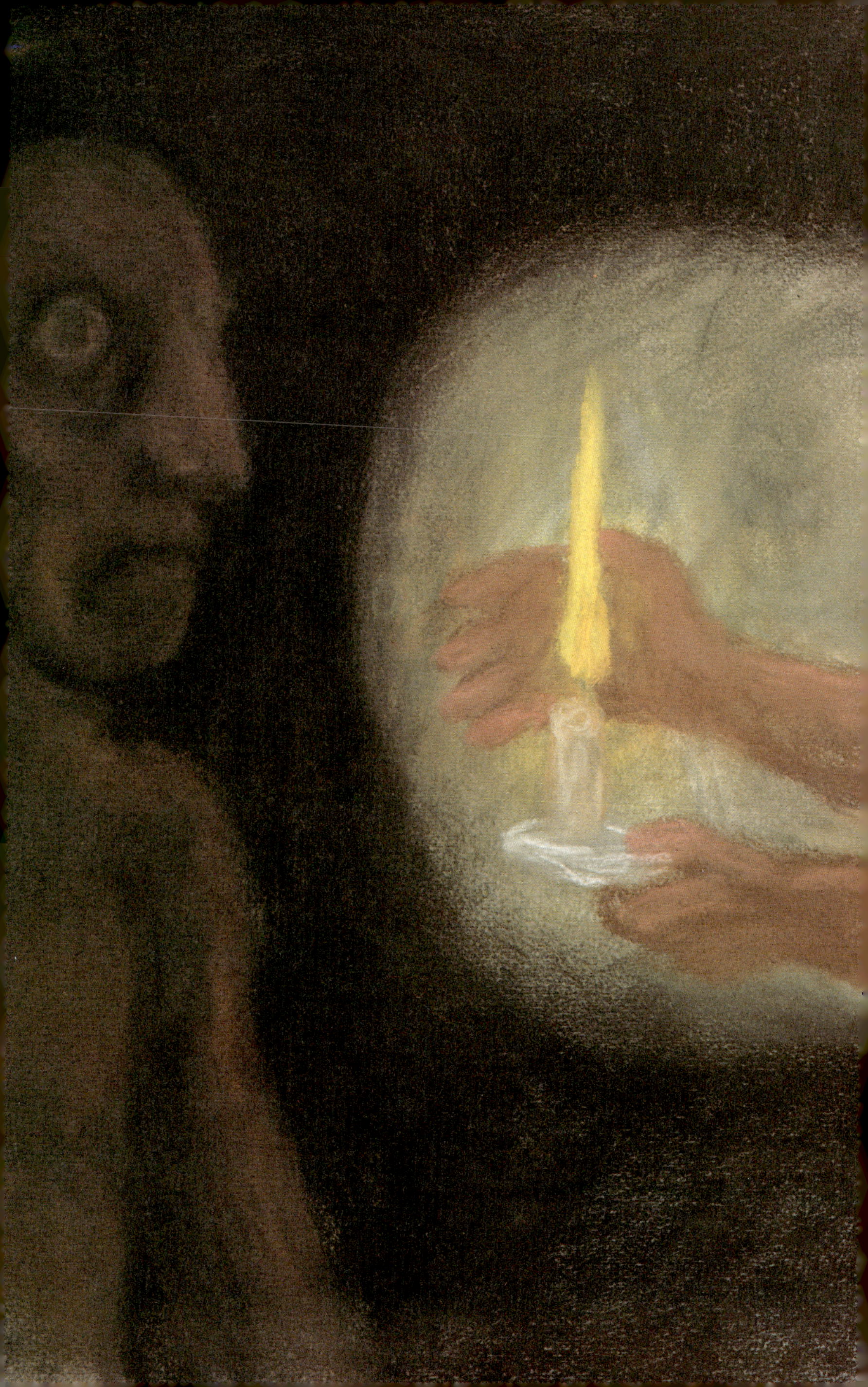

'See can you find milk anywhere now!' said the man.
She searched but couldn't find any milk.
'See is there water, if there isn't any milk!' said the man.
She looked everywhere for water, but there was none.
'There isn't a drop of water in the house,' said she.
'Light a candle!' said he.
She did so.
'Hold that candle for me now!' said he.

He made off to a room where two sons of the man of the house were asleep. He took a knife and cut their throats, and drew their blood. He took away the blood, mixed it with the oatmeal, and began to eat it. He urged the girl to eat it also, and when he came near her, she pretended to eat it, while at the same time she was letting it fall into her apron.

"Tis a great pity,' said she, 'that this should happen to those two boys.'

'It wouldn't have happened to them,' said the man, 'if they had kept some clean water in the house; but they didn't, and they must take what has happened to them!'

'Is there anything to bring the two young men to life again?' she asked.

'No,' said he, 'because you and I have eaten what would have revived them. If some of the oatmeal which was mixed with their blood was put into their mouths, life would come back to them, as it had been before. And the two of them would have a good life, if they had lived,' said he. 'Do you see that field that their father owns?'

'I do,' said she.

'Nobody knows all the gold there is in it near the bushes over there,' said the man. 'You must take me back now to where you found me,' said he.

She took him on her back, and when she was going through a muddy gap which led out from the yard, she let the oatmeal which she had hidden in her apron, fall down near a fence. She took him along and never stopped till she took him to the grave out of which she had taken him.

'Put me into the coffin!' said he.
She did so.
'I'll be going home now,' said she.
'You won't!' said he. 'You must cover up my coffin with earth, as you found it.'

She started to fill in the grave, and after a while, the cock crowed at some house near the graveyard.

'I'll go now, the cock is crowing,' said she.

'Don't take any notice of that cock!' said he. 'He isn't a March cock. Work away and finish your task!'

She had to keep on filling in the grave. After another while, a second cock crowed.

'I'll go now,' said she. 'The cock is crowing.'

'You may go now,' said he. 'That's a true March cock, and if he hadn't crowed just now, you'd have to stay with me altogether.'

She went off home, and by that time, the dance was over. She went to bed, and slept late until her mother called her.

''Tis a great shame for you to be sleeping and the bad news we have near us at our neighbours!' said her mother.

'What news is that?' asked the girl.

'This neighbour of ours found his two sons dead in the one bed this morning!' said her mother.

'How can I help that?' asked the girl.

'I know you can't,' said her mother. 'But put on your clothes and go to the wake.'

She went off to the wake. She remembered every word that the man had said to her. All the people at the wake were crying, but she didn't cry at all.

'Would you give me one of them as a husband, if I brought them to life again?' she asked their father.

The young man who had sent her to the graveyard for the blackthorn stick was at the wake and he heard what she said.

'I thought you'd marry me,' said he.

'Don't talk at all!' said she. 'I'm tired enough after all I have gone through on account of you last night! Nobody knows what I have suffered on account of your blackthorn stick!'

'Joking me you are!' said the man of the house. 'I know well that you couldn't put the life into them again. I'm troubled enough without you making fun of me!'

''Tisn't making fun of you I am at all!' said the girl. 'I'll put life into them, if I get one of them as a husband, and all I'll ask along with him is that field above the house, the Field of the Bushes. You can give the rest of the farm to the other fellow.'

'I'd give you that field gladly,' said their father, 'if I saw that you had put the life into them again, as they were before.'

She went out and found the oatmeal that she had let fall near the fence. She took it in and put some of it into the mouth of each of them. As soon as she did that, the two of them rose up, alive, as well as they had ever been.

After a while, she married one of them and she told him the whole story about her meeting with the dead man. When they were married, she told her husband to go and dig near the bushes—that he might find something there. He did and found a potful of gold. He took it home and emptied the gold out of it, and put it into the bank or some other place to keep. The old pot happened to remain in the house, and there was some kind of writing on it that no one could read. A few years later, a poor scholar called to the house and he saw the pot.

'Who put that writing on the pot?' he asked.

'We don't know,' they said. 'We don't notice it much.'

'I don't either,' said he, 'but I know what the writing says.'

'That's more than we do,' said they. 'What is written on it?'

'It says that on the other side there is three times as much,' said he.

That put them thinking, and they remembered where they had found the pot and how much gold was in it. So when the night came, out went the girl and her husband, and they started to dig at the eastern side of where they found the pot. There they found three other pots, all full of gold! You may be sure that they weren't short of anything then! They built a fine house in the corner of that field. And that's how that girl got her money because of the man of the oatmeal.

THE HUNTED SOUL

There were an old Goodwife that lived down to Coleford Water, and she used to come into Crowcombe market with her bits and her pieces, but she were a very stout old body, and her pony old Smart he was getting on in years now—reckon he was nearly forty—and so they used to get ready quite early in the morning, round about four o'clock, and start on. Well, one time, old Goody she mistook the time; she got up, she got her things ready, put in the stockings, and the apples, and the eggs into the pannier, and she loaded her old Smart, and then she gets up herself on upping stock, and on to his back, and away they goes afore midnight.

Well, bye and bye, old Goody she began to feel a bit sleepy-like. Old Smart he was a-plodding on as he'd done all these years, and she began to nod, and must have slept a bit, 'cos, when she woke up— summat waked she, and there was old Smart, a-standing in the middle o' sixty-acre, and he was a-trembling with fear. Ah! Sweat were behind his ears, and his mane and his tail they were stiff with fright; and Granny, she looked around like and there she saw a little white rabbit hopping towards her, all terrified, and there came the sound of hounds behind. But they weren't real hounds, oh! no, they ain't no real hounds; best not say too much about them. Well, when Granny sees this little white rabbit, she were that sorry for her, she forgot white rabbits were witch-souls, and she took off lid o' the pannier, and white rabbit hopped in, and Granny clapped down the lid tight. Then she tried to get old Smart to move on, but he wasn't doing no moving, not he; he kept his eyes on a bit o' grass did old Smart—he knowed a bit—he wasn't going to look up. When Granny sees that, she remembered, and she got out her knitting-needles, see, and went on with her stocking, and she heard them there dogs coming nearer and a clatter o' hoofs, and a great fine black rider he come up alongside her. His horse had horns, and there was a green light round them, and those dogs had green fire coming out o' their mouths.

''Ave 'e seen a rabbit go by?' says the rider.

She heard the dogs coming nearer.

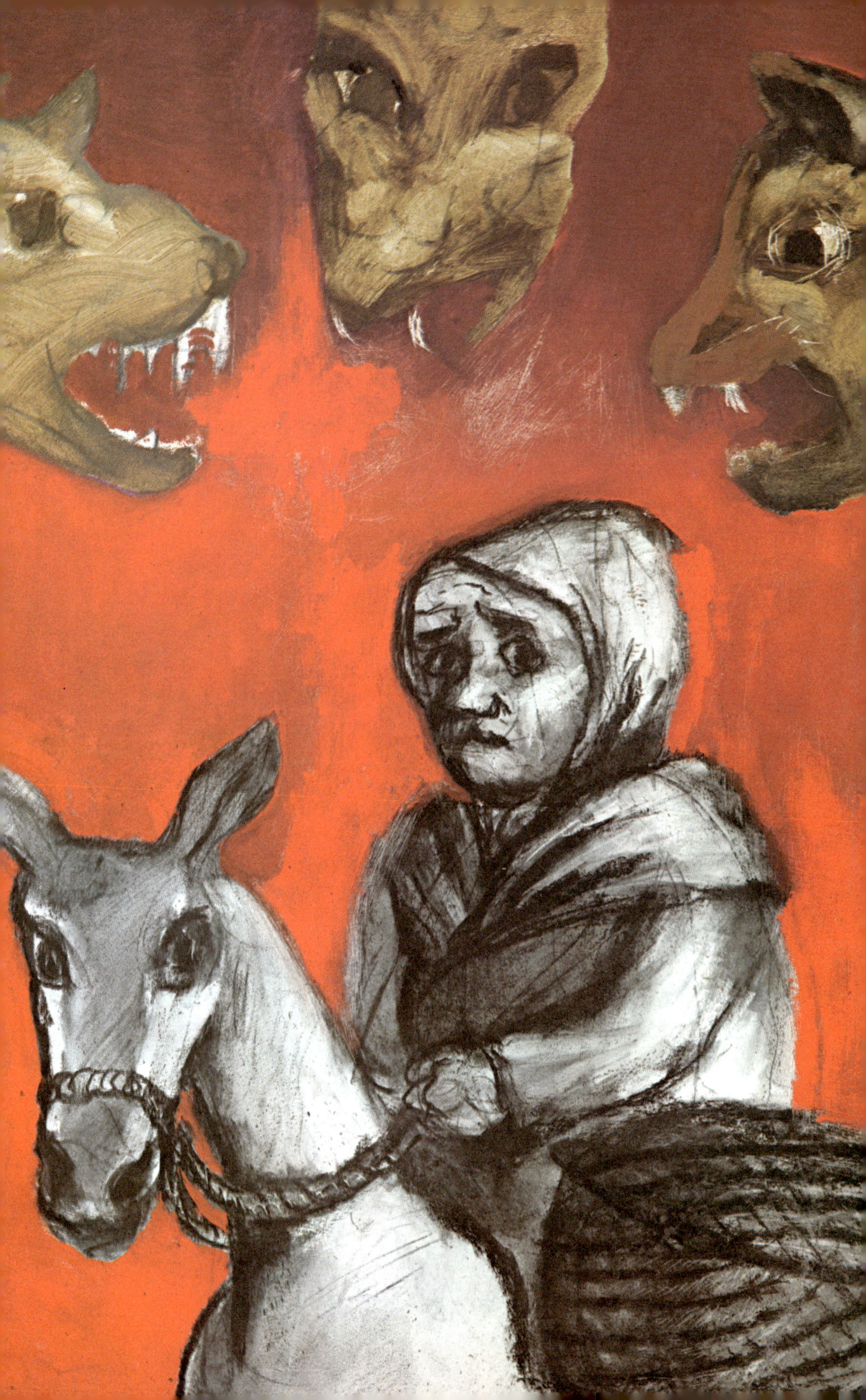

Well! Granny knew better than to answer him, so she just shook her head; and that wasn't wrong neither, 'cos rabbit was in pannier! And away the whole hunt went up towards Will's Neck. You could hear their howls on the wind. And then old Smart, he got up, and he lumbered up at a canter—a thing he hadn't done for about twenty year, and he never stopped till he came to Roebuck Ford, and then he do stop. I said he knowed a thing or two, 'cos nothing can harm thee if you be in the middle of running water. No witches nor devils nor nothing. Then Granny she lifted up the lid o' her pannier, and out came the most beautiful lady.

'Oh!' says she, 'how can I thank thee? When I was young, I was a witch, and when I died, I was condemned to be hunted forever by the Devil and his pack of Yeth-hounds, until I could get behind them. And now you've saved my soul.'

And then she gave a most beautiful smile, all lit up like sunlight, and then she was gone. Well, Granny and old Smart, they made their way up along to Crowcombe. When they got to Butter Cross, church clock was striking three! So they set theirselves down by the Cross, and they finished their sleep. It had been a hard night for old folks, but the dogs couldn't harm them, on account the horse was shod, see?

WILD ALASDAIR OF ROY BRIDGE

This Wild Alasdair lived at Roy Bridge. He was a very rough kind of man. That's why he was called Wild Alasdair. It was a custom in the district to have dances at times, especially at Christmas. They used to collect money to buy the drinks. This year they collected a sum to buy drinks for their Christmas dance. There was no one more suitable to go to get the drink than Alasdair.

Alasdair went off with his pony. In those days men always used to carry a big stick or wooden staff. Alasdair arrived at the inn. There were people drinking there, and he spent a while along with them. Then he bought the whisky for the dance and tied it on the pony's back.

When Alasdair reached Roy Bridge on his way home, the pony stopped, and refused to go any farther, but began to back. Alasdair was cursing the pony, and beating it, but the pony would not go on. Alasdair then looked to see what was keeping the pony back. There was a man sitting at the far end of the bridge. Alasdair shouted to him to clear out or he would split him against the bridge. The man paid no heed. Alasdair went over and hit him across the back with his stick, and the stick flew into pieces off his back as if it had struck an iron bar. The man got up and came to grips with Alasdair. Though Alasdair was big and brave, he could not stand up to the man on the bridge, and he was beaten until he was unable to walk.

The pony went home. When it arrived, Alasdair's wife raised the alarm that Alasdair was dead somewhere. A search was made for him. He met them on the road crawling home on his hands and

Alasdair was big and brave but he could no stand up to the man the bridge.

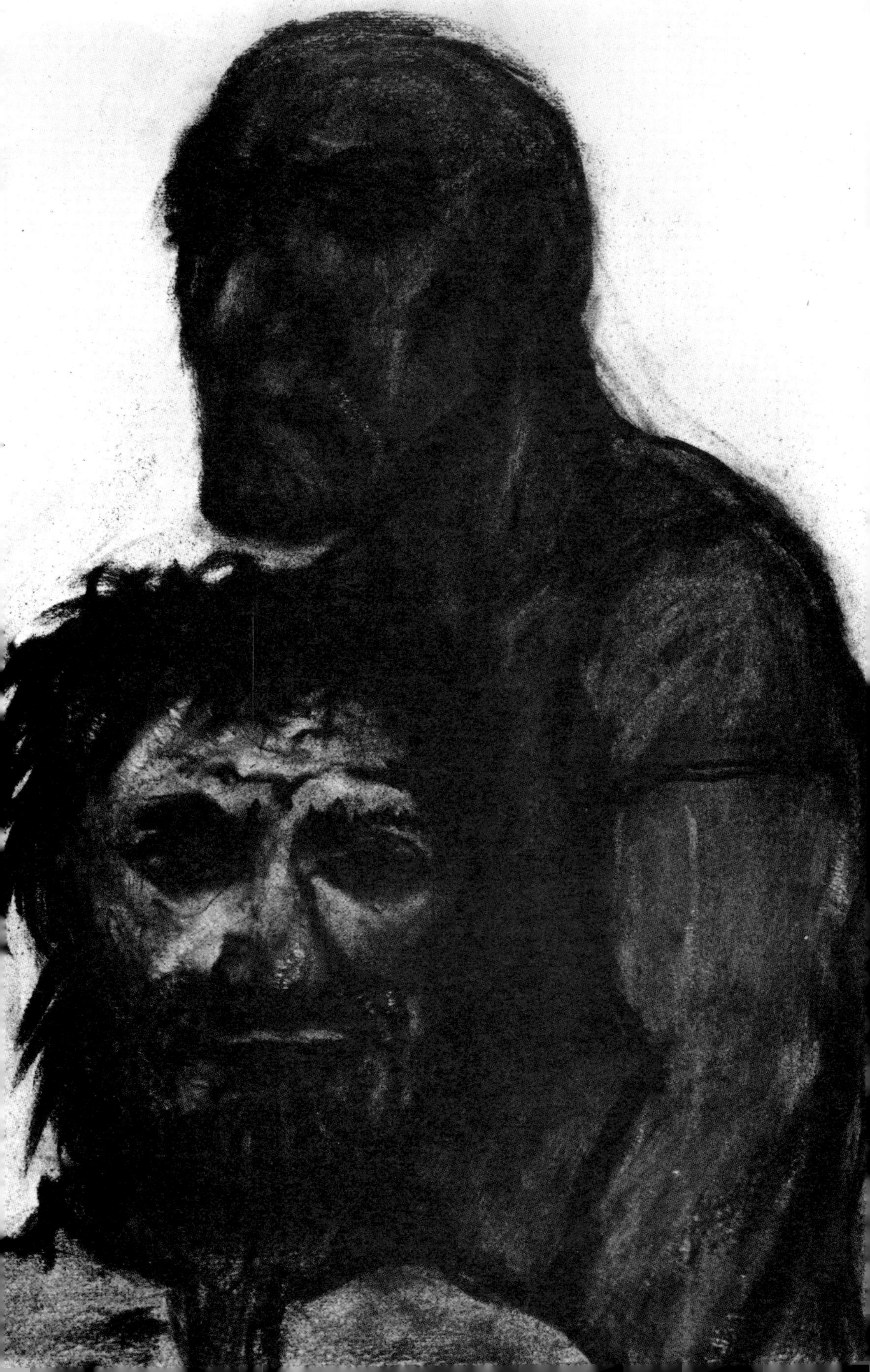

knees; he couldn't stand. They took him home. They thought there was nothing wrong with him but the drink, something which had happened before often enough. Alasdair spent a fortnight in bed, and recovered. He didn't say a word about what had happened to him.

One night after he and his wife had gone to bed, they heard the cows lowing in the byre, which was behind the house.

'Goodness,' said his wife, 'one of the cows has got loose, you'd better get up in case she kills the others.' 'Oh'—Alasdair thought of something else—'they'll be all right.' The cows kept on lowing. At last his wife said, 'I'd better get up myself.'

When Alasdair saw she was going to get up, he said to himself that she mustn't go out, anyway. 'Stay where you are then, I'll go out.' He put on his clothes and went out, and when he got out, the man was before him in the door of the byre. What Alasdair had got at Roy Bridge, he got again that night, until he was left lying half dead there.

When his wife got tired of waiting for him, she went out herself. Alasdair was stretched out unable to move. She managed to drag him into the house and put him in bed. Afterwards he told her that this was what had happened to him at Roy Bridge the night he was bringing back the whisky. From that time he was always called 'Alasdair of the Ghost'. He was afraid to go outside the house after dark. He thought he would clear out of the place entirely, sell his belongings and go to America. So he did. He went to America, and when he got there he found it was but a wild place, nothing but forest. He managed to make a cabin in the forest, which was very thick. He began to cut a track through the forest to the cabin, so he could find his way there any time. He was only spending what little he had, there wasn't a penny coming in.

One night when he was coming home, what did he see but a man in front of him in this tunnel who looked like the man who had met him at Roy Bridge. Alasdair didn't know whether to keep on or to turn back. Then the man spoke to him.

'Well, you think I'm the man who met you at Roy Bridge!'

'Yes,' said Alasdair.

'I'm he, right enough,' said the man, 'and it's just as easy for me to give you tonight what I gave you at Roy Bridge. You thought I wouldn't come to America at all, since you came over; but I came with you. But I'll not touch you tonight, as I think you've been through enough. The best thing you can do now is to return where you came from while you have enough to take you back. I shall not trouble you again. You were taking to do with a lot of things you had no business to. Neither will you learn who I am.'

Alasdair didn't want to return. He could barely afford the fare. When he got back to Roy Bridge there was nothing for him there. The people there had such pity on him, that everyone who had bought anything at his roup, gave it back to him to make him up as he was before. That's what happened to 'Alasdair of the Ghost'.

'KINTAIL AGAIN'

Once there was a crofter-fisherman in Kintail, who used to go to sea to fish every day with his sons. One day when they were out fishing, the weather became very bad. They had to clear a headland before they could get into harbour. The old man saw that the boat could not clear the headland, and that the only way they could save themselves was to let her run ashore. Some people saw them, and got together, and helped them to get ashore. But the boat's keel was broken.

After they had gone home and had a meal, the old man thought it would be just as necessary for them to go out fishing tomorrow as it had been today; so he went to the wood to see if he could find a tree that would make a new keel for the boat, taking an axe with him. He searched the wood, but he couldn't find a tree that satisfied him. Even if he had found one, he would still have had to get a carpenter to saw it, and he didn't know when it would have been ready. The tree he found that was of the right size, had a bend in it; he couldn't find one that suited him.

At last night fell. He was trying to get out of the wood, and some time during the night he succeeded. He didn't know where to go; but then he saw a light some way off, and he made straight for the light. When he reached it, he found a neat little house there, and he went in. There were three old women inside; one of them, who was sitting by the fire, was extremely old. Another was tidying the house. He asked them if he could stay until the morning. They looked at each other, and one of them said reluctantly that he could.

They asked where he had come from, and he told them. They told him how far he was from his home, and said he had gone a distance on the wrong way.

After a while, the one who was at the fireside got up and joined the others, and they were talking to each other on the other side of the room. The fisherman thought they were talking about him, but he didn't attach much importance to it. One of the old women turned to him and said that he had better go down to the room at the other end of the house, where there was a bed in which he could sleep until the morning. He said that he didn't need a bed, he could manage at the fireside.

'Oh, you'd better go to bed, you'll feel better for walking tomorrow. Take the light, you can leave it burning,' she said.

He got up and went. In the room he found nothing but a bed and a table, and a big chest over beneath the window. He went to bed, but he didn't fall asleep; he was worried about his family at home, thinking they might be looking for him. He put out the light. Then he noticed one of the old women come to the door. He pretended to be asleep, and she came in, and went over to the chest, and took out a bonnet, and tied it on her head. 'London again!' said the old woman. Away she went; he didn't get another glimpse of her! Then he heard another of the old women come to the door. She didn't wait so long at the door as the first; she went over and took a bonnet out of the chest and tied it on her head, and all she said was 'London again!' just like the first one. Then he noticed the third old woman at the door. She was afraid she was late; she went straight to the chest and took out another bonnet and put it on her head and said 'London again!' following the others, and he was left alone.

He thought he would not stay there any longer, but start on his way home. He got up and dressed. When he was ready to go, he thought he would look to see what was in the chest, since he had such a good chance. He opened the chest, but all there was inside was one or two of the bonnets he had seen the old women put on. He tried one on his head, and it fitted him very well. 'London again!' he said. Out he went and in a twinkle he was standing in a whisky cellar in London. The three old women were there, stretched out dead drunk. He didn't bother about the old women, but he turned off the spigots—which were running as the old women hadn't closed them, being drunk. He then tried a mouthful of every kind of whisky there—he needed it all right!

He thought he would sit down, as the cellar was so close. He took off the bonnet, and put it in his pocket. His first awakening was someone kicking him! There was no sign of the old women.

'You rascal, you've been coming here long enough! You've ruined me! But at last we've got you!'

The police were sent for, and the poor fisherman was taken away to prison. Then he was tried in court. He told the court what had happened to him, and how he came to be there. Who'd believe that? No one! He didn't need to be telling such lies. The loss had been going on a long time, and it wasn't what had been drunk by any means, but what had been spilt. All the policemen and all the detectives in London had been unable to catch the thief, until they caught the fisherman. He was sentenced to be hanged.

The day he was to be hanged, a large crowd collected near the gallows. The hangman brought the fisherman out and took him on to the scaffold and put the noose round his neck, and told him that he had now ten minutes in which to say anything he wanted to say.

'Oh, I haven't anything to say that I haven't said already,' said the fisherman. 'You are hanging an innocent man.'

'You're anything but that,' said the hangman.

The fisherman put his hand in his pocket, and what did he find but the bonnet.

'May I put this bonnet on my head before you hang me?' he said.

'Oh, you can put anything you like on your head,' said the hangman.

The fisherman tied the bonnet on his head. 'Kintail again!' he said. Away he went with the gallows through the sky! On the way he threw the hangman off the gallows into the sea, and the hangman was drowned. The fisherman with the gallows came to Kintail; and he had a fine straight plank that would make a keel for his boat!

*Away he went with t[he]
gallows through the s[ky]*

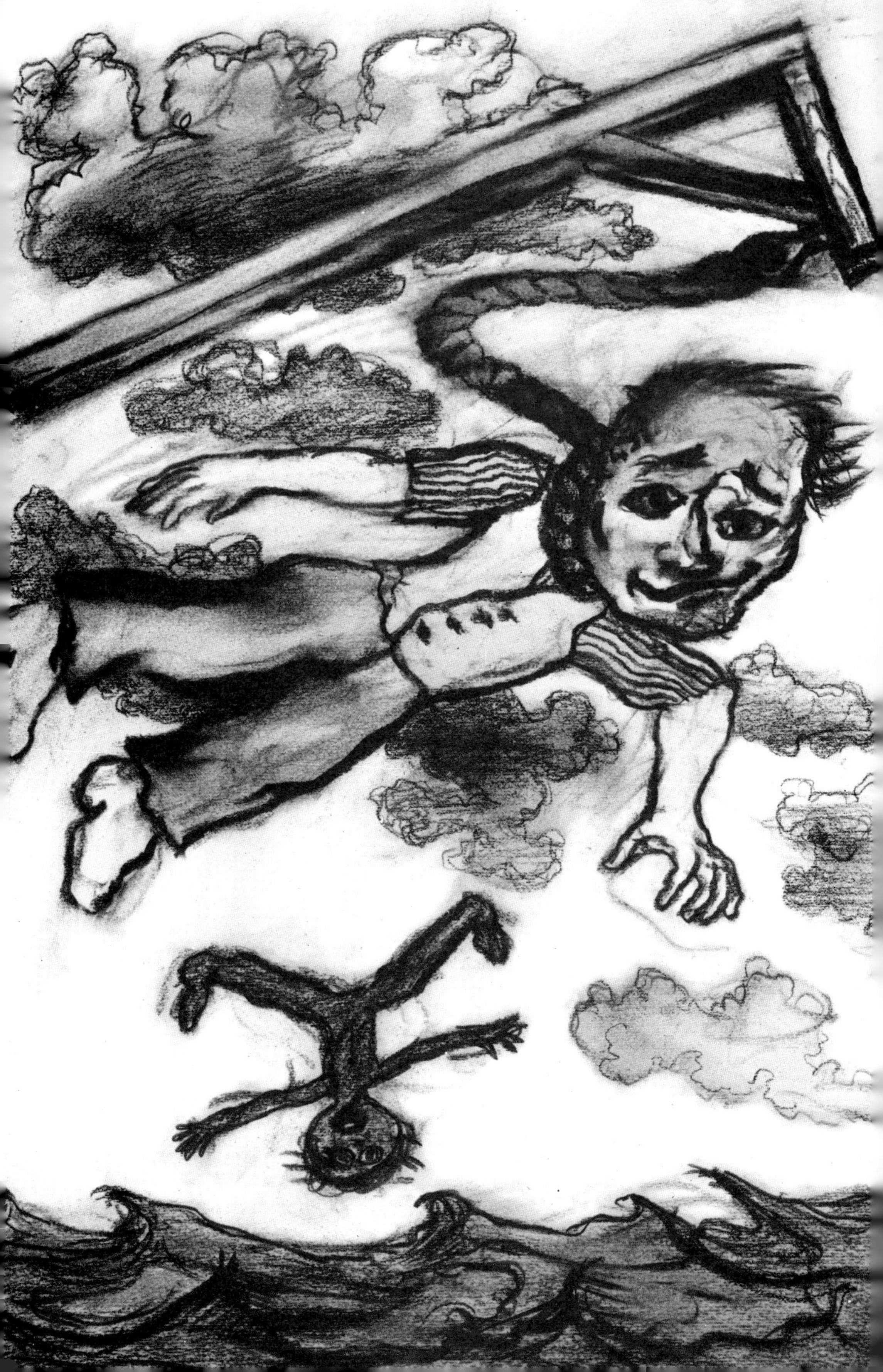

BREWERY OF EGGSHELLS

In Treneglwys there is a certain shepherd's cot known by the name of Twt y Cymrws because of the strange strife that occurred there. There once lived there a man and his wife, and they had twins whom the woman nursed tenderly. One day she was called away to the house of a neighbour at some distance. She did not much like going and leaving her little ones all alone in a solitary house, especially as she had heard tell of the good folk haunting the neighbourhood.

Well, she went and came back as soon as she could, but on her way back she was frightened to see some old elves of the blue petticoat crossing her path though it was midday. She rushed home, but found her two little ones in the cradle and everything seemed as it was before.

But after a time the good people began to suspect that something was wrong, for the twins didn't grow at all.

The man said: 'They're not ours.'

The woman said: 'Whose else should they be?'

And so arose the great strife so that the neighbours named the cottage after it. It made the woman very sad, so one evening she

She cleaned out the shell of a hen's egg.

made up her mind to go and see the Wise Man of Llanidloes, for he knew everything and would advise her what to do.

So she went to Llanidloes and told the case to the Wise Man. Now there was soon to be a harvest of rye and oats, so the Wise Man said to her, 'When you are getting dinner for the reapers, clear out the shell of a hen's egg and boil some potage in it, and then take it to the door as if you meant it as a dinner for the reapers. Then listen if the twins say anything. If you hear them speaking of things beyond the understanding of children, go back and take them up and throw them into the waters of Lake Elvyn. But if you don't hear anything remarkable, do them no injury.'

So when the day of the reap came the woman did all that the Wise Man ordered, and put the eggshell on the fire and took it off and carried it to the door, and there she stood and listened. Then she heard one of the children say to the other:

> Acorn before oak I knew,
> An egg before a hen,
> But I never heard of an eggshell brew
> A dinner for harvest men.

So she went back into the house, seized the children and threw them into the Llyn, and the goblins in their blue trousers came and saved their dwarfs and the mother had her own children back and so the great strife ended.

TEIG O'KANE AND THE CORPSE

There was once a grown-up lad in the County Leitrim, and he was strong and lively, and the son of a rich farmer. His father had plenty of money, and he did not spare it on the son. Accordingly, when the boy grew up he liked sport better than work, and, as his father had no other children, he loved this one so much that he allowed him to do in everything just as it pleased himself. He was very extravagant, and he used to scatter the gold money as another person would scatter the white. He was seldom to be found at home, but if there was a fair, or a race, or a gathering within ten miles of him, you were dead certain to find him there. And he seldom spent a night in his father's house, but he used to be always out rambling, and it's many's the kiss he got and he gave, for he was very handsome, and there wasn't a girl in the country but would fall in love with him.

It happened one day that the old man was told that the son had ruined the character of a girl in the neighbourhood, and he was greatly angry, and he called the son to him, and said to him, quietly and sensibly—'Settle with yourself now whether you'll marry that girl and get my land as a fortune with her, or refuse to marry her and give up all that was coming to you; and tell me in the morning which of the two things you have chosen.'

'Isn't my father a great fool,' says he to himself. 'I was ready enough, and only too anxious to marry Mary; and now since he threatened me, faith I've a great mind to let it go another while.'

His mind was so much excited that he remained between two notions as to what he should do. He walked out into the night at last to cool his heated blood, and went on to the road. He walked on for nearly three hours, when he suddenly remembered that it was late in the night, and time for him to turn. 'Musha! I think I forgot myself,' says he; 'it must be near twelve o'clock now.'

The word was hardly out of his mouth, when he heard the sound of many voices, and the trampling of feet on the road before him. 'I don't know who can be out so late at night as this, and on such a lonely road,' said he to himself.

He stood listening, and then he saw well enough by the light of the moon a band of little people coming towards him, and they were carrying something big and heavy with them. 'Oh, murder!' says he to himself, 'sure it can't be that they're the good people that's in it!'

He looked at them again, and perceived that there were about twenty little men in it, and there was not a man at all of them higher than about three feet or three feet and a half, and some of them were grey, and seemed very old. Then they all stood round about him. They threw the heavy thing down on the road, and he saw on the spot that it was a dead body.

He became as cold as the death, and there was not a drop of blood running in his veins when an old little grey man came up to him and said, 'Isn't it lucky we met you, Teig O'Kane?'

Poor Teig could not bring out a word at all, and so he gave no answer.

'Teig O'Kane,' said the little grey man again, 'isn't it timely you met us?'

Teig could not answer him.

'Teig O'Kane,' says he, 'the third time, isn't it lucky and timely that we met you?'

But Teig remained silent, for he was afraid to return an answer.

The little grey man turned to his companions, and there was joy in his bright little eye. 'And now,' says he, 'Teig O'Kane hasn't a word, we can do with him what we please. Teig, Teig,' says he, 'you're living a bad life, and we can make a slave of you now, and you cannot withstand us, for there's no use in trying to go against us. Lift that corpse.'

Teig was so frightened that he was only able to utter the two words, 'I won't;' for as frightened as he was, he was obstinate and stiff.

'Teig O'Kane won't lift the corpse,' said the little man, with a wicked little laugh. 'Make him lift it.'

Teig tried to run from them, but they followed him, and they held him tight, in a way that he could not stir, with his face against the ground. Six or seven of them raised the body then, and pulled it over to him, and left it down on his back. The breast of the corpse was squeezed against Teig's back and shoulders, and the arms of the corpse were thrown around Teig's neck. Then they stood back from him a couple of yards, and let him get up. He rose, foaming at the mouth and cursing, and he shook himself, thinking to throw the corpse off his back. But his fear and his wonder were great when he found that the two arms had a tight hold round his own neck, and strongly he tried, he could not throw it off.

The little grey man came up to him again, and said he to him, 'Now, little Teig,' says he, 'you didn't lift the body when I told you to lift it, and see how you were made to lift it; perhaps when I tell you to bury it you won't bury it until you're made to bury it!'

'Anything at all that I can do for your honour,' said Teig, 'I'll do it,' for he was getting sense already.

The little man laughed a sort of laugh again. 'You're getting quiet now, Teig,' says he. 'I'll go bail but you'll be quiet enough before I'm done with you. Listen to me now, Teig O'Kane, and if you don't obey me in all I'm telling you to do, you'll repent it. You must carry with you this corpse that is on your back to Demus Church, and you must bring it into the church with you, and make a grave for it in the very middle of the church, and you must raise up the flags and put them down again the very same way, and you must carry the clay out of the church and leave the place as it was when you came, so that no one could know that there had been anything changed. But that's not all. Maybe that the body won't be allowed to be buried in that church; perhaps some other man has the bed, and, if so, it's likely he won't share it with this one. If you don't get leave to bury it in Demus Church, you must carry it to Rock of Orus' Son, and bury it in the churchyard there; and if you don't get it into that place, take it with you to St Ronan's Church; and if that churchyard is closed on you, take it to Long Imlogue; and if you're not able to bury it there, you've no more to do than to take it to Kill-Breedya, and you can bury it there without hindrance. I cannot tell you what one of those churches is the one where you will have leave to bury that corpse under the clay, but I know that it will be allowed you to bury him at some church or other of them. If you do this work rightly, we will be thankful to you, and you will have no cause to grieve; but if you are slow or lazy, believe me we shall take satisfaction of you.'

When the grey little man had done speaking, his comrades laughed and clapped their hands together. 'Glic! Glic!' they all cried; 'go on, go on, you have eight hours before you till daybreak, and if you haven't this man buried before the sun rises, you're lost.' They struck a fist and a foot behind on him, and drove him on in the road. He was obliged to walk, and to walk fast, for they gave him no rest.

He thought himself that there was not a wet path, or a dirty lane, or a crooked contrary road in the whole county, that he had not walked that night. The night was at times very dark, and he used often to fall. Sometimes he was hurt, and sometimes he escaped, but he was obliged always to rise on the moment and to hurry on. Sometimes the moon would break out clearly, and then he would look behind him

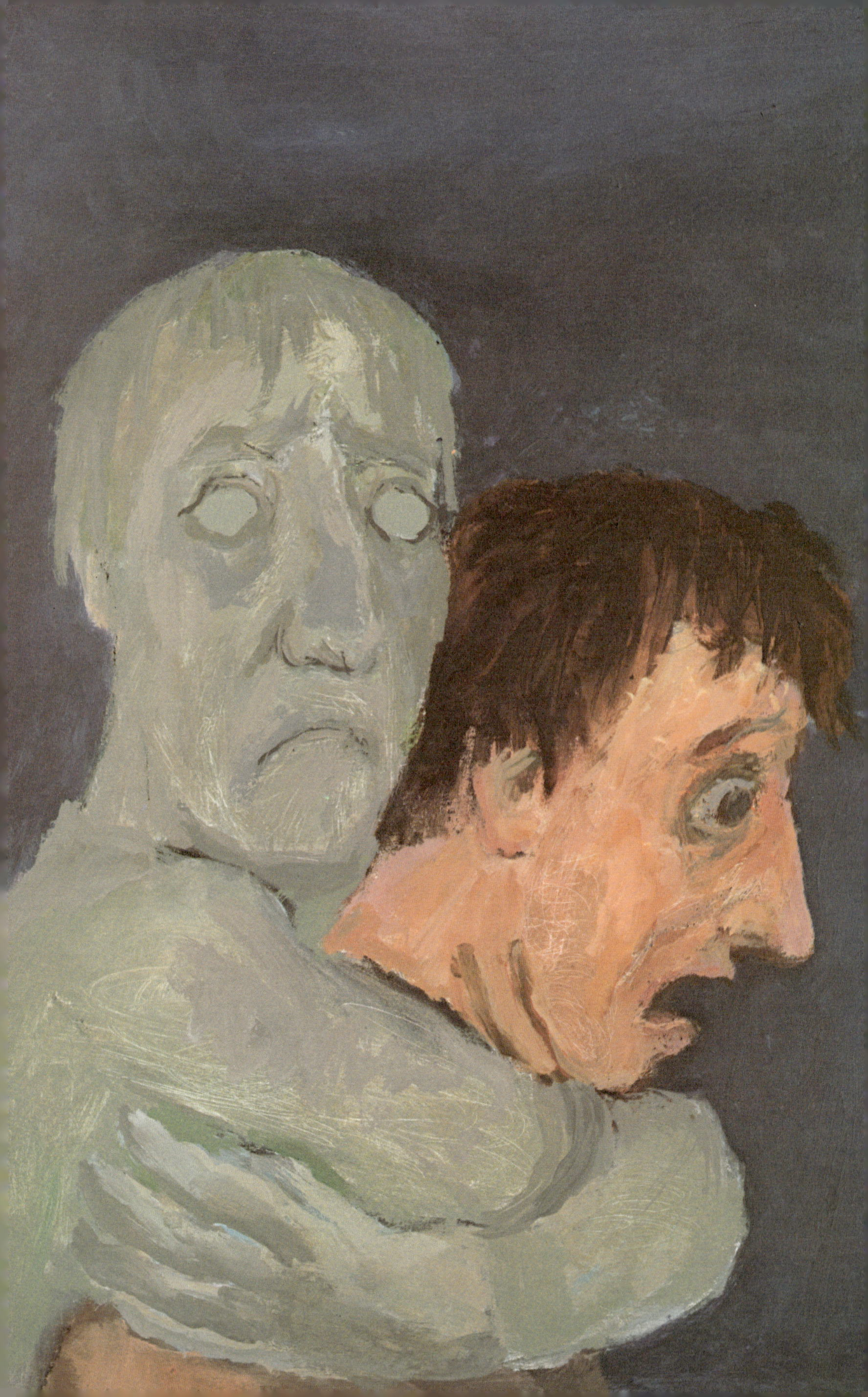

and see the little people following at his back.

He did not know how far he had walked, when at last one of them cried out to him, 'Stop here!' He stood, and they all gathered round him.

'Do you see those withered trees over there?' says the old boy to him again. 'Demus Church is among those trees, and you must go in there by yourself, for we cannot follow you or go with you'.

Teig went into the churchyard, and he walked up the old grassy pathway leading to the church. When he reached the door, he found it locked. The door was large and strong, and he did not know what to do. At last he drew out his knife with difficulty, and stuck it in the wood to try if it were not rotten, but it was not.

'Now,' said he to himself, 'I have no more to do; the door is shut, and I can't open it.'

Before the words were rightly shaped in his own mind, a voice in his ear said to him, 'Search for the key on the top of the door, or on the wall.'

He started. 'Who is that speaking to me?' he cried, turning round; but he saw no one. The voice said in his ear again, 'Search for the key on the top of the door, or on the wall.'

'What's that?' said he, and the sweat running from his forehead; 'who spoke to me?'

'It's I, the corpse, that spoke to you!' said the voice.

'Can you talk?' said Teig.

'Now and again,' said the corpse.

Teig searched for the key, and he found it on the top of the wall. He was too much frightened to say any more, but he opened the door wide, and as quickly as he could, and he went in, with the corpse on his back.

'Light the candle,' said the corpse.

'Bury me now, bury me now; there is a spade and turn the ground.' When the first flag was raised it was not hard to raise the others near it, and Teig moved three or four of them out of their places. The clay that was under them was soft and easy to dig, but he had not thrown up more than three or four shovelfuls, when he felt the iron touch something soft like flesh. He threw up three or four more shovelfuls from around it, and then he saw that it was another body that was buried in the same place.

'I am afraid I'll never be allowed to bury the two bodies in the same hole,' said Teig, in his own mind. 'You corpse, there on my back,' says he, 'will you be satisfied if I bury you down here?' But the corpse never answered him a word.

'That's a good sign,' said Teig to himself. 'Maybe he's getting quiet,' and he thrust the spade down in the earth again. Perhaps he hurt the flesh of the other body, for the dead man that was buried there stood up in the grave, and shouted an awful shout. 'Hoo! hoo!! hoo!!! Go! go!! go!!! or you're a dead, dead, dead man!' And then he fell back in the grave again. Teig's hair stood upright on his head like the bristles of a pig, the cold sweat ran off his face, and then came a tremor over all his bones, until he thought that he must fall.

But after a while he became bolder, when he saw that the second corpse remained lying quietly there, and he threw in the clay on it again, and he smoothed it overhead, and he laid down the flags carefully as they had been before. 'It can't be that he'll rise up any more,' said he.

He went down the aisle a little further, and drew near to the door, and began raising the flags again, looking for another bed for the corpse on his back. He was not long digging until he laid bare an old woman without a thread upon her but her shirt. She was more lively than the first corpse, for he had scarcely taken any of the clay away from about her, when she sat up and began to cry, 'Ho, you clown! Ha, you clown! Where has he been that he got no bed?'

Poor Teig drew back, and when she found that she was getting no answer, she closed her eyes gently, lost her vigour, and fell back quietly and slowly under the clay. Teig did to her as he had done to the man—he threw the clay back on her, and left the flags down.

He began digging again near the door, but before he had thrown up more than a couple of shovelfuls, he noticed a man's hand laid bare by the spade. 'By my soul, I'll go no further, then,' said he to himself; 'what use is it for me?' And he threw the clay in again on it, and settled the flags as they had been before.

He left the church then, and he laid his face between his two hands, and cried for grief and fatigue. He made another attempt to loosen the hands of the corpse that were squeezed round his neck, but they were as tight as if they were clamped; and the more he tried to loosen them, the tighter they squeezed him. He was going to sit down once more, when the cold, horrid lips of the dead man said to him, 'Rock of Orus' Son,' and he remembered the command of the good people.

He rose up, and looked about him. 'I don't know the way,' he said.

As soon as he had uttered the word, the corpse stretched out suddenly its left hand that had been tightened round his neck, and kept it pointing out, showing him the road he ought to follow. Teig followed that road, and whenever he came to a path or road meeting it, the corpse always stretched out its hand and pointed with its fingers, showing him the way he was to take.

Many was the cross-road he turned down, and many was the crooked lane he walked, until he saw from him an old burying ground at last, beside the road, but there was neither church nor chapel nor any other building in it. The corpse squeezed him tightly, and he stood. 'Bury me, bury me in the burying ground,' said the voice.

Teig drew over towards the old burying-place, and he was not more than about twenty yards from it, when, raising his eyes, he saw hundreds and hundreds of ghosts—men, women, and children—sitting on the top of the wall round about, or standing on the inside of it, or running backwards and forwards, and pointing at him, while he could see their mouths opening and shutting as if they were speaking, though he heard no word, nor any sound amongst them at all.

He was afraid to go forward, so he stood where he was, and the moment he stood, all the ghosts became quiet, and ceased moving. Then Teig understood that it was trying to keep him from going in, that they were. He then heard the voice of the corpse in his ear, saying 'St Ronan's Church,' and the skinny hand was stretched out again, pointing him out the road.

As tired as he was, he had to walk, and the road was neither short nor even. Many was the toss he got, and many a bruise they left on his body. At last he saw St Ronan's Church from him in the distance, standing in the middle of the burying ground. He moved over to the gate, but as he was passing in, he tripped on the threshold. Before he could recover himself, something that he could not see seized him by the neck, by the hands, and by the feet, and bruised him, and shook him, and choked him, until he was nearly dead; and at last he was lifted up, and carried more than a hundred yards from that place, and then thrown down in an old dyke, with the corpse still clinging to him.

'You corpse, up on my back,' said he, 'shall I go over again to the churchyard?'—but the corpse never answered him. 'That's a sign you don't wish me to try it again,' said Teig.

He was now in great doubt as to what he ought to do, when the corpse spoke in his ear, and said 'Long Imlogue.'

'Oh, murder!' said Teig, 'must I bring you there? If you keep me long walking like this, I tell you I'll fall under you.'

He went on, however, in the direction the corpse pointed out to him. He could not have told, himself, how long he had been going, when the dead man behind suddenly squeezed him, and said, 'There!'

Teig looked from him, and he saw a little low wall, that was so broken down in places that it was no wall at all. It was in a great wide field, in from the road; and only for three or four great stones at the corners, that were more like rocks than stones, there was nothing to show that there was either graveyard or burying ground there.

'Is this Long Imlogue? Shall I bury you here?' said Teig.

'Yes,' said the voice.

'But I see no grave or gravestone, only this pile of stones,' said Teig.

The corpse did not answer, but stretched out its long fleshless hand, to show Teig the direction in which he was to go. He went on, but when he came to within fifteen or twenty yards of the little low square wall, there broke out a flash of lightning, bright yellow and red, with blue streaks in it, and went round about the wall in one course, and it swept by as fast as the swallow in the clouds, and the longer Teig remained looking at it the faster it went, till at last it became like a bright ring of flame round the old graveyard, which no one could pass without being burnt by it.

Teig was amazed; he was half dead with fatigue, and he had no courage left to approach the wall. There fell a mist over his eyes, and there came a swooning in his head, and he was obliged to sit down upon a great stone to recover himself.

As he sat there on the stone, the voice whispered once more in his ear, 'Kill-Breedya;' and the dead man squeezed him so tightly that he cried out. He rose again, and went forwards as he was directed.

At last the corpse stretched out its hand, and said to him, 'Bury me there.'

'This is the last burying-place,' said Teig in his own mind; 'and the little grey man said I'd be allowed to bury him in some of them, so it must be this; it can't be but they'll let him in here.'

The first faint streak of the ring of day was appearing in the east. 'Make haste, make haste!' said the corpse; and Teig hurried forward as well as he could to the graveyard, which was a little place on a bare hill, with only a few graves in it. He came to the middle of the ground, and then stood up and looked round him for a spade or shovel to make a grave. As he was turning round and searching, he suddenly perceived what startled him greatly—a newly-dug grave right before him. He moved over to it, and looked down, and there at the bottom he saw a black coffin. He clambered down into the hole and lifted the lid, and found that the coffin was empty. He had hardly mounted up out of the hole, and was standing on the brink, when the corpse, which had clung to him for more than eight hours, suddenly relaxed its hold of his neck, and loosened its shins from round his hips, and sank down with a *plop* into the open coffin.

Teig fell down on his two knees at the brink of the grave, and gave thanks to God. He made no delay then, but pressed down the coffin lid in its place, and threw in the clay over it with his two hands; and when the grave was filled up, he stamped and leaped on it with his feet, until it was firm and hard, and then he left the place. He was more than twenty-six miles from home where he was, and he had come all that way with the dead body on his back in one night.

He was a changed man from that day. He never drank too much; he never lost his money over cards; and especially he would not take the world and be out late by himself of a dark night.

He was not a fortnight at home until he married Mary, the girl he had been in love with; and it's at their wedding the sport was, and it's he was the happy man from that day forward, and it's all I wish that we may be as happy as he was.

LITTLE PEOPLE
OF THE
OTHERWORLD

THE LITTLE PEOPLE

Our family diminished very much till at last there were but three brothers left, and they separated. One went to Ennis and another came here and the other to your own place beyond. It was a long time before they could make one another out again. It was my uncle used to go away among *them*. When I was a young chap, I'd go out in the field working with him, and he'd bid me go away on some message, and when I'd come back it might be in a faint I'd find him. It was he himself was taken; it was but his shadow or some thing in his likeness was left behind. He was a very strong man. My father had no notion at all of managing things. He lived to be eighty years, and all his life he looked as innocent as that little chap turning the hay. My uncle had the same innocent look; I think they died quite happy.

One time the wife got a touch of the little people, and she got it again, and the third time she got up in the morning and went out of the house and never said where she was going. But I had her watched, and I told the boy to follow her and never to lose sight of her, and I gave him the sign to make if he'd meet any bad thing. So he followed her, and she kept before him, and while he was going along the road something was up on top of the wall with one leap—a red-haired man it was, with no legs and with a thin face. But the boy made the sign and got hold of him and carried him till he got to the bridge. At the first he could not lift the man, but after he made the sign he was quite light. And the woman turned home again, and never had a touch after. It's a good job the boy had been taught the sign. Make that sign with your thumbs if ever when you're walking out you feel a sort of shivering in the skin, for that shows there's some bad thing near, but if you hold your hands like that, if you went into a stream itself, it couldn't harm you. And if you should any time feel a sort of pain in your little finger, the surest thing is to touch it with human dung. Don't neglect that, for if they're glad to get one of us, they'd be seven times better pleased to get the like of you.

Youngsters they take mostly to do work for them, and they are death on handsome people, for they are handsome themselves. To all sorts of work they put them, and digging potatoes and the like, and they have wine from foreign parts, and cargoes of gold coming in to them. Their houses are ten times more beautiful and ten times grander than any house in this world. And they could build one of them up in that field in ten minutes. Clothes of all colours they wear, and crowns like that one in the picture, and of other shapes. They have different queens, not always the same. The people they bring away must die some day; as to themselves, they were living from past ages, and they can never die till the time when God has His mind made up to redeem them.

And those they bring away are always glad to be brought back again. If you were to bring a heifer from those mountains beyond and to put it into a meadow, it would be glad to get back again to the

A red-haired man was, with no legs.

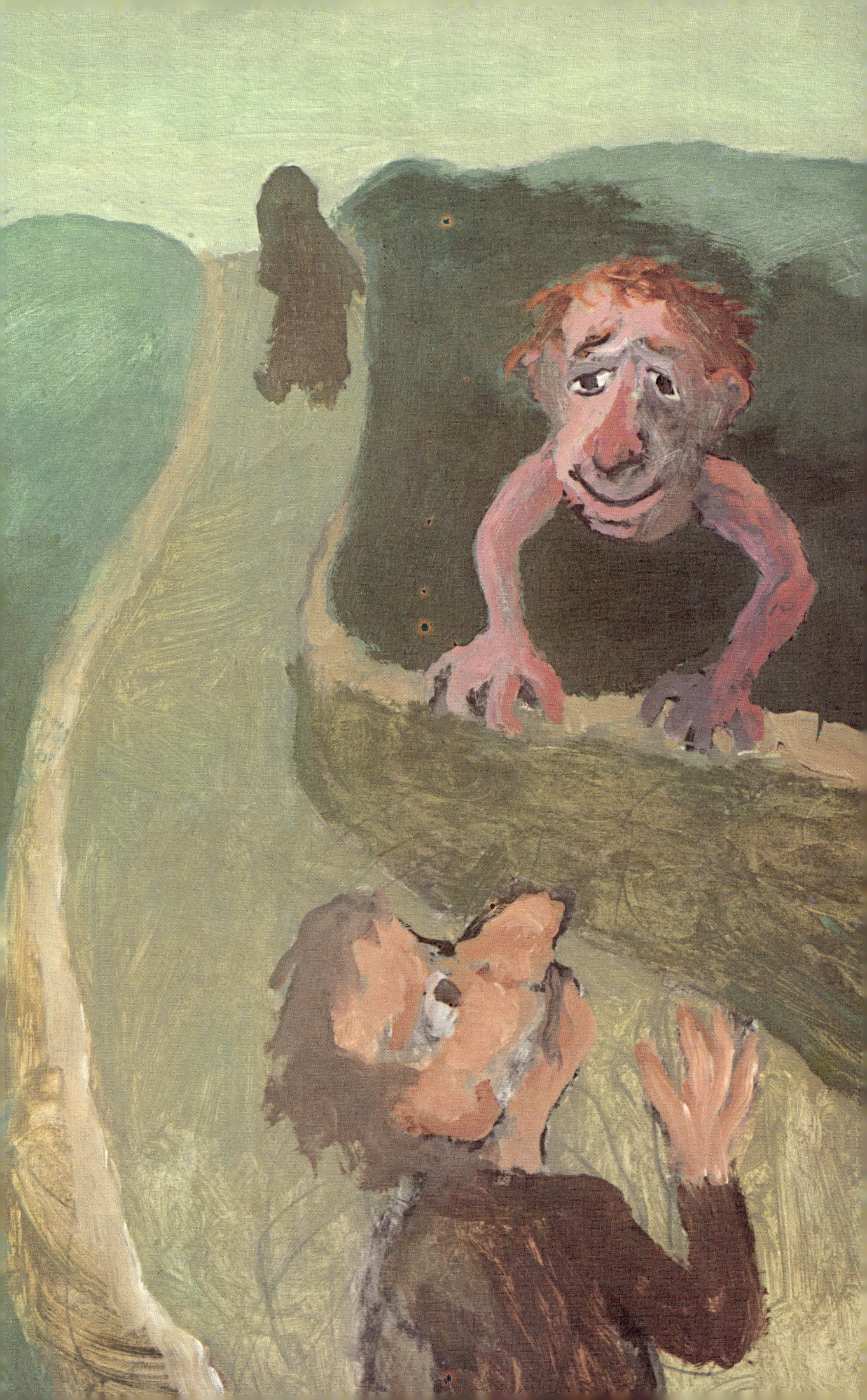

mountain, because it is the place it knows.

Coaches they make up when they want to go driving, with wheels and all, but they want no horses. There might be twenty of them going out together sometimes, and all full of them.

They are everywhere around us, and may be within a yard of us now in the grass. But if I ask you, 'What day is tomorrow,' and you said, 'Thursday,' they wouldn't be able to overhear us. They have the power to go in every place, even on to the book the priest is using.

There was one John Curran lived over there towards Bunahowe, and he had a cow that died, and they were striving to rear the calf—boiled hay they were giving it, the juice the hay was boiled in. And you never saw anything to thrive as it did. And one day some man was looking at it and he said, 'You may be sure the mother comes back and gives it milk.' And John Curran said, 'How can that be, and she dead?' But the man said, 'She's not dead, she's in the stream beyond. And if you go towards it half an hour before sunrise you'll find her, and you should catch a hold of her and bring her home and milk her, and when she makes to go away again, take a hold of her tail and follow her.' So he went out next morning, half an hour before sunrise, up toward the stream, and brought her home and milked her, and when the milking was done she started to go away and he caught a hold of the tail and was carried along with her. And she brought him into the stream, through a door. And behind the door stood a barrel, and what was in the barrel is what they put their finger in, and touch their forehead with when they go out, for if they didn't do that all people would be able to see them. And as soon as he got in, there were voices from all sides. 'Welcome, John Curran, welcome, John Curran.' And he said: 'The devil take you, how well you know my name; it's not a welcome I want, it's my cow to bring home again.' So in the end he got the cow and brought her home. And he saw there a woman that had died out of the village about ten years before, and she suckling a child.

They hate me because I do cures. My wife got a touch from them, and they have a watch on her ever since. It was the day after I married and I went to the fair at Clarenbridge. And when I came back the house was full of smoke, but there was nothing on the hearth but cinders, and the smoke was more like the smoke of a forge. And she was within lying on the bed, and her brother was sitting outside the door crying. So I went to the mother and asked her to come in, and she was crying too. And she knew well what had happened, but she didn't tell me, but she sent for the priest. And when he came he sent me for Geoghegan and that was only an excuse to get me away, and what he and the mother tried to bring her to do was to face death, and they knew I wouldn't allow that if I was there. But the wife was very stout and she wouldn't give in to them. So the priest read more, and he asked would I be willing to lose something, and I said, so far as a cow or a calf I wouldn't mind losing that. Well, she partly recovered, but from that day, no year went by but I lost ten lambs maybe or other things. And twice they took my children out of the bed, two of them I have lost. And the others they gave a touch to. That girl there—see the way she is, and can't walk. In one minute it came on her out in the field, with the fall of a wall.

It was one among *them* that wanted the wife. A woman and a boy we often saw come to the door, and she was the matchmaker. And when we would go out, they would have vanished.

You can cure all things brought about by *them*, but not any common ailment. But there is no cure for the stroke given by a queen or a fool. There is a queen in every house or regiment of them. It is of those they steal away they make queens for as long as they live or that they are satisfied with them.

There were two women fighting at a spring of water, and one hit the other on the head with a can and killed her. And after that her children began to die. And the husband went to Biddy Early and as soon as she saw him she said, 'There's nothing I can do for you, your wife was a wicked woman, and the one she hit is a queen among them, and she is taking your children one by one and you must suffer till twenty-one years are up.' And so he did.

The stroke of a fool, there's no cure for either. There are many fools among them dressed in strange clothes like one of the mummers that used to be going through the country. But it might be the fools are the wisest after all. There are two classes, the Dundonians that are like ourselves, and another race, more wicked and more spiteful. Very small they are and wide, and their belly sticks out in front, so that what they carry they don't carry it on the back, but in front, on the belly in a bag.

As to their treasure, it's best to be without it. There was a man living by a stream, and where his house touched the stream, he built a little room and left it for them, clean and in good order, the way they'd like it. And whenever he'd want money, for a fair or the like, he'd find it laid on the table in the morning. And when he had it again, he'd leave it there, and it would be taken away in the night. But after that going on for a time he lost his son. You should do that in your own big house. Set a little room for them—with spring water in it always—and wine you might leave—no, not flowers—they wouldn't want so much as that—but just what would show your good will.

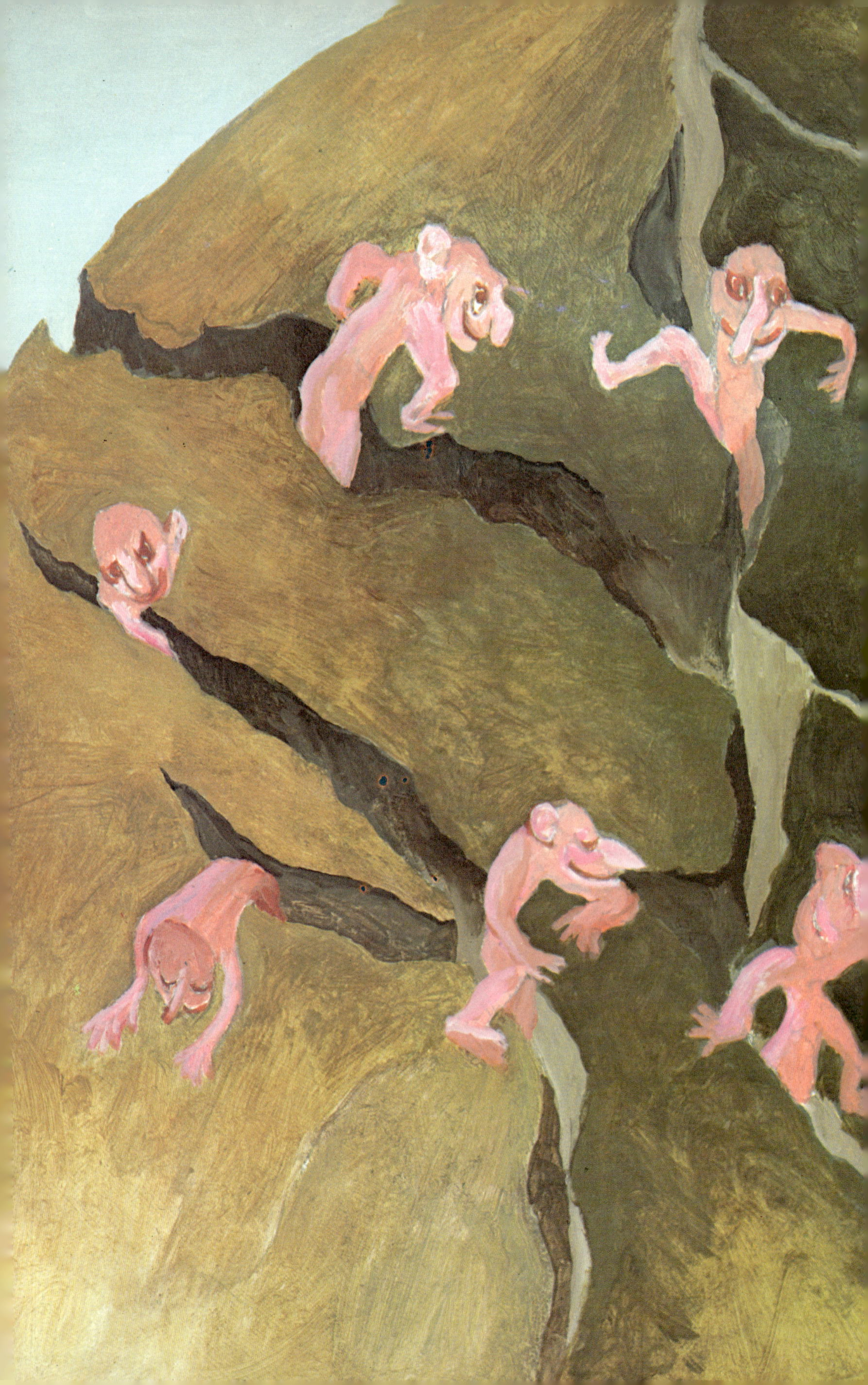

GOBLIN COMBE

There was a parcel of children and they was a-picking primroses, see, and one poor little dear her wandered away on her lone self right down into Goblin Combe. She were only a little trot, see, and didn't know no better. Well, when she do find she's a-lost she cries, and the tears do run down her dear little face, and drop on her pinafore like summer rain, and she do throw her little self a-down in her grief and the primroses they knock against a rock. Then the rock opens and there's the fairises all come to comfort her tears. They do give her a gold ball and they lead the dear little soul safe home—on account she was carrying primroses, see.

Well, 'twas the wonder of the village and the conjuror he gets the notion he'd get his fists on more than one gold ball when next the fairises opened the hill. So he do pick a bunch of primroses and he go on up Goblin Combe, and he was glad enough to get in to the rock after all he see and hear on the way up. Well, 'twasn't the right day, nor the right number of primroses, and he wasn't no dear little soul—so they took him!

THE THREE COWS

There was a farmer, and he had three cows, fine fat beauties they were. One was called Facey, the other Diamond, and the third Beauty. One morning he went into his cowshed, and there he found Facey so thin that the wind would have blown her away. Her skin hung loose about her, all her flesh was gone, and she stared out of her great eyes as though she'd seen a ghost; and what was more, the fireplace in the kitchen was one great pile of wood-ash. Well, he was bothered with it; he could not see how all this had come about.

Next morning his wife went out to the shed, and see! Diamond was for all the world as wisht a looking creature as Facey—nothing but a bag of bones, all the flesh gone, and half a rick of wood was gone, too; but the fireplace was piled up three feet high with white wood ashes. The farmer determined to watch the third night; so he hid in a closet which opened out of the parlour, and he left the door just ajar, that he might see what passed.

Tick, tick, went the clock, and the farmer was nearly tired of waiting; he had to bite his little finger to keep himself awake, when suddenly the door of his house flew open, and in rushed maybe a thousand pixies, laughing and dancing and dragging at Beauty's halter till they had brought the cow into the middle of the room. The farmer really thought he should have died with fright, and so perhaps he would had not curiosity kept him alive.

Tick, tick, went the clock, but he did not hear it now. He was too intent staring at the pixies and his last beautiful cow. He saw them throw her down, fall on her, and kill her; and then with their knives they ripped her open, and flayed her as clean as a whistle. Then out ran some of the little people and brought in firewood and made a roaring blaze on the hearth, and there they cooked the flesh of the cow—they baked and they boiled, they stewed and they fried.

'Take care,' cried one, who seemed to be the king, 'let no bone be broken.'

Well, when they had all eaten, and had devoured every scrap of beef on the cow, they began playing games with the bones, tossing them one to another. One little leg-bone fell close to the closet door, and the farmer was so afraid lest the pixies should come there and find him in their search for the bone, that he put out his hand, and drew it in to him. Then he saw the king stand on the table and say, 'Gather the bones!'

Round and round flew the imps, picking up the bones. 'Arrange them,' said the king; and they placed them all in their proper positions in the hide of the cow. Then they folded the skin over them, and the king struck the heap of bone and skin with his rod. Whisht! up sprang the cow and lowed dismally. It was alive again; but, alas! as the pixies dragged it back to its stall, it halted in the off fore-foot, for a bone was missing.

> The cock crew,
> Away they flew

And the farmer crept trembling to bed.

PEERIFOOL

There was once a widowed Queen in Rousay, who was living in a small house with a kail-yard and a cow, and they found all their cabbages were being taken.

The eldest daughter said to the Queen she would put a blanket round her, and watch all night in the kail-yard. So after night fell, a very big giant came into the yard, and he began to cut the cabbages and put them into a creel.

The Princess said what was he doing with her mother's kail, and he said if she was not quiet, he would take her too. But she would not be quiet, so he flung her into the creel, and carried her away with the creel. When he got home he told her the work she had to do; she had to milk the cow, and take her up to the hills called Bloodfield, then she had to take wool, and wash, and tease, and comb, and card and spin it, and make it into cloth. When the giant had gone, she milked the cow, and drove her into the high hills, then she made a bowl of porridge for herself. As she was supping it, a crowd of little yellow-heads, the peerie folk, came running in, asking for some.

She said:

> Little for one, and less for two,
> And never a grain have I for you.

A crowd of peerie folk asking for some.

So they went away, and she set to on her wool, but she could do nothing with it. At night the giant came back, and he was very angry, and took a strip of skin off her, from the crown of her head to the sole of her foot, and threw her up over the rafters, among the hens, where she could neither move nor speak. And the same thing happened to the second daughter.

The third night the youngest Princess sat down to watch, and the giant carried her off as he had done her sisters, and set her the same tasks. She drove the cow up to the high hills, and she made herself a bowl of porridge, but when the peerie folk came in, she told them to get something to sup with.

Some got heather cows, and some got broken dishes, but they all got a share of her porridge. When they had gone, a peerie yellow-headed boy came in, and asked if she had any work for him. He could do anything with wool. She said she had plenty of work, but nothing to pay him with, but he said he would do it for nothing if she would tell him his name. So she got him the wool and he went out. When it was getting dark, an old woman came to the door and asked her for lodging. She dared not grant it, so the old woman went out to the high knowe, and lay under it for shelter. But it was hot, and she climbed up to the top for air. There was a crack at the top, and light coming out, and the old woman heard a voice saying: 'Tease, teasers, tease; card, carders, card; spin, spinners, spin; for Peerifool, Peerifool, is my name.' She looked in, and there she saw the peerie folk working and the peerie boy running round them. The old woman thought she had news worth a lodging, and went back to tell the Princess. When the peerie boy came back with the cloth, the Princess guessed one name, and then another, and at last she said: 'Peerifool is your name.' He threw down the wool, and ran off very angry. As the giant was coming home that night, he met a great number of peerie folk, with their tongues hanging out of their mouths, and their eyes hanging out in their cheeks. He asked them what was the matter, and they said it was pulling out the wool so fine. The giant said he had a bonnie goodwife at home, and if she had done her work this time, he would never make her work so again. When he came home, she had a great store of cloth, and he was very pleased with her. Next day when the giant went out, the Princess found her sisters, and she took them down from the rafters, and put the strips of skin back on them, and she hid the eldest in a big creel, and put some fine things in with her, and grass on top, and in the evening she asked the giant to carry it to her mother's to feed the cow. The giant would do anything for her now, so he carried it, and the next night he carried the second sister in the same way. The third day she told the giant that one more creel would do, and she would have it ready, but she might be out herself for a short while. So then she hid herself in the basket, with all the fine things she could find, and pulled grass over herself, and the giant carried her home. But the Queen and her two daughters had a great boiler of boiling water ready, and when he had set down the basket, they poured it over him from the upper window, and that was the end of the giant.

REWARDS AND PUNISHMENT

TATTERCOATS

In a great palace by the sea there once dwelt a very rich old lord, who had neither wife nor children living, only one little granddaughter, whose face he had never seen in all her life. He hated her bitterly, because at her birth his favourite daughter died; and when the old nurse brought him the baby, he swore, that it might live or die as it liked, but he would never look on its face as long as it lived.

So he turned his back, and sat by his window looking out over the sea, and weeping great tears for his lost daughter, till his white hair and beard grew down over his shoulders and twined round his chair and crept into the chinks of the floor, and his tears, dropping on to the window-ledge, wore a channel through the stone, and ran away in a little river to the great sea. And, meanwhile, his granddaughter grew up with no one to care for her or clothe her; only the old nurse, when no one was by, would sometimes give her a dish of scraps from the kitchen, or a torn petticoat from the rag-bag; while the other servants of the palace would drive her from the house with blows and mocking words, calling her 'Tattercoats', and pointing at her bare feet and shoulders, till she ran away crying, to hide among the bushes.

And so she grew up, with little to eat or wear, spending her days in the fields and lanes, with only the gooseherd for a companion, who would play to her so merrily on his little pipe, when she was hungry, or cold, or tired, that she forgot all her troubles, and fell to dancing, with his flock of noisy geese for partners.

But, one day, people told each other that the king was travelling through the land, and in the town near by was to give a great ball, to all the lords and ladies of the country, when the prince, his only son, was to choose a wife.

One of the royal invitations was brought to the palace by the sea, and the servants carried it up to the old lord, who still sat by his window, wrapped in his long white hair and weeping into the little river that was fed by his tears.

But when he heard the king's command, he dried his eyes and bade them bring shears to cut him loose, for his hair had bound him a fast prisoner and he could not move. And then he sent them for rich clothes, and jewels, which he put on; and he ordered them to saddle the white horse, with gold and silk, that he might ride to meet the king.

Meanwhile Tattercoats had heard of the great doings in the town, and she sat by the kitchen-door weeping because she could not go to see them. And when the old nurse heard her crying she went to the lord of the palace, and begged him to take his granddaughter with him to the king's ball.

But he only frowned and told her to be silent, while the servants laughed and said: 'Tattercoats is happy in her rags, playing with the gooseherd, let her be—it is all she is fit for.'

A second, and then a third time, the old nurse begged him to let the girl go with him, but she was answered only by black looks and fierce words, till she was driven from the room by the jeering servants, with blows and mocking words.

Weeping over her ill success, the old nurse went to look for Tattercoats; but the girl had been turned from the door by the cook, and had run away to tell her friend the gooseherd how unhappy she was because she could not go to the king's ball.

But when the gooseherd had listened to her story, he bade her

*beard and hair crept
over his shoulders
twined around the*

cheer up, and proposed that they should go together into the town to see the king and all the fine things; and when she looked sorrowfully down at her rags and bare feet, he played a note or two upon his pipe, so gay and merry that she forgot all about her tears and her troubles, and before she well knew, the herdboy had taken her by the hand, and she, and he, and the geese before them, were dancing down the road towards the town.

Before they had gone very far, a handsome young man, splendidly dressed, rode up and stopped to ask the way to the castle where the king was staying; and when he found that they, too, were going thither, he got off his horse and walked beside them along the road.

The herdboy pulled out his pipe and played a low sweet tune, and the stranger looked again and again at Tattercoats's lovely face till he fell deeply in love with her, and begged her to marry him.

But she only laughed, and shook her golden head.

'You would be finely put to shame if you had a goosegirl for your wife!' said she; 'go and ask one of the great ladies you will see tonight at the king's ball, and do not flout poor Tattercoats.'

But the more she refused him the sweeter the pipe played, and the deeper the young man fell in love; till at last he begged her, as a proof of his sincerity, to come that night at twelve to the king's ball, just as she was, with the herdboy and his geese, and in her torn petticoat and bare feet, and he would dance with her before the king and the lords and ladies, and present her to them all, as his dear and honoured bride.

So when night came, and the hall in the castle was full of light and music, and the lords and ladies were dancing before the king, just as the clock struck twelve, Tattercoats and the herdboy, followed by his flock of noisy geese, entered at the great doors, and walked straight up the ballroom, while on either side the ladies whispered, the lords laughed, and the king seated at the far end stared in amazement.

But as they came in front of the throne, Tattercoats's lover rose from beside the king, and came to meet her. Taking her by the hand, he kissed her thrice before them all, and turned to the king.

'Father!' he said, for it was the prince himself, 'I have made my choice, and here is my bride, the loveliest girl in all the land, and the sweetest as well!'

Before he had finished speaking, the herdboy put his pipe to his lips and played a few low notes that sounded like a bird singing far off in the woods; and as he played, Tattercoats's rags were changed to shining robes sewn with glittering jewels, a golden crown lay upon her golden hair, and the flock of geese behind her became a crowd of dainty pages, bearing her long train.

And as the king rose to greet her as his daughter, the trumpets sounded loudly in honour of the new princess, and the people outside in the street said to each other:

'Ah! now the prince has chosen for his wife the loveliest girl in all the land!'

But the gooseherd was never seen again, and no one knew what became of him; while the old lord went home once more to his palace by the sea, for he could not stay at court, when he had sworn never to look on his granddaughter's face.

So there he still sits by his window, if you could only see him, as you some day may, weeping more bitterly than ever, as he looks out over the sea.

THREE HEADS OF THE WELL

There was a king and a queen, and the king had a daughter, and the queen had a daughter. And the king's daughter was bonny and good-natured, and everybody liked her; and the queen's daughter was ugly and ill-natured, and nobody liked her. And the queen didn't like the king's daughter, and wanted her away. So she sent her to the well at the world's end, to get a bottle o' water. Well, she took her bottle, and she went and she went till she came to a pony that was tethered, and the pony said to her:

Flit me, flit me, my bonny May,
For I haven't been flitted this seven year and a day.

And the king's daughter said: 'Ay will I, my bonny pony, I'll flit ye.' So the pony gave her a ride over the moor o' hecklepins.

Well, she went far and far and further than I can tell, till she came to the well at the world's end; and when she came to the well it was awful deep, and she couldn't get her bottle dipped. And as she was looking down, thinking what to do, there looked up to her three shaggy heads, and they said to her:

Wash me, wash me, my bonny May,
And dry me wi' yer clean linen apron.

And she said: 'Ay will I; I'll wash ye.' So she washed the three old men's heads, and dried them with her clean linen apron; and then they took and dipped her bottle for her.

And the shaggy heads said the one to the other:

Weird, brother, weird, what'll ye weird?

And the first one said: 'I weird that if she was bonny afore, she'll be ten times bonnier.' And the second one said: 'I weird that every time she speaks, a diamond and a ruby and a pearl drop out of her mouth.' And the third one said: 'I weird that every time she combs her head, she'll get a peck o' gold and a peck o' silver out of it.'

Well, she came home to the king's court again, and if she was bonny before, she was ten times bonnier. And the queen was that vexed, she didn't know what to do, but she thought she would send her own daughter to see if she could fall in with the same luck. So she gave her a bottle and sent her away to the well at the world's end.

Well the queen's daughter went and went until she came to the pony, and the pony said:

Flit me, flit me, my bonny May,
For I haven't been flitted this seven year and a day.

And the queen's daughter said: 'O ye nasty beast, do ye think I'll flit ye? Do ye ken who ye're speaking till? I'm a queen's dochter.' Well, she wouldn't flit the pony, and the pony wouldn't give her a ride over

She saw three sh
heads in the wel

the moor o' hecklepins. And she had to go on her bare feet, and the hecklepins cut at her feet, and she could hardly go at all.

Well, she went far and far and further than I can tell, till she came to the well at the world's end. And the well was deep, and she couldn't get her bottle dipped; and as she was looking down, thinking what to do, there looked up to her three shaggy heads, and they said to her:

> Wash me, wash me, my bonny May,
> And dry me wi' yer clean linen apron.

And she said: 'O ye nasty dirty beasts, di' ye think I'm going to wash ye? Di' yer ken who ye're speaking till? I'm a queen's dochter.' And she wouldn't wash them, and they wouldn't dip her bottle for her.

And the old men's heads said the one to the other:

> Weird, brother, weird, what'll ye weird?

And the first one said: 'I weird that if she was ugly afore, she'll be ten times uglier.' And the second said: 'I weird that every time she speaks, a frog and a toad jump out o' her mouth.' And the third one said: 'I weird that every time she combs her head, she'll get a peck o' lice and a peck o' fleas out of it.'

So she went away home again, and if she was ugly before, she was ten times uglier. And there was a bonny young prince came and married the king's daughter; and the queen's daughter had to put up with an old cobbler, and he beat her every day with a leather strap.
She knew there were only three other drops in the green bottle and she was afraid. She ran as fast as she could to the Black Well, but who should be there before her but the wee ugly bogle himself, singing:

> O gie me my water, my honey, my hert,
> O gie me my water, my ain kind dearie;
> For don't you mind upon the time
> We met in the wood at the Well so wearie?

She gave him the water, not forgetting the three drops from the green bottle. But he had scarcely drunk the witched water when he vanished, and there was a fine young prince, who spoke to her as if he had known her all her days.

They sat down beside the Black Well.

'I was born the same night as you,' he said, 'and I was carried away by the fairies the same night as you were found on the lip of the Well. I was a bogle for so many years because the fairies were scared away. They made me play many tricks before they would let me go, and return to my father, the King of France, and make the bonniest lass in all the world my bride.'

'Who is she?' said the maiden.

'The miller of Cuthilldorie's daughter,' said the young Prince.

Then they went home and told their stories over again, and that very night they were married. A coach came for them, and the miller and his wife, and the Prince and the Princess, drove away singing:

O but we're happy, my honey, my hert,
  O but we're happy, my ain kind dearie;
For don't you mind upon the time
  When we met in the wood at the Well so wearie?

THAT'S ENOUGH TO GO ON WITH

There was a little boy and a little girl, and they lived in a poor little hut, and they never had enough to eat, but their granny taught them good manners, and people liked them for it, and sometimes they'd give them a bite here and there—old cabbage leaves, a little scrumpy, or turnip for the pot, even a few bones for soup, or stale crusts the hens left over, and they always said: 'No more, please. That's enough to go on with, thank you kindly,' when they got it, so they did fairly well.

Now there was a fat rich farmer who lived close by, with fine orchards, and corn ricks, and a herd of cows, but he sold every cabbage leaf, and he counted all his turnips, he never had any meat (it cost money) and there weren't any crusts left over either—so he grew richer and richer, and fatter and fatter. When the little boy and the little girl took their little goat to grass, they had to go along a lane near his fields, and his dog chased them away. And he came and threw stones at their old granny picking up twigs in her own little plot, and said she was a witch and stole his cows' milk, and that was a terrible lie. Their little goat did give just one sup of milk among them. So the little boy and girl and the goat had to go farther away to find grass the farmer couldn't call his, and one day the poor hungry little goat broke its tether and ran away into the Little Men's Wood, where the grass grew thick. The little boy and the little girl ran after the goat, for they knew no one ever went there and they were very frightened, but they remembered their good manners and they called out, 'Please forgive our hungry goat—may we come into your wood and catch her? Thank you kindly', and on they went. But the little goat wasn't eating grass, she was eating strawberries as fast as she could. The wood was red with them. The little boy and the little girl looked and looked and then they said, 'We are very hungry, and so is our granny at home. May we pick a handful?'

And the mischievous little men called out: 'Pick all you want.' For the strawberries were magic ones and you had to go on eating and eating unless you gave thanks. But the granny had taught them well, and they only picked a double handful to take home to her and ate far less than the goat, then they said, 'No more, please—that's enough to go on with, and thank you kindly,' and the goat was able to stop gobbling and go with them safe out of the wood.

They never went short of rich milk after that, and ripe strawberries grew in their bit of garden all the year round, so they never went hungry either. Now one day the fat farmer spied their strawberries

The strawberries w
magic ones.

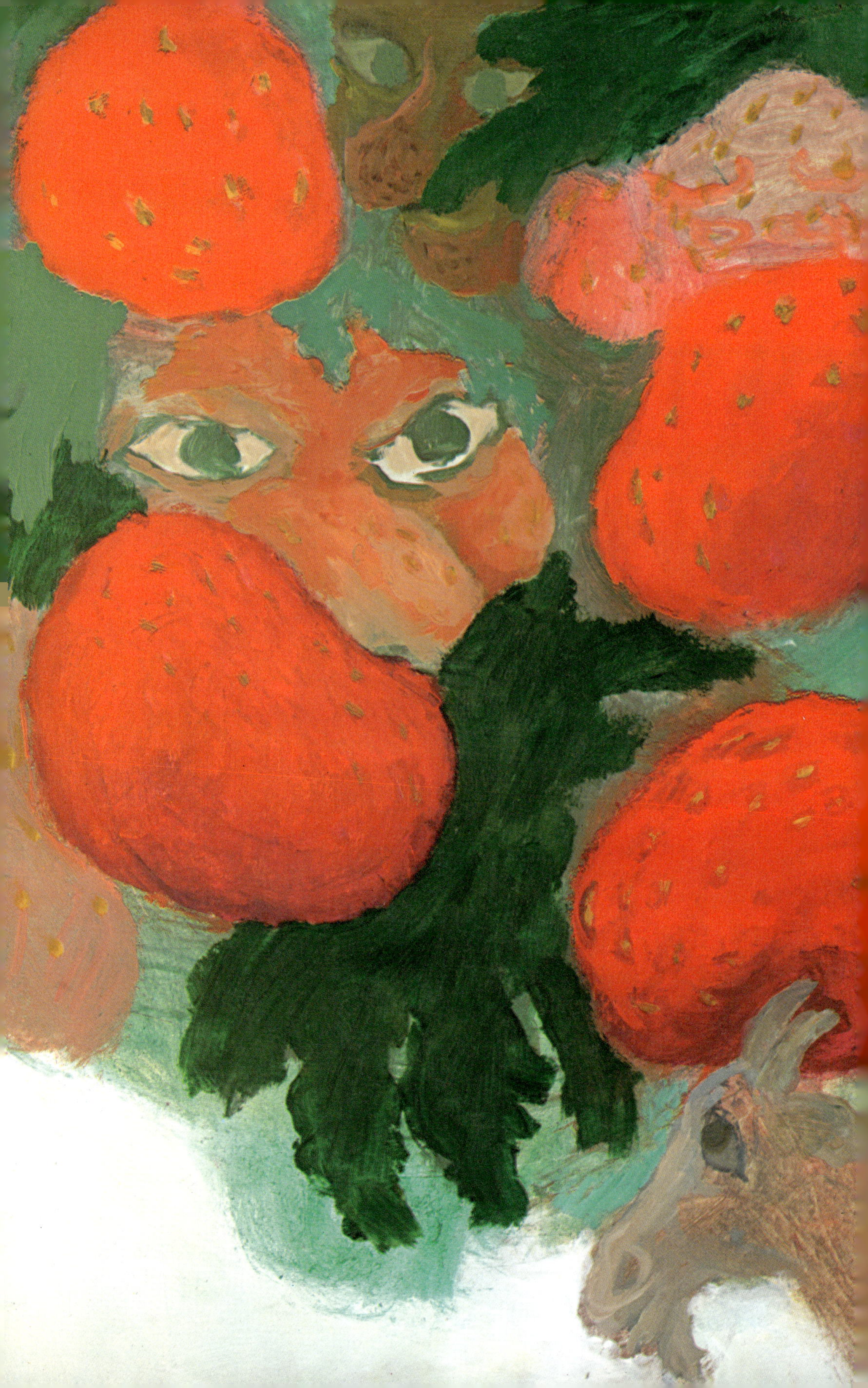

all red in the snow and he up and oped their gate and in he came.

'Where did you steal the strawberries I grow to sell?' he shouted and *that* was a terrible lie.

But they told him they must have come from the Little Men's Wood.

'That wood is mine too!' he yelled, and *that* was a worse lie still, for the Little Men heard him.

Then he picked every strawberry in the garden, and began to eat them, while the children watched quietly. They knew when he went another crop would ripen again for their supper time—but the farmer, he raved for more.

'They grow in the Little Men's Wood,' said they, and off he rushed as fast as he could to get there. There were hundreds of berries growing in the snow and he ate, and he ate, and he couldn't stop to say 'Please', and he ate, and he ate, and he didn't ask leave, and he ate, and he ate, and he didn't know how to say 'That's enough' or 'Thank you kindly', so he ate and he ate all day, and all night, and all the week thro', and when Sunday came he burst with a bang.

THE FAIRY WIFE

There was a young man below in the Rosses long ago. He was living alone. One day as he was straining potatoes at the doorway, a woman came up to him, and he spoke to her.

'Come in,' said he.

'I won't go in today,' said she.

Next day, she came to the door again when he was straining potatoes.

'Come in,' said he.

'I won't go in today,' said she.

On the third day, he was straining potatoes again when the woman came.

'Come in,' said he.

'Very well, I'll go in today,' said she.

She went in and lived there with him. About a year later, she gave birth to a son. A good while after that, the harvest fair was to be held in Glenties.

'I think I'll go to the fair today,' said the young man. 'I want to meet my friends from around Glenties. I have uncles living there.'

'Do, of course,' said his wife.

He set out for the fair. He saw his uncles there, but instead of coming to speak to him, it was as though they were avoiding him. At last he went up and stood in front of one of them and asked what was wrong.

'What crime have I committed?' he asked. 'I haven't met ye for a long time, and all ye do is avoid me.'

'Why shouldn't we avoid you,' said the uncle, 'when we hear that you have married a fairy woman? If you had come to us first, we

A door opened in the and a boy came out.

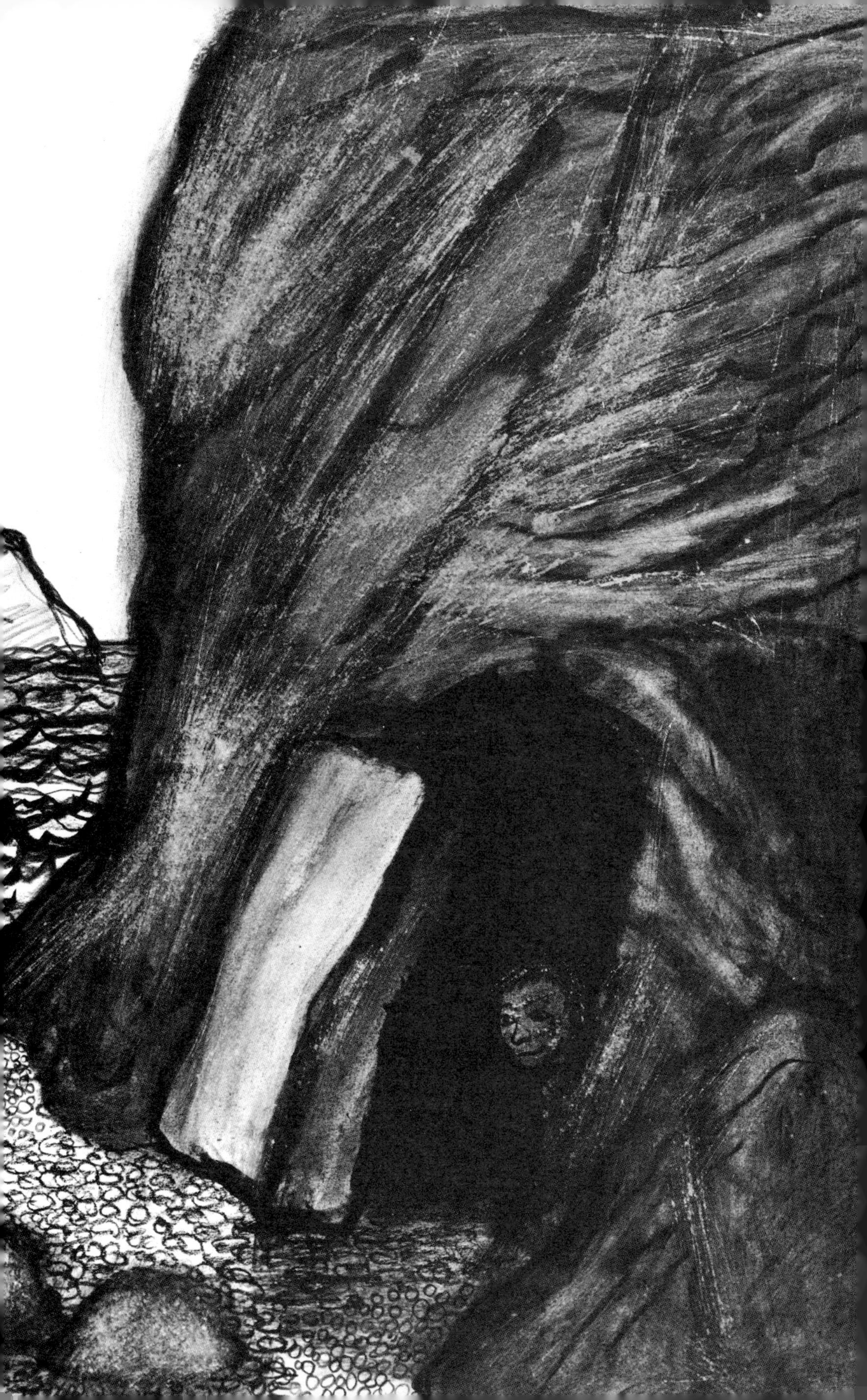

would have got a good wife for you, and you needn't have taken up with her at all. Now,' said the uncle, 'I'm going to buy a knife for you to kill her with when you go home.'

The uncle bought a knife for him. The young man took it home, but even if he did, he had no wish to kill her. There was a field of corn near the house, and as he passed it on his way home, he threw the knife into it as far as he could. His wife was sitting in the kitchen when he got home.

'Well, how did you put in the day?' she asked.

'Very well,' said he.

'What humour were your uncles in?'

'Good,' said he.

'You should tell the truth,' said she. 'They were in a bad humour. One of them told you you had married a fairy woman, and that if you had gone to them first, they would have picked a good wife for you. And didn't he buy a knife for you to kill me with?'

'He did, surely,' said the husband.

'And you threw it away from you into the corn?'

'I did.'

''Tis well that you did,' said she. 'I'm going to leave you altogether now, and you can go to your uncles, and let them pick a wife for you.'

She left and took the child with her.

'Now,' said she, as she was leaving, 'it won't be long until you marry again. Every night when you are going to bed, I want you to leave a light burning and some food on the table for me. The child and myself will come to eat it.'

And so it happened. It wasn't long after till he got married. Late one night when he and his wife were in bed in the kitchen, she turned her head and saw the woman and her child having a good meal. Then they left. Some time later, she saw the woman and child at the table again. The woman in bed gave a laugh that echoed through the house. Then the woman at the table spoke.

'That's a laugh that you will cry for yet,' said she.

She left the house and never came back.

The husband was well off and wanted for nothing. But after a while, all his cattle began to die on him, and in the end, he was left with only a mare and foal. The foal was almost reared. One day when he was putting them out to graze, the mare galloped over a cliff and was killed. All he had then was the foal. He took her and put her on an island to keep her from harm.

When the foal was a year or two old, the man said to his wife one day, 'I think I'll go for the foal today and take her to the fair and sell her.'

He took the foal off the island. As he was taking her along the road to the fair, he came to where there was a cliff at the side of the road. As they were passing by, a door opened in the cliff, and a boy came out.

'What are you asking for the foal?' said he.

The man named the price.

'I'll give you five pounds for her,' said the boy.

'That's not enough,' said the man.

'Take her to the fair then,' said the boy, 'and if you are offered more for her, take it. If you don't get more, come back this way, and I'll give you the five pounds.'

He reached the fair with the foal and kept her there till the evening. But if he did, he got no offer more than five pounds; so he decided that the first person that had made him that offer should get her. He brought the foal back home the same way. The boy was waiting for him and he gave him the foal.

'Come in now, and I'll give you the money,' said the boy.

He went in and saw his first wife sitting near the fire. As the boy was giving him the money, she spoke.

'Give him five pounds more,' said she.

The boy did so.

'And five more now,' said she.

The boy obeyed.

The man knew well that she was his first wife.

'Go home now,' said she. 'You have cried enough now for the laugh your wife gave the last night I was in your house. Go home now and buy cattle and sheep with the price of the foal. That's your son, who bought her from you. It won't be long until you are well off again.'

He went home and bought cattle and sheep with the price of the foal, and it wasn't long till he was as rich as he had been before. He prospered from day to day and was snug till the day of his death.

ORANGE AND LEMON

There were once a mother and a father who had two daughters, Orange and Lemon. The mother liked Lemon best, and the father Orange. The mother used to make Orange do all the dirty work, as soon as the father had turned his back. One day, she sent her to fetch milk, and said, 'If you break the pitcher, I'll kill you.' As Orange returned, she fell down and broke the pitcher, and so when she came home, she hid herself in the passage. When the mother came out, she saw the broken pitcher, and the girl, and took her into the house, when the girl cried:

'Oh, mother! Oh, mother! don't kill me!'

The mother said, 'Close the shutters in.'

'Oh, mother! Oh, mother! don't kill me!'

'Light the candle.'

'Oh, mother! Oh, mother! don't kill me!'

'Put the pan on.'

'Oh, mother! Oh, mother! don't kill me!'

'Fetch the block we chop the wood on.'

'Oh, mother! Oh, mother! don't kill me!'

'Bring the axe.'

'Oh, mother! Oh, mother! don't kill me!'

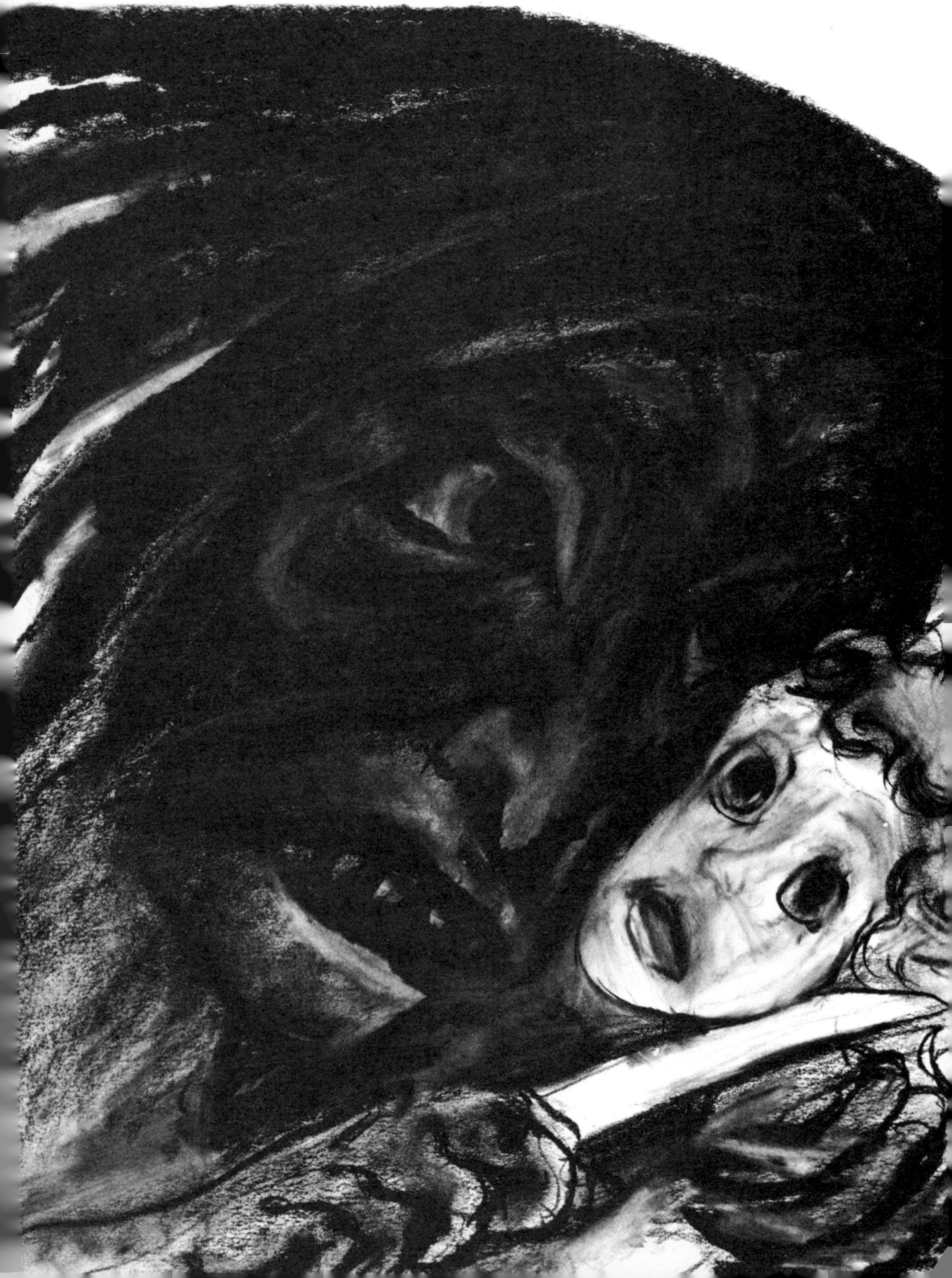

'Put your head on the block.'
'Oh, mother! Oh, mother! don't kill me!'
But the mother chopped off her head, and cooked it for dinner. When the father came home, he asked what there was for dinner.
'Sheep's head,' replied the mother.
'Where's Orange?'
'Not come from school yet.'
'I don't believe you,' said the father. Then he went upstairs and found fingers in a box, whereupon he was so overcome that he fainted. Orange's spirit flew away to a jeweller's shop and said:

> My mother chopped my head off,
> My father picked my bones,
> My little sister buried me,
> Beneath the cold marble stones.

The jewellers said: 'If you say that again we will give you a gold watch.' So she said it again, and they gave her a gold watch. Then she went off to a bootshop, and said:

> My mother chopped my head off,
> My father picked my bones,
> My little sister buried me,
> Beneath the cold marble stones.

And the bootmakers said: 'If you say it again, we will give you a pair of boots.' So she said it again, and they gave her a pair of boots. Then she went to the stonemason's and said:

> My mother chopped my head off,
> My father picked my bones,
> My little sister buried me,
> Beneath the cold marble stones.

And the stonemasons said, 'If you say it again, we will give you a piece of marble as big as your head.' So she said it again, and they gave her a piece of marble as big as her head.

She took the things, and flew home, and sat at the top of the chimney, and shouted down:

> Father, father, come to me,
> And I will show thee what I've got for thee!

So he came, and she gave him a gold watch.
    Then she shouted down:

> Sister! sister! come to me,
> And I will show thee what I've got for thee.

So she came, and she gave her a pair of boots.
    Then she shouted down:

> Mother! Mother! come to me,
> And I will show thee what I've got for thee.

The mother put her head right up the chimney, when the big block of marble came down and killed her. Then Orange came down and lived with her father and Lemon happily ever after.

THE OLD MAN AT THE WHITE HOUSE

There was once a man who lived in a white house in a certain village, and he knew everything about everybody who lived in the place.

In the same village there lived a woman who had a daughter called Sally, and one day she gave Sally a pair of yellow gloves and threatened to kill her if she lost them.

Now Sally was very proud of her gloves, but she was careless enough to lose one of them. After she had lost it she went to a row of houses in the village and inquired at every door if they had seen her glove. But everybody said 'No,' and she was told to go and ask the old man that lived in the white house.

So Sally went to the white house and asked the old man if he had seen her glove. The old man said, 'I have thy glove, and I will give it to thee if thou wilt promise me to tell nobody where thou hast found it. And remember, if thou tells anybody I shall fetch thee out of bed when the clock strikes twelve at night.'

So he gave the glove back to Sally.

But Sally's mother got to know about her losing the glove, and said, 'Where did you find it?'

Sally said, 'I daren't tell, for if I do the old man will fetch me out of bed at twelve o'clock at night.'

Her mother said, 'I will bar all the doors and fasten all the windows and then he can't get in and fetch thee.' And she made Sally tell her where she had found her glove.

So Sally's mother barred all the doors and fastened all the windows, and Sally went to bed at ten o'clock that night and began to cry. At eleven she began to cry louder, and at twelve o'clock she heard a voice saying in a whisper, but gradually getting louder and louder:

'Sally, I'm up one step.'
'Sally, I'm up two steps.'
'Sally, I'm up three steps.'
'Sally, I'm up four steps.'
'Sally, I'm up five steps.'
'Sally, I'm up six steps.'
'Sally, I'm up seven steps.'
'Sally, I'm up eight steps.'
'Sally, I'm up nine steps.'
'Sally, I'm up ten steps.'
'Sally, I'm up eleven steps.'
'Sally, I'm up twelve steps!'
'Sally, I'm at thy bedroom door!'
'SALLY, I HAVE HOLD OF THEE!'

He knew everything about everybody.

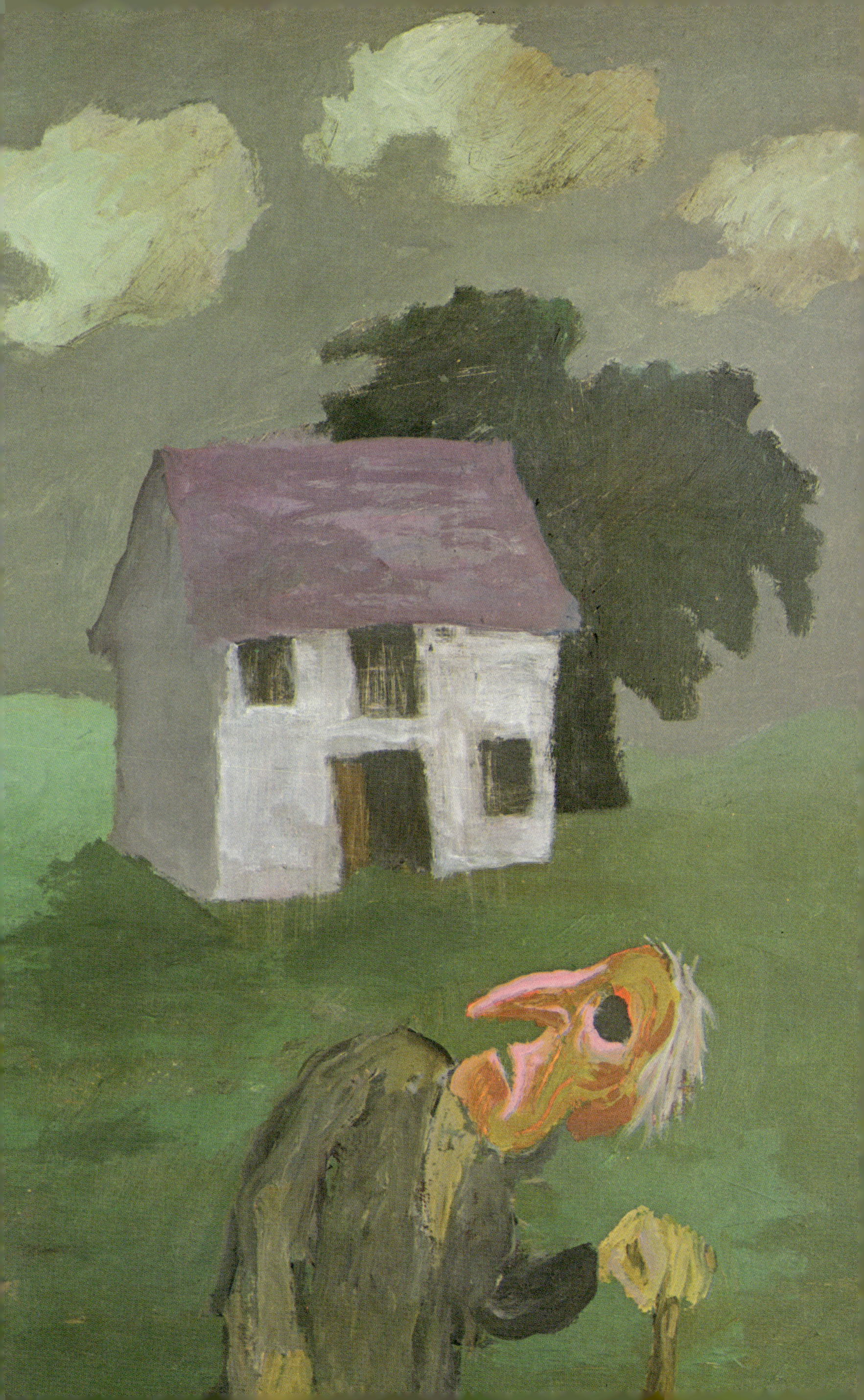

THE FAIRY FOLLOWER

There was once a lad, and he loved a girl with all his heart, and all he wanted was health and wealth to marry her. His love was so hot that he could not bear to wait, but set to get help from the fairies. It was an unchancy thing to do, and he set about it the wrong way. First he took a fair white cloth without asking the farmer's wife's leave, and no good could come of that. Then he filled a pail of river water, and that wouldn't do. Then he tried a pail of well water, and that wouldn't do. At last, he filled a pail of clear spring water, and that was right enough, but he stood it outside the door on the night of the new moon, instead of inside, so nothing came of that. So he had to wait a whole month, till the next new moon, and for two nights running, he set the pail inside the door, but that wasn't good enough, and still nothing happened. So he waited another month; it was May by this time, and he swept the hearth, and put the pail of water to stand on it, two nights, before the new moon, and that was right. Just after midnight, he tiptoed down to the pail, and there was a thin gold oil on top of the water. He skimmed it off, and made a cake of it, with meal, and set it down on the fair white cloth. He made a circle and said the words and waited.

The door opened, and a dark fairy came in, and stretched out her hand for the cake.

'Not for thee,' he said, and he shouldn't have spoken.

Then a fair fairy came in, and stretched out her hand. He tapped her on the wrist and said, 'Not for thee.' But he shouldn't have touched her.

Then came a most beautiful lady in green, and she said, 'For me,' and ate the cake.

After that she was always with him, and he told her his wishes. She granted them right enough, but in a back-handed way that turned them all to bitterness. He wanted marriage, and he got it, but with a cruel old woman, the richest in the parish. So he had his money too, and small good it did him. Then a great pestilence came on the place, and people died to the right and left of him, and his poor pretty sweetheart, whom he had loved all his life, was the first to die. But the lad's great strength bore him through everything, and it seemed he could not die. But at length the fairy at his elbow, meddling and urging him this way and that, though no one else could see her, wore him down to a thread and he died. As he lay in his coffin, a dark, cloudy shadow came down over it, and out of the darkness a voice said, very cold and clear, 'For me.'

He waited till the new moon.

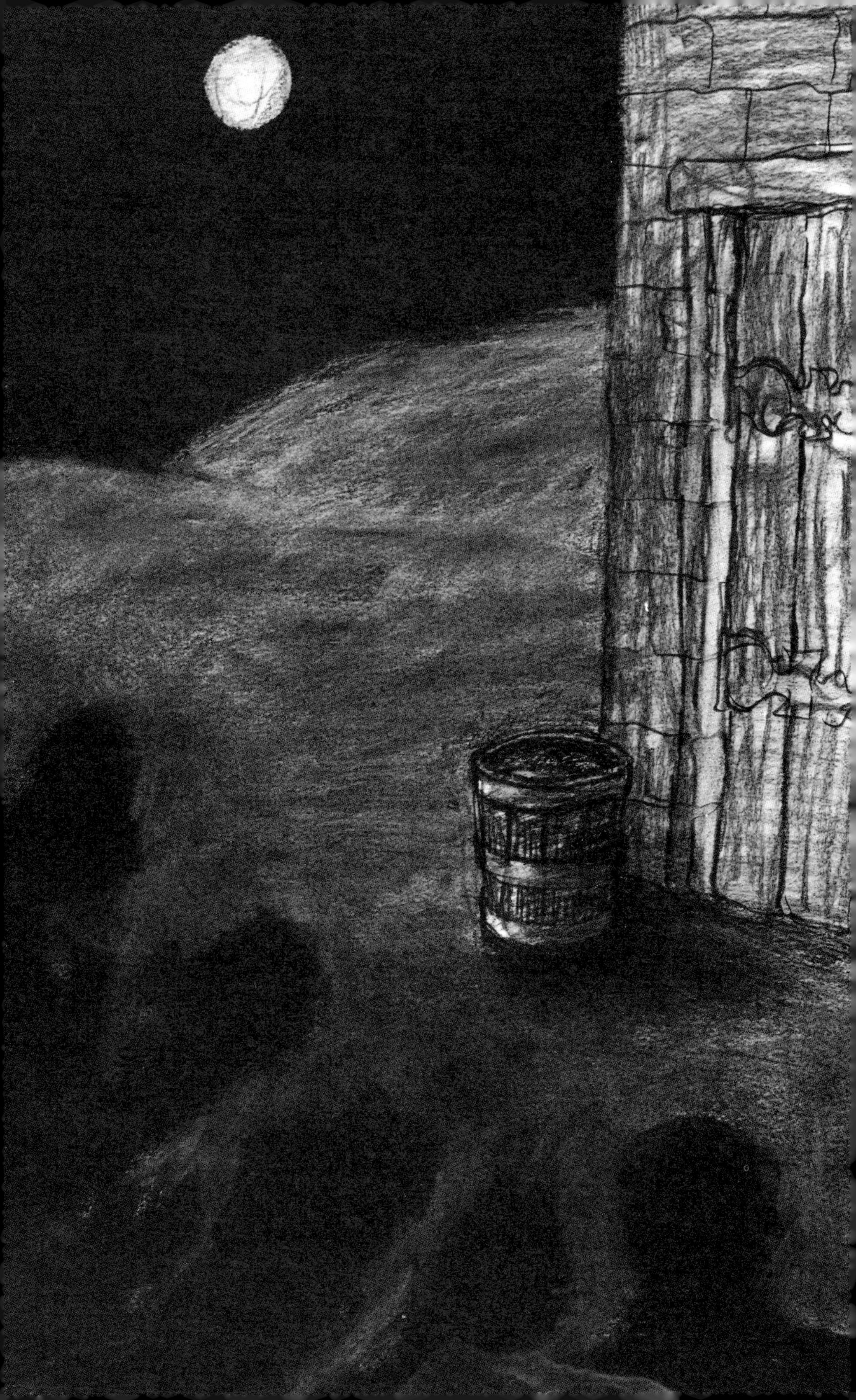

SILKEN JANET OR MUCKETTY MEG

> Blue eye beauty,
> Brown eye bonny,
> Grey eye grumpy,
> Green eye greedy,
> Black eye pick the pie,
> Lie in bed and tell a lie.

There was a pretty lass they called Jane, but she was proud and greedy and very poor. She thought her looks made a lady of her, and she wouldn't lift a finger to sweep or dust or clean herself, or help on the farm, or mind the sheep.

She said they were dirty, and when they answered her, 'Dirty beast,' she didn't like it.

She wouldn't milk the cows, she said they were mucky, and when they answered her 'Mucky Minny,' she didn't like that either.

As for the pigs, she said they smelled, and when they answered, 'Stinking slut,' she liked it no better.

One day she stole some silk from a Ladies' Bower on the Fairy Knoll and made herself a fine gown over her old rags, but she didn't wash; then she went to walk on the Fairy Knoll, and when they saw her on *their* land, in all her dirt and stolen finery, they had a mind to punish her. So all the beasts began to call out at her:

> Silken Janet she wears a fine gown,
> She stole it, she stole it from Down a Down,
> She never paid a penny,
> Because she hadn't any.

They made such a racket that people heard, and they caught Silken Janet, and were going to take away her fine dress, but it was so dirty they said she should be hanged in it. Then she cried out to the beasts to help her, but they all answered:

> Nobody likes a grimy lass,
> Nobody wants a stinking slut,
> Nobody needs a dirty beast,
> Go away and roll in the muck.

Well, she couldn't anyway, even if she wanted to.

Then she cried out to the lads, 'Will you not help a pretty lass?' But they answered her:

> Nobody likes a grimy lass,
> Nobody likes a stinking slut,
> Nobody wants a dirty beast,
> Go away and roll in the muck.

And she couldn't anyway, and the hangman got the rope round her neck—and then she saw a fine gentleman in green, and called out to him, 'Will you not save a pretty lass?'

The hangman got rope round her neck

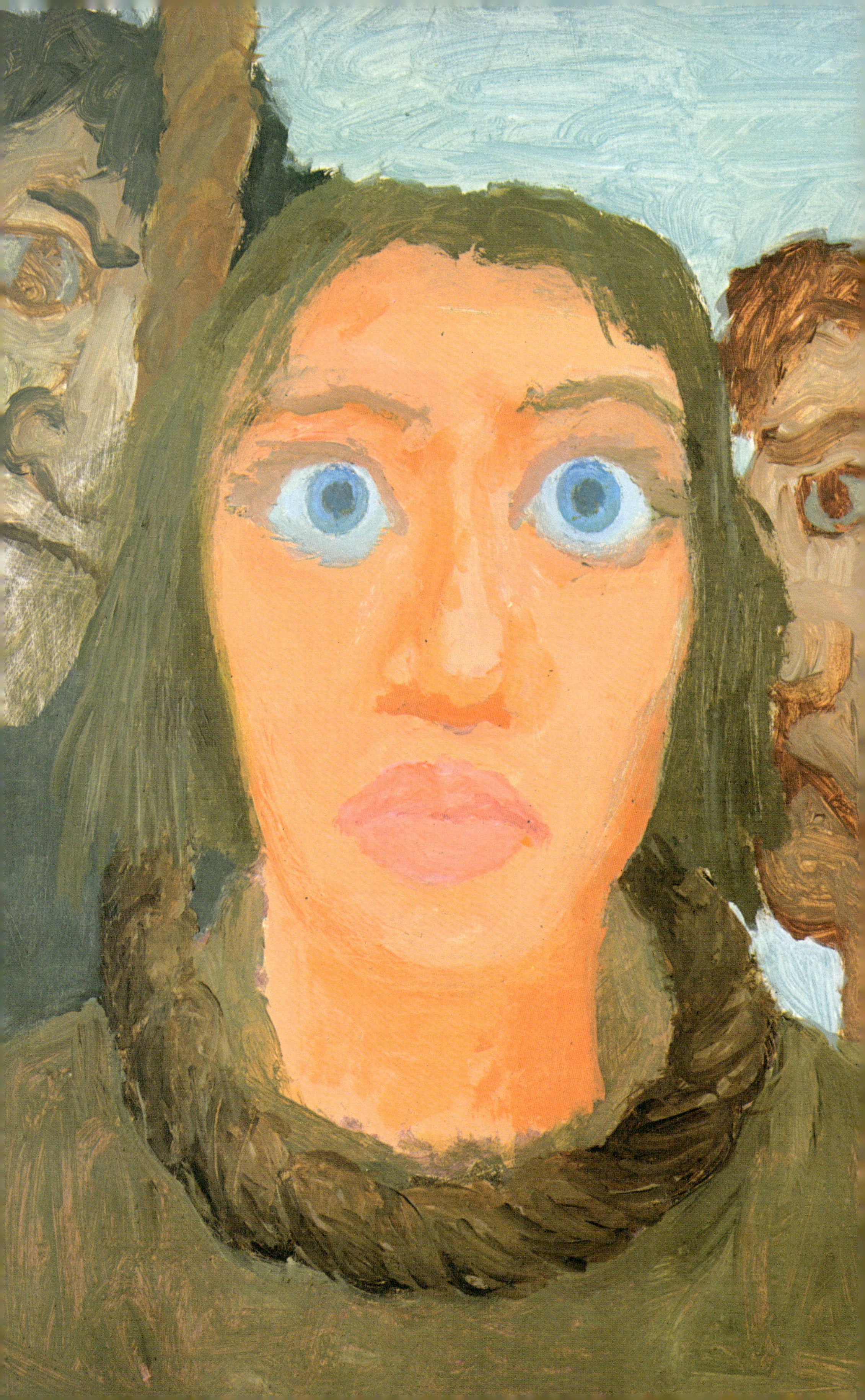

And he said, 'Leave it to me, but you must pay me your two blue eyes.'

'What will I see with?' she begged.

'Green ones,' said he, and took away her blue ones, and left her with green.

Well, she cried, but the rope was still there. 'I'll give you my fine golden gown,' she said.

'It's stolen! I'll not touch it. I want real gold,' he said.

'I have none,' she cried.

'There's all your pretty gold hair under the dirt. I'll take that.'

And he cut it all off.

'Now go and wash it in the river.'

And she got out of the rope and the crowd, and ran down to the river so fast she fell right in.

When she climbed out, she had lost the tresses of hair, so she sat and cried. But nobody came to hang her, and when she looked down, the golden gown had been washed off her, and her rags were clean as a daisy.

Then the pig came by. 'Good morning, clean lass,' said he.

Then a sheep came by. 'Pretty clean curly locks,' said she.

Then a cow came by with a pail on her horns. 'I'll let you milk me, my clean pretty lass,' she said. 'There's a crowd looking for a dirty golden slut that was to be hanged, and I don't want them to have my milk.'

So she set to milking, and did it quite well. And when the crowd came by, she kept her face hid against the cow. But the gentleman in green took her by the hair and looked at her. 'This is a clean lass,' he said. 'She's got a lint white linen gown, and curly lint white locks. She's got green eyes!' They were so disappointed they threw her in the river again.

When she climbed out this time, she couldn't see any crowd, or any gallows, or any gentleman in green. She was all in her washed rags, and her long golden hair hung down to dry about her, and she was on the Fairy Knoll.

'I best be out of here,' she said, and ran for home. She ran till her dry rags fluttered in the wind, and her golden hair streamed out around her and she met a young farmer.

'Good morning, blue eyes,' he said. 'I'm looking for a clean pretty wife to work all her days. Will you marry me?'

'That I will gladly,' said Silken Janet.

HUMOUR

THE MAN WHO HAD NO STORY

There was a man one time, and his name was Rory O'Donoghue. His wife was a great woman for knitting stockings, and Rory's job was to go from town to town, selling them.

There was to be a fair in Macroom on a certain day, and Rory left home the evening before with his bag of stockings to sell them at the fair next day. Night came on him before he reached the town. He saw a light in a house at the roadside, and he went in. There was no one inside before him but a very old man.

'You're welcome, Rory O'Donoghue,' said the old man.

Rory asked him for lodgings for the night and told him that he was on his way to the fair at Macroom. The old man said he could stay and welcome. A chair that was at the bottom of the kitchen moved up toward the fire, and the old man told Rory to sit on it.

'Now,' said the old man, 'Rory O'Donoghue and myself would like to have our supper.'

A knife and a fork jumped up from the dresser and cut down a piece of meat that was hanging from the rafters. A pot came out of the dresser, and the meat hopped into it. Up rose the tongs that were at the side of the hearth; they pulled out some sods of turf and made a fire. Down jumped the hangers and hooked the pot over the fire. A bucket of water rose up, and water was poured over the meat. The cover jumped onto the pot. A wickerwork sieve filled itself with potatoes, threw them into the bucket of water, and washed them. The potatoes then rose up and went into a second pot. The knife and fork went up to the first pot and the lid rose up. Up came a plate from the dresser. The knife and fork took out the meat from the pot and put it on the plate. The hangers took the pot off the fire and hung the pot of potatoes on it. When the potatoes were boiled, they strained off the water into the sieve. A tablecloth spread itself on the table. Up rose the sieve and spread the potatoes out on the table. The plate of meat jumped onto the table and so did two other plates as well as two knives and forks. A knife and fork cut the meat into two portions and put some on each plate.

'Get up, Rory O'Donoghue,' said the old man. 'Let us start eating!'

When they had eaten their supper, the tablecloth rose up and cleared off what was left into a bucket. Rory and the old man rose from the table and sat at either side of the fire. Two slippers came up to Rory O'Donoghue and two others to the old man.

'Take off your shoes, Rory, and put on those slippers,' said the old man. 'Do you know, Rory, how I spend my nights here? I spend one-third of each night eating and drinking, one-third telling stories or singing songs, and the last third sleeping. Sing a song for me now, Rory.'

'I never sang a song in my life,' said Rory.

'Tell a story, then.'

'I never told a story of any kind,' said Rory.

A knife and fork jump up from the dresser.

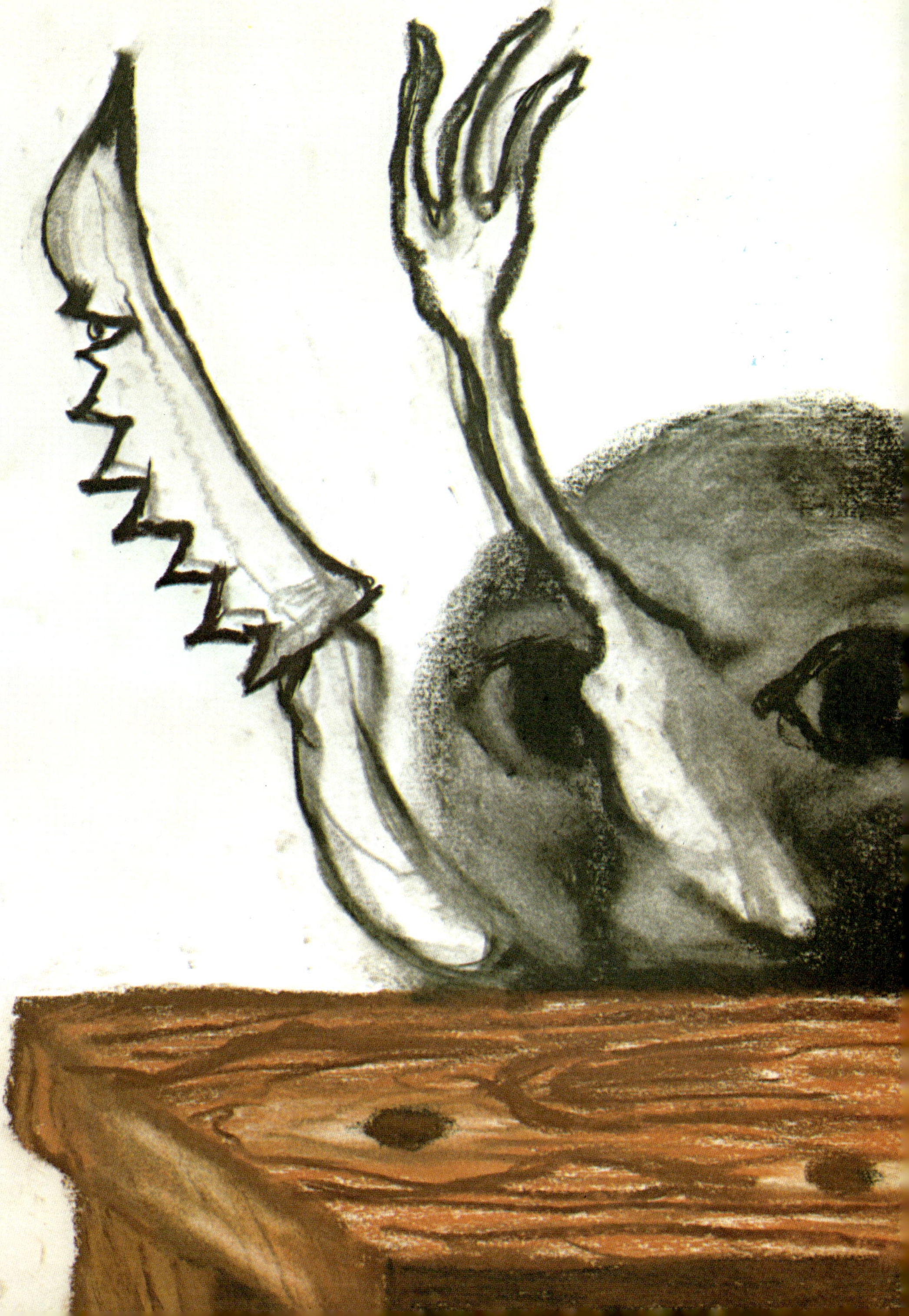

'Well, unless you tell a story or sing a song, you'll have to go off out the door,' said the old man.

'I can't do any of the two,' said Rory.

'Off out the door with you, then,' said the old man.

Rory stood up and took hold of his bag of stockings. No sooner had he gone out than the door struck him a blow on the back. He went off along the road, and he hadn't gone very far when he saw the glow of a fire by the roadside. Sitting by the fire was a man, who was roasting a piece of meat on a spit.

'You're welcome, Rory O'Donoghue,' said the man. 'Would you mind, Rory, taking hold of this spit and turning the meat over the fire? But don't let any burnt patch come on it.'

No sooner had Rory taken hold of the spit than the man left him. Then the piece of meat spoke.

'Don't let my whiskers burn,' it shouted.

Rory threw the spit and the meat from him, snatched up his bag of stockings, and ran off. The spit and the piece of meat followed him, striking Rory O'Donoghue as hard as they could on the back. Soon Rory caught sight of a house at the side of the road. He opened the door and ran in. It was the same house he had visited earlier, and the old man was in bed.

'You're welcome, Rory O'Donoghue,' said the old man. 'Come in here to bed with me.'

'Oh, I couldn't,' said Rory. 'I'm covered with blood!'

'What happened to you since you left here?' asked the old man.

'Oh, the abuse I got from a piece of meat that a man was roasting by the roadside,' said Rory. 'He asked me to turn the meat on the spit for a while, and 'twasn't long till the meat screamed at me not to burn its whiskers. I threw it from me, but it followed me, giving me every blow on the back, so that I'm all cut and bruised.'

'Ah, Rory,' said the old man. 'If you had a story like that to tell me, when I asked you, you wouldn't have been out until now. Lie in here on the bed now, and sleep the rest of the night.'

Rory went into the bed and fell asleep. When he awoke in the morning, he found himself on the roadside, with his bag of stockings under his head, and not a trace of a house or dwelling anywhere around him.

RAT'S CASTLE

Tom Tinker was on his way home with a load of new tins. There was rain and storms and a bad night for any Christian to be out. Broomsticks and queer laughings and all. 'I'll shelter a bit,' says Tom Tinker, 'and save my tins from rust, that's what I'll do. I'll wait up in Rat's Castle. It still has a good roof and four walls, for all it's got a queer name.'

So in he went.

There was a bogey three heads lifting roof.

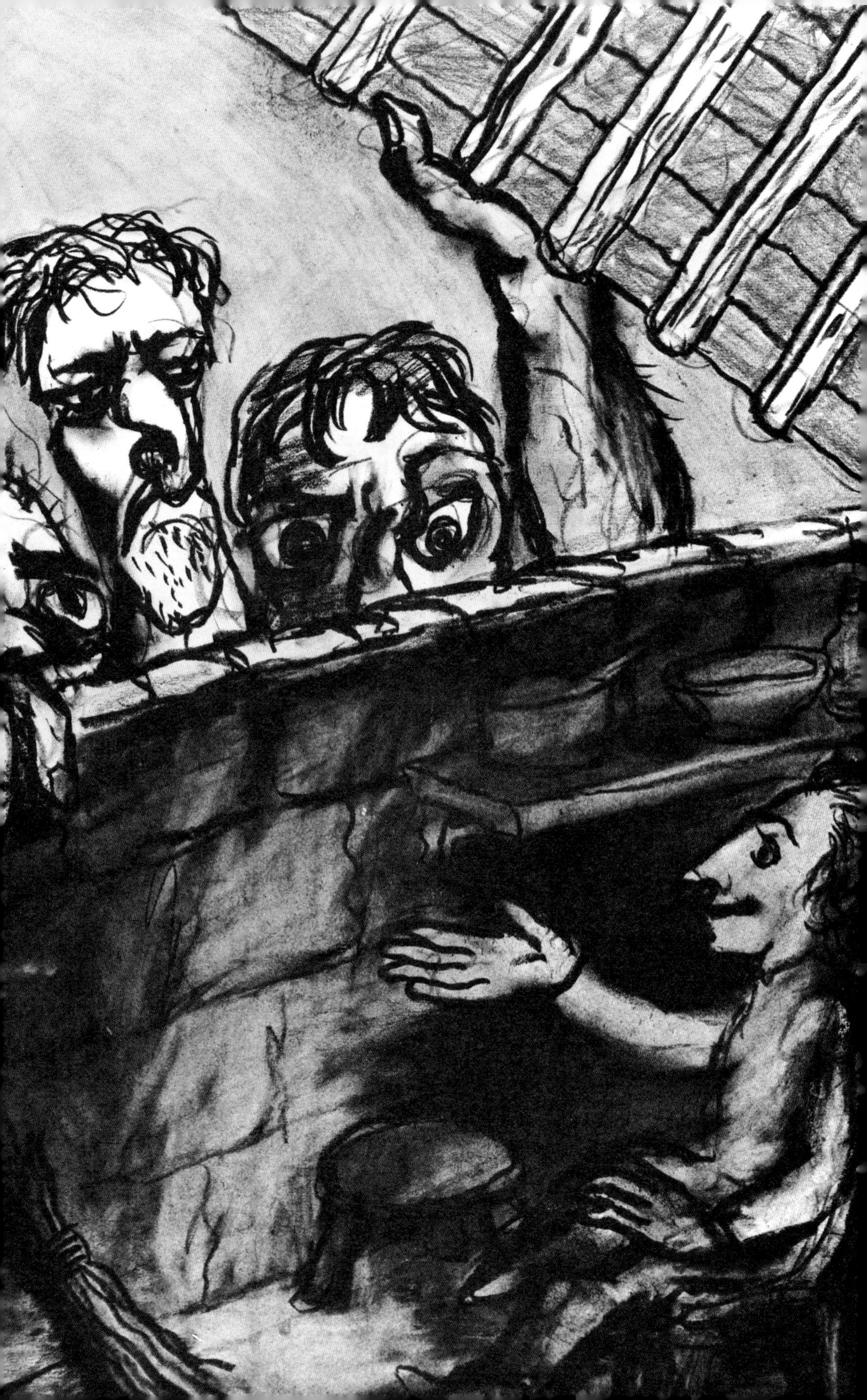

First thing he noted is there's no iron bar to door.

'I'll be ready for that,' says Tom Tinker, so he lit a good fire, made a brew of tea and put his tins to dry off and his tools all a-row, hot and handy. Then he filled a tin or two with tea and set them as near the fire as no matter, and he started on his own welcome drink.

He heard a nasty laugh and there was a grinning, hairy bogey sat opposite. Horrible sight he was. 'Aren't you frittened?' says he.

'Not exackly,' answers Tom Tinker. 'Just intrusted. Have a cup of tea.' And he handed out the boiling tea in the red-hot tin on his pincers.

The bogey takes it and tossed it off, relishing, then he crumpled the tin into a red-hot ball, and bunged it back straight at Tom Tinker's face.

Now Tom he was a master hand with a bat so up come the pincers and he slammed the red-hot ball straight back into the bogey's grin. That settled it. There was teeth all over the floor and he didn't wait for no more.

'Ruining my pincers,' says Tom and took a well-earned swig of his own tea, and there was another bogey bigger than the first and he'd got two heads to grin with.

'Aren't you frittened?' says he. 'Not exackly,' says Tom Tinker. 'Just intrusted. Have a cup of tea.' And this time the tin was white hot and the pincers steamed, but the tea went down easy and back came the tin in a white-hot ball straight at Tom Tinker.

He was ready and waiting for the bowling with his soldering-iron. Couldn't say whether ball hit one head or both but there was ten-inch teeth all scattered abroad and that one didn't wait for no more. 'I hope I'll get to finish my tea,' says Tom Tinker, but no, it wasn't to be. A huge hairy hand came clutching down the chimney and Tom let it have a stroke of his best with his hammer and there was a yell that shook the walls.

Tom Tinker he just heaved his dry sack of tins and his tools at the ready and he felt a draught of wind. He looked up and there was a bogey with three heads lifting off the roof.

'Not enough tea left,' says Tom, and he edged to the door.

It was part open and there was a long, scaly tail propping it wide.

Tom he took his tin-cutting shears to it and pinned it where it was.

'Aren't you frittened?' says Three Heads.

'Not exackly,' says Tom. 'You just bide there nicely. I'm going home to fetch my sledge-hammer.'

WHUPPITY STOORIE

There was once a gentleman that lived in a very grand house, and he married a young lady that had been delicately brought up. In her husband's house she found everything that was fine—fine tables and chairs, fine looking-glasses, and fine curtains; but then her husband expected her to be able to spin twelve hanks o' thread every day, besides attending to her house; and, to tell the even-down truth, the

Each mouth was away to one side

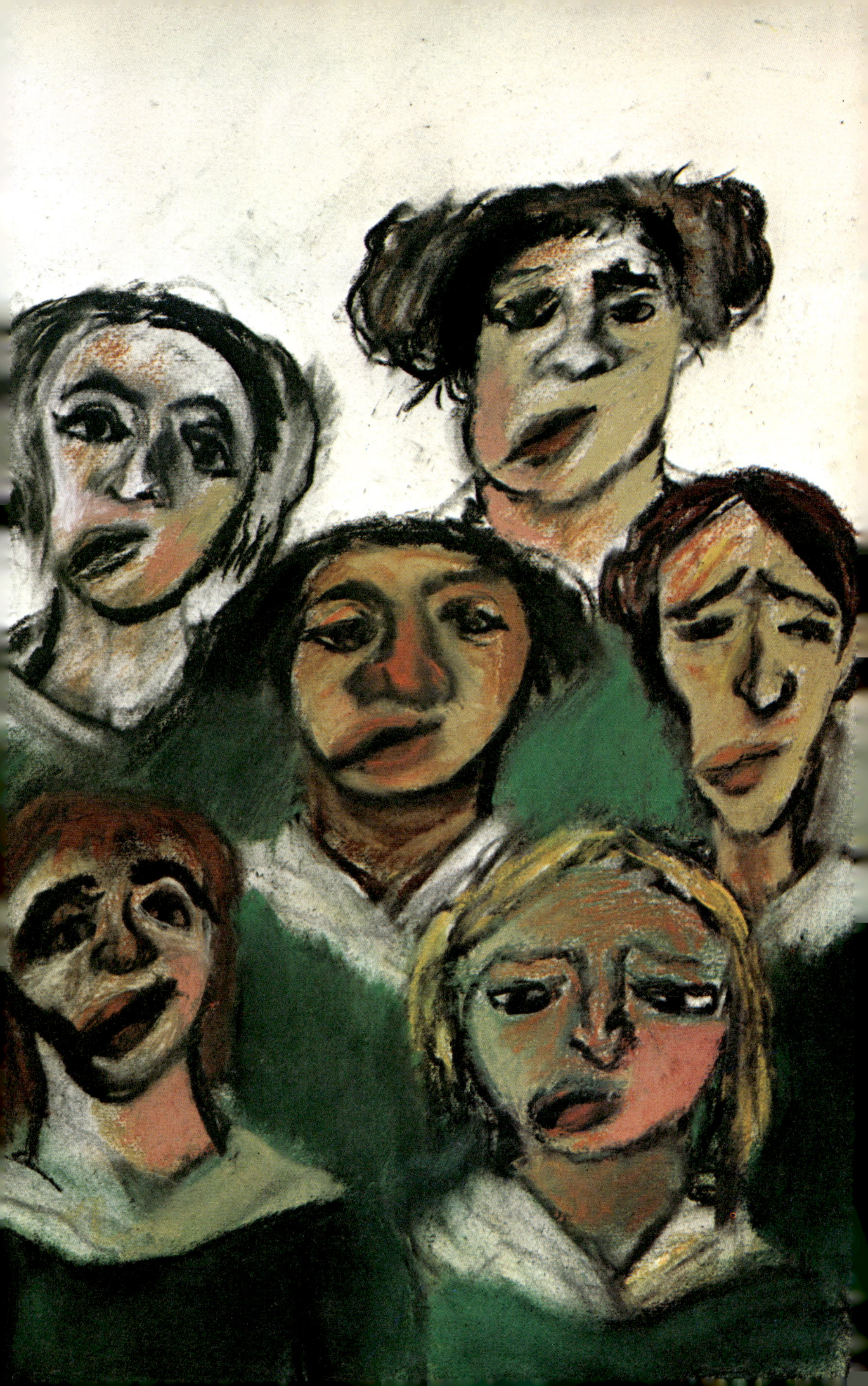

lady could not spin a bit. This made her husband glunchy with her, and before a month had passed, she found herself very unhappy.

One day the husband gaed away upon a journey, after telling her that he expected her, before his return, to have not only learned to spin, but to have spun a hundred hanks o' thread. Quite downcast, she took a walk along the hill-side, till she came to a big flat stone, and there she sat down and groaned. By-and-by, she heard a strain o' fine small music, coming as it were frae aneath the stone, and on turning it up, she saw a cave below, where there were sitting six wee ladies in green gowns, every one o' them spinning on a little wheel, and singing:

>   Little kens my dame at hame
>   That Whuppity Stoorie is my name.

The lady walked into the cave, and was kindly asked by the wee bodies to take a chair and sit down, while they still continued their spinning. She observed that each mouth was thrown away to one side, but she didna venture to ask the reason. They asked why she looked so unhappy, and she telt them that it was because she was expected by her husband to be a good spinner, when the plain truth was, that she could not spin at all, and found herself quite unable for it, having been so delicately brought up; neither was there any need for it, as her husband was a rich man. 'Oh, is that a'?' said the little wifies, speaking out at their cheeks all crooked like.

'Yes, and is it not a very good all too?' said the lady, her heart like to burst with distress.

'We could easily quit ye o' that trouble,' said the wee women. 'Just ask us a' to dinner for the day when your husband is to come back. We'll then let you see how we'll manage him.'

So the lady asked them all to dine with herself and her husband on the day when he was to come back.

When the goodman came home, he found the house so occupied with preparations for dinner, that he had no time to ask his wife about her thread; and before ever he had once spoken to her on the subject, the company was announced at the hall door. The six little ladies all came in a coach-and-six, and were as fine as princesses, but still wore their gowns of green. The gentleman was very polite, and shewed them up the stair with a pair of wax candles in his hand. And so they all sat down to dinner, and conversation went on very pleasantly, till at length the husband, becoming familiar with them, said: 'Ladies, if it be not an uncivil question, I should like to know how it happens that all your mouths are turned away to one side, all crooked like?'

'Is that the case?' cried the gentleman. 'Then, John, Tam, and Dick, fye, go haste and burn every rock, and reel, and spinning-wheel in the house, for I'll not have my wife to spoil her bonny face with spin-spin-spinning.'

And so the lady lived happily with her goodman all the rest of her days.

SUMMAT QUEER ON BATCH

There was an old widow body who had a little cottage up on Batch, on the common land. She came to market with her bits to sell, and she wouldn't go home no how. Well, they axed her, and all she'd say was, 'There's Summat Queer on Batch!' and not a word more. Well, Job Ash, he says to her, 'Never 'e mind, my dear, I'll go up Batch for 'e, no fear.' And he up and went.

'Twas a bit of a weary way up to Batch, road was lonely, and wind whistled and blew. He got to cottage, and 'twas a little cottage like, with a front door and back door opposite each other, and kitchen was one side o' passage, sitting-room was t'other side, and stairs was in cupboard. In he goes, front door was wide open, and he swings the bar across, and he goes to back door and he swings the bar across there. Then he takes a look-see in sitting-room. Wasn't no one there. Then he gave a look-see to kitchen. No one there neither. Then he rubs his hands together, and he thinks of the drubbing them lads was going to have.

He opens door to bedroom upstairs. Wasn't no one there neither. 'Where be they to?' said Job, and he come down and front door was open—back door was open too. Well, Job he took a quick look-see outside back door, and it slammed to behind him, and bar slid across. Well, Job, he took off round corner, gets round by front door as fast as he could, and that slams in his face too, and bar slid across. Well, Job, he took a deep breath, he did, and then he takes a look over his shoulder, and there was Summat Queer standing right behind him. At that, Job he took off down that road like he was at Shepton Mallet races. He was a great fleshy fellow, and when he'd got about a mile or so, he sat down on a heap of stones, and he puffs like a pair o' bellows, and got out his neckerchief, and he rubs his face, thankful. And then he looks down, and there's a great flat foot aside of his one. Then he looks up a little further, and there's a great hairy hand by his knee. And then he looks up a little further still, and there's a great wide grin.

'That were a good race, weren't it?' says it.

'Ar,' says Job, 'and when I've got my breath back, we'll have another!'

THE OLD WOMAN WHO LIVED IN A VINEGAR BOTTLE

Once upon a time there was an old woman who lived in a vinegar bottle. One day a fairy was passing that way, and she heard the old woman talking to herself.

'It is a shame, it is a shame, it is a shame,' said the old woman. 'I didn't ought to live in a vinegar bottle. I ought to live in a nice little cottage with a thatched roof, and roses growing all up the wall, that I ought.'

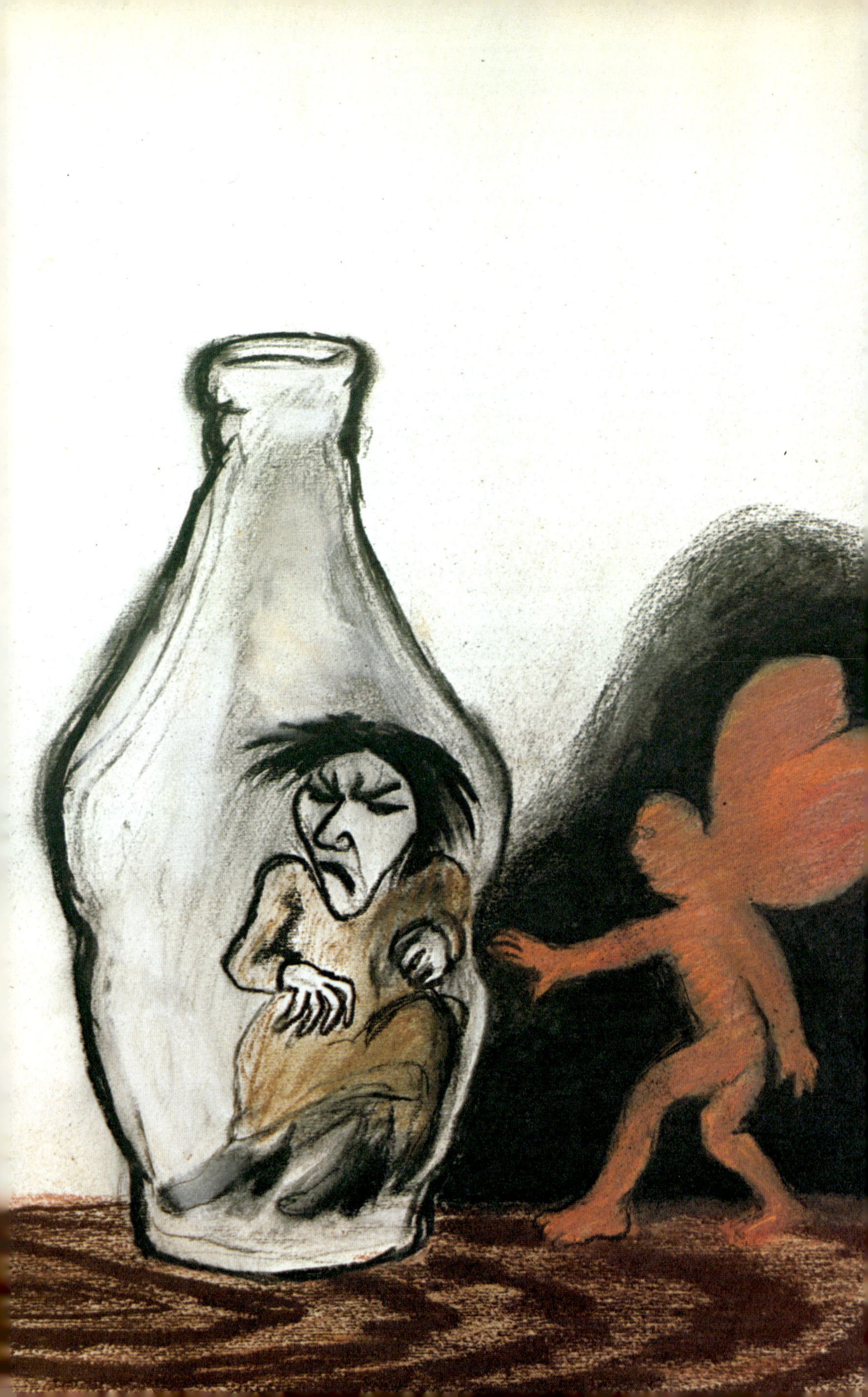

So the fairy said, 'Very well, when you go to bed to-night you turn round three times, and shut your eyes, and in the morning you'll see what you will see.'

So the old woman went to bed, and turned round three times and shut her eyes, and in the morning there she was, in a pretty little cottage with a thatched roof, and roses growing up the walls. And she was very surprised, and very pleased, but she quite forgot to thank the fairy.

And the fairy went north, and she went south, and she went east, and she went west, all about the business she had to do. And presently she thought, 'I'll go and see how that old woman is getting on. She must be very happy in her little cottage.'

And as she got up to the front door, she heard the old woman talking to herself.

'It is a shame, it is a shame, it is a shame,' said the old woman. 'I didn't ought to live in a little cottage like this, all by myself. I ought to live in a nice little house in a row of houses, with lace curtains at the windows, and a brass knocker on the door, and people calling mussels and cockles outside, all merry and cheerful.'

The fairy was rather surprised; but she said: 'Very well. You go to bed to-night, and turn round three times, and shut your eyes, and in the morning you shall see what you shall see.'

So the old woman went to bed, and turned round three times and shut her eyes, and in the morning there she was in a nice little house, in a row of little houses, with lace curtains at the windows, and a brass knocker on the door, and people calling mussels and cockles outside, all merry and cheerful. And she was very much surprised, and very much pleased. But she quite forgot to thank the fairy.

And the fairy went north, and she went south, and she went east, and she went west, all about the business she had to do; and after a time she thought to herself, 'I'll go and see how that old woman is getting on. Surely she must be happy now.'

And when she got to the little row of houses, she heard the old woman talking to herself. 'It is a shame, it is a shame, it is a shame,' said the old woman. 'I didn't ought to live in a row of houses like this, with common people on each side of me. I ought to live in a great mansion in the country, with a big garden all round it, and servants to answer the bell.'

And the fairy was very surprised, and rather annoyed, but she said: 'Very well, go to bed and turn round three times and shut your eyes, and in the morning you will see what you will see.'

And the old woman went to bed, and turned round three times, and shut her eyes, and in the morning there she was, in a great mansion in the country, surrounded by a fine garden, and servants to answer the bell. And she was very pleased and very surprised, and she learned how to speak genteelly, but she quite forgot to thank the fairy.

And the fairy went north, and she went south, and she went east, and she went west, all about the business she had to do; and after a time she thought to herself, 'I'll go and see how that old woman is getting on. Surely she must be happy now.'

But no sooner had she got near the old woman's drawing-room window than she heard the old woman talking to herself in a genteel voice.

'It certainly is a very great shame,' said the old woman, 'that I should be living alone here, where there is no society. I ought to be a duchess, driving in my own coach to wait on the Queen, with footmen running beside me.'

The fairy was very much surprised, and very much disappointed, but she said: 'Very well. Go to bed to-night, and turn round three times and shut your eyes; and in the morning you shall see what you shall see.'

So the old woman went to bed, and turned round three times, and shut her eyes; and in the morning, there she was, a duchess with a coach of her own, to wait on the Queen, and footmen running beside her. And she was very much surprised, and very much pleased. BUT she quite forgot to thank the fairy.

And the fairy went north, and she went south, and she went east, and she went west, all about the business she had to do; and after a while she thought to herself: 'I'd better go and see how that old woman is getting on. Surely she is happy, now she's a duchess.'

But no sooner had she come to the window of the old woman's great town mansion, than she heard her saying in a more genteel tone than ever: 'It is indeed a very great shame that I should be a mere Duchess, and have to curtsey to the Queen. Why can't I be a queen myself, and sit on a golden throne, with a golden crown on my head, and courtiers all around me.'

The fairy was very much disappointed and very angry; but she said: 'Very well. Go to bed and turn round three times, and shut your eyes, and in the morning you shall see what you shall see.'

So the old woman went to bed, and turned round three times, and shut her eyes; and in the morning there she was in a royal palace, a queen in her own right, sitting on a golden throne, with a golden crown on her head, and her courtiers all around her. And she was highly delighted, and ordered them right and left. But she quite forgot to thank the fairy.

And the fairy went north, and she went south, and she went east, and she went west, all about the business she had to do; and after a while she thought to herself: 'I'll go and see how that old woman is getting on. Surely she must be satisfied now!'

But as soon as she got near the Throne Room, she heard the old woman talking.

'It is a great shame, a very great shame,' she said, 'that I should be Queen of a paltry little country like this instead of ruling the whole round world. What I am really fitted for is to be Pope, to govern the minds of everyone on Earth.'

'Very well,' said the fairy. 'Go to bed. Turn round three times, and shut your eyes, and in the morning you shall see what you shall see.'

So the old woman went to bed, full of proud thoughts. She turned round three times and shut her eyes. And in the morning she was back in her vinegar bottle.

SIR GAMMERS VAN

Last Sunday morning at six o'clock in the evening as I was sailing over the tops of the mountains in my little boat, I met two men on horseback riding on one mare: so I asked them 'Could they tell me whether the little old woman was dead yet who was hanged last Saturday week for drowning herself in a shower of feathers?' They said they could not positively inform me, but if I went to Sir Gammer Vans he could tell me all about it. 'But how am I to know the house?' said I. 'Ho, 'tis easy enough,' said they, 'for 'tis a brick house, built entirely of flints, standing alone by itself in the middle of sixty or seventy others just like it.' 'Oh, nothing in the world is easier,' said I. 'Nothing *can* be easier,' said they; so I went on my way. Now this Sir G. Vans was a giant, and bottle-maker. And as all giants who *are* bottle-makers usually pop out of a little thumb-bottle from behind the door, so did Sir G. Vans. 'How d'ye do?' says he. 'Very well, I thank you,' says I. 'Have some breakfast with me?' 'With all my heart,' says I. So he gave me a slice of beer, and a cup of cold veal; and there was a little dog under the table that picked up all the crumbs. 'Hang him,' says I. 'No, don't hang him,' says he; 'for he killed a hare yesterday. And if you don't believe me, I'll show you the hare alive in a basket.' So he took me into his garden to show me the curiosities. In one corner there was a fox hatching eagle's eggs; in another there was an iron apple-tree, entirely covered with pears and lead; in the third there was the hare which the dog killed yesterday alive in the basket; and in the fourth there were twenty-four *hipper switches* threshing tobacco, and at the sight of me they threshed so hard that they drove the plug through the wall, and through a little dog that was passing by on the other side. I, hearing the dog howl, jumped over the wall; and turned it as neatly inside out as possible, when it ran away as if it had not an hour to live. Then he took me into the park to show me his deer: and I remembered that I had a warrant in my pocket to shoot venison for his majesty's dinner. So I set fire to my bow, poised my arrow, and shot amongst them. I broke seventeen ribs on one side, and twenty-one and a-half on the other; but my arrow passed clean through without ever touching it, and the worst was I lost my arrow: however, I found it again in the hollow of a tree. I felt it; it felt clammy. I smelt it: it smelt honey. 'Oh, ho!' said I, 'here's a bee's nest,' when out sprang a covey of partridges. I shot at them; some say I killed eighteen; but I am sure I killed thirty-six, besides a dead salmon which was flying over the bridge, of which I made the best apple-pie I ever tasted.

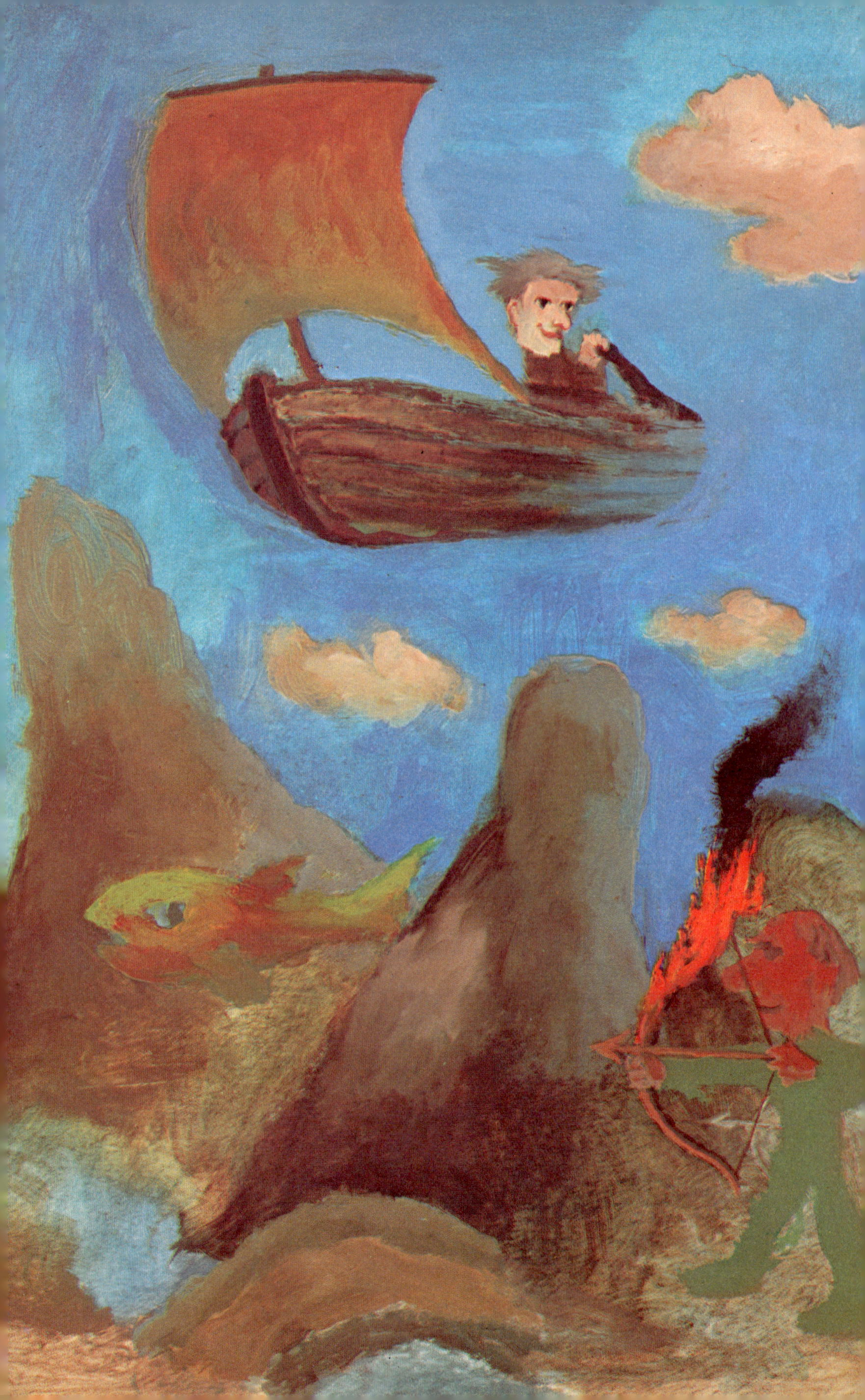

FORCES OF NATURE

THE APPLE TREE MAN

There was a hard-working chap that was eldest of a long family, see, so when his dad died there wasn't anything left for him. Youngest gets it all, and he gave bits and pieces to all his kith; but he don't like eldest, see, so all he lets him have is his dad's old donkey, and an ox that was gone to a skeleton, and a tumbledown cottage with two or three ancient old apple-trees where his dad had lived with his

Sure enough the don
was talking to the o...

granfer. The chap doesn't grumble, but he goes cutting grass along the lane, and the old dunk began to fatten, and he rubs the ox with herbs and says the words, and old ox he perks himself up and walks smart, and then he turns his beasts into orchard, and those old apple-trees flourish a marvel.

But it doesn't leave him time to find the rent. Oh yes, the youngest was bound to have his rent. On the dot too!

Then one day the youngest comes into the orchard and says, ''Twill be Christmas Eve come tomorrow, when beasts do talk. There's a treasure hereabouts we've all heard tell, and I'm set to ask your dunk. He mustn't refuse to tell me. You wake me just afore midnight and I'll take a whole sixpence off the rent.'

Come Christmas Eve the chap he gave old dunk and ox a bit extra and he fixed a bit of holly in the cattle-shed, and he got his last mug of cider, and mulled it in the ashes, and went out to the orchard to give it to the apple-trees. Then the Apple-Tree Man calls to the chap and he says, 'You take a look under this great diddicky root of ours.' And there was a chest full of finest gold. ''Tis yours, and no one else,' says the Apple-Tree Man. 'Put it away safe and bide quiet about it.' So he did that. 'Now you can go call your dear brother,' says Apple-Tree Man, ''tis midnight.'

Well, youngest brother he ran out in a terrible hurry-push and sure enough the dunk's a-talking to the ox. 'You know this great greedy fool that's a-listening to us, so unmannerly, he wants us to tell him where treasure is.'

'And that's where he won't ever get it,' says the ox. ''Cause someone has a-taken it already.'

THE SOUL AS A BUTTERFLY

There were two men searching for sheep one time in a glen. There was a stream running through it. They were tired and exhausted from their travels, so in the evening they stretched themselves down in the glen-side. The evening was delightful, and one of them fell fast asleep. The other remained awake. As he was watching the sleeper, he noticed his mouth widening, and out of it came a white butterfly! It went down along his body and along one of his legs, before alighting on the grass, and then went on for about six yards. The man who was awake rose to his feet and followed the butterfly until it reached a small, uneven pathway. It went along the pathway until it came to the edge of the stream. There was a stone flag, under which the water flowed, across the stream, and the butterfly went across by the flag to the other side. It continued on until it came to a small clump of sedges, and it went in and out through the clump several times. The man followed it for twenty yards or so further, until the butterfly came to an old horse-skull, which was white and weather-beaten. The butterfly went in through one of the eye-sockets, and the man

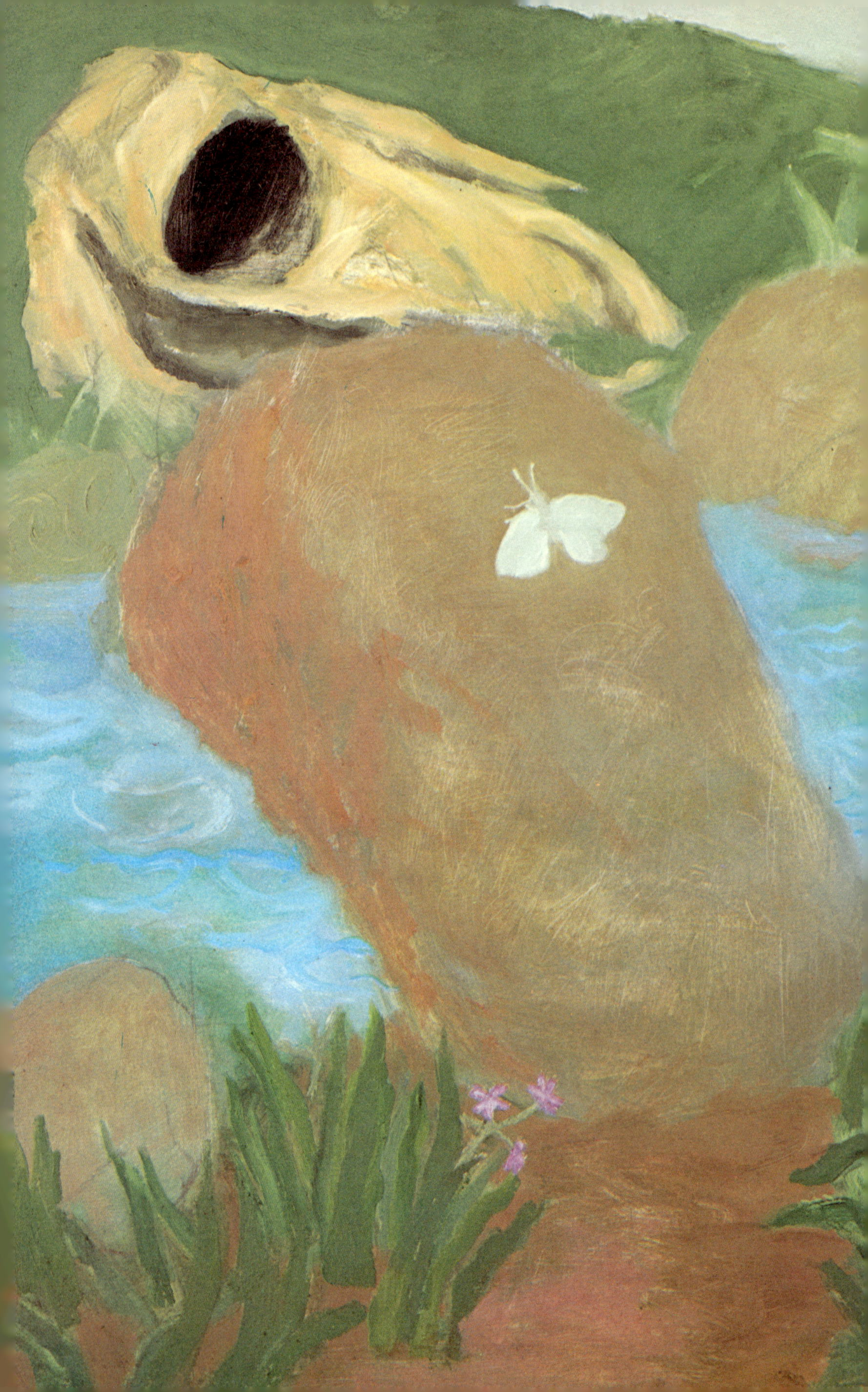

watched as it went into, and searched, every corner of the skull. It then went out again through the other socket.

The butterfly then went back by the same route: in and out through the clump of sedges, across the stream by the stone flags then along the uneven pathway, until it reached the sleeper's body. It made its way up along his right leg, and never stopped until it closed his mouth. The next moment he sighed and yawned and opened his eyes. He glanced around and saw his companion looking at him.

'It must be late in the evening by now,' said he.

'Whether 'tis late or early,' replied his companion, 'I have seen some wonders just now.'

'"Tis I who have seen the wonders!' said the sleeper. 'I dreamt that I was going along a fine, wide road, with trees and flowers at either side of me, until I came to a great river. Across the river was the finest and most ornamental bridge I had ever seen. Soon after crossing the bridge, I came to the most wonderful wood I had ever seen. I walked through it for a long time, until at the other side of it I came to a splendid palace. I went into it. There was nobody to be seen. I walked from one room to another until I grew tired. I was making up my mind to stay there, when an eerie feeling came over me. I left the palace and travelled along the same route home. I felt very hungry when I arrived, and then when I was going to eat some food, I woke up.'

'It looks as if the soul wanders around while the body is sleeping,' said his companion. 'Come with me now, and I'll show you all the fine places you passed through in your sleep.'

He told him about the butterfly, and showed him the uneven, little pathway, the stone flag across the stream, the clump of sedges and the horse-skull.

'That skull,' said he, 'is the fine palace you were in a while ago. That clump of sedges is the wonderful wood you saw, and that stone flag is the ornamental bridge you crossed. And that rough, little path is the fine, wide road you travelled, with flowers at every side!'

Both of them had seen wonders.

THE DEAD MOON

Long ago the Lincolnshire Cars were full of bogs and it was death to walk through them, except on moonlight nights, for harm and mischance and mischief, Bogles and Dead Things and crawling horrors came out at nights when the moon did not shine. At length the Moon heard what things went on in the bog-land when her back was turned, and she thought she would go down to see for herself, and find what she could do to help. So at the month's end she wrapped a black cloak round her, and hid her shining hair under a black hood, and stepped down into the bog-lands. It was all dark and watery, with quaking mud, and waving tussocks of grass, and no light except what

he man followed the tterfly for twenty rds.

came from her own white feet. On she went, deep into the bogland and now the witches rode about her on their great cats, and the will-o'-the-wykes danced with the lanterns swinging on their backs, and dead folks rose out of the water, and stared at her with fiery eyes, and the slimy dead hands beckoned and clutched. But on she went, stepping from tuft to tuft, as light as the wind in summer, until at length a stone turned under her, and she caught with both hands at a snag nearby to steady herself; but as soon as she touched it it twisted round her wrists like a pair of handcuffs and held her fast. She struggled and fought against it but nothing would free her. Then, as she stood trembling she heard a piteous crying, and she knew that a man was lost in the darkness, and soon she saw him, splashing after the will-o'-the-wykes, crying out on them to wait for him, while the Dead Hands plucked at his coat, and the creeping horrors crowded round him, and he went further and further from the Path.

The Moon was so sorry and so angry that she made a great struggle, and though she could not loose her hands, her hood slipped back, and the light streamed out from her beautiful golden hair, so that the man saw the bog-holes near him and the safe path in the distance nearly as clear as by day. He cried for joy, and floundered across, out of the deadly bog and back to safety, and all the bogles and evil things fled away from the moonlight, and hid themselves. But the Moon struggled in vain to free herself, and at length she fell forward, spent with the struggle, and the black hood fell over her head again, and she had no strength to push it off. Then all the evil things came creeping back, and they laughed to think they had their enemy the Moon in their power at last. All night they fought and squabbled about how best they should kill her, but when the first grey light before dawn came they grew frightened, and pushed her down into the water. The Dead Folk held her, while the Bogles fetched a great stone to put over her, and they chose two will-o'-the-wykes to guard her by turns, and when the day came the Moon was buried deep, until someone should find her, and who knew where to look?

The days passed, and folk put straws in their caps, and money in their pockets against the coming of the new Moon, and she never came. And as dark night after dark night passed, the evil things from the bog-land came howling and screeching up to men's very doors, so that no one could go a step from the house at night, and in the end folk sat up all night, shivering by their fires, for they feared if the lights went out, the things would come over the thresholds.

At last they went to the Wise Woman who lived in the old mill, to ask what had come of their Moon. She looked in the mirror, and in the brewpot, and in the Book, and it was all dark, so she told them to set straw and salt and a button on their door-sills at night, to keep them safe from the Horrors, and to come back with any news they could give her.

Well, you can be sure they talked, at their firesides and in the Garth and in the town. So it happened one day, as they were sitting on the settle at the Inn, a man from the far side of the bog-land cried out all of a sudden, 'I reckon I know where the Moon is, only I was so mazed I never thought on it.' And he told them how he had been all astray one night, and like to lose his life in the bog-holes, and all of a sudden a clear bright light had shone out, and showed him the way home. So off they all went to the Wise Woman, and told what the man had said. The Wise Woman looked in the Book, and in the pot, and at last she got some glimmer of light and told them what they must do.

*slimy dead hands
ned and clutched.*

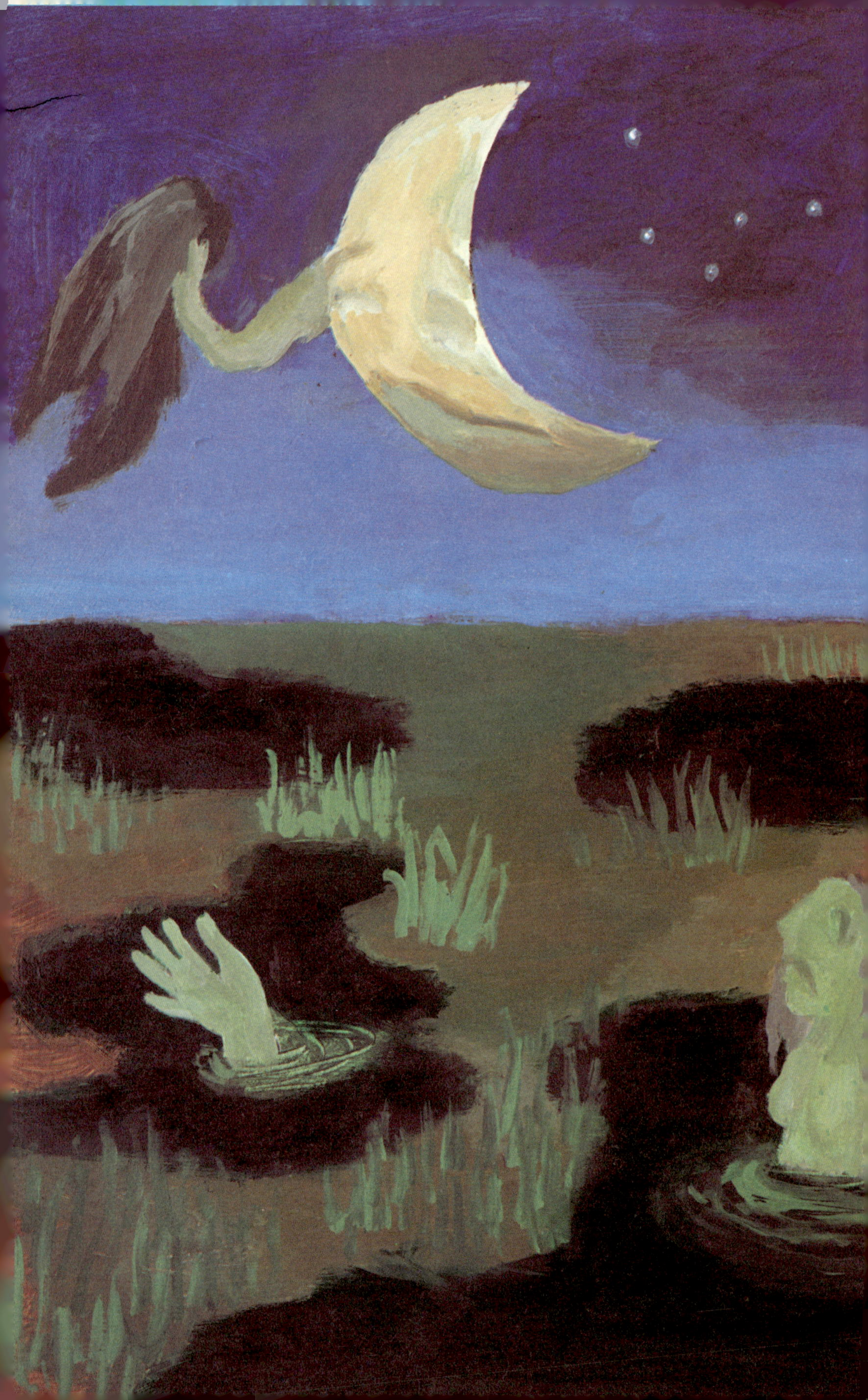

They were to set out together in the darkness with a stone in their mouths and a hazel twig in their hands, and not a word must they speak till they got home; and they must search through the bog till they found a coffin, and a cross, and a candle, and that was where the Moon would be. Well, they were main feared, but next night they set out and went on and on, into the midst of the bog.

They saw nothing, but they heard a sighing and whispering round them and slimy hands touching them, but on they went, shaking and scared, till suddenly they stopped, for half in, and half out of the water they saw a long stone, for all the world like a coffin, and at the head of it stood a black snag stretching out two branches, like a gruesome cross, and on it flickered a tiddy light. Then they all knelt down and they crossed themselves and said the Lord's Prayer, forward for the sake of the cross, and backward against the Bogles, but all silently, for they knew they must not speak. Then all together they heaved up the stone. For one minute they saw a strange beautiful face looking up at them and then they stepped back mazed with the light, and with a great shrieking wail from all the horrors, as they fled back to their holes, and the next moment the full moon shone down on them from the Heavens, so that they could see their path near as clear as by day.

And ever since then the Moon has shone her best over the boglands, for she knows all the evil things that are hid there and she remembers how the Car men went out to look for her when she was dead and buried.

THE SPECKLED BULL

Once upon a time, and a long time ago it was, there was a king and a queen in Ireland. That wasn't in your time or in my time but in the time of people who are long since dead and gone.

They had one son, the finest man that ever walked on green grass. Every woman in the country was after him, each thinking that she would get him. The daughters of the gentry came to see him, but he didn't give them a second look. There were two sisters living near the palace, one of them about seven years older than the other, and whenever the prince went out walking or hunting, he used to call upon these girls on his way home. The upshot of it was that they became friendly. The eldest girl took a great notion for him and thought that he might marry her, but he paid no attention at all to her. Needless to say, he preferred the young sister, and the end of it was that he married her. Sisters and all though they were, the marriage made the eldest very jealous, and she wouldn't mind if she saw her sister drowned in a pool of water.

At the end of a year or so, the prince's wife gave birth to a son. Her husband happened to be out hunting at the time, and the only one with her was the jealous sister. She made up her mind to get rid of the child and to tell the prince, when he came home, that his wife had given birth to a kitten. That might cause trouble between them. So what did she do but wrap the child up in a dirty piece of cloth and throw him into the river. The prince returned home at twilight, went to his wife's room, and saw her lying in bed.

'What's wrong with her?' he asked the sister, who was minding her.

'I don't know,' said she. 'That's a nice wife you married. I thought she was going to have a child, and what had she but a kitten.'

'And what did you do with it?' said the prince.

'What would I do but throw it in the river?' said she.

The prince was very sad at what he heard, but he said nothing and kept his troubles to himself. He remained as friendly as before with his wife, and when she got well again, they lived happily. A year later, while the prince was hunting one day, didn't his wife give birth to another son. And the sister tried the same trick again. She placed the child in a small box and threw the little creature, alive and all, out into the river.

'Now,' said she, 'when he comes home this evening, I'll tell him 'twas a strange wife he married, who could only give birth to animals, like the pup today.'

When the prince returned in the evening, he didn't see his wife about the house, so he went to her room and found her lying asleep in bed. Her sister was with her, and he asked her what was wrong.

'Well,' said the sister, 'if you wanted to marry, you had all the women in the world to choose from. And look whom you married. Your wife has just given birth to a pup.'

'And what did you do with it?'

'What would I do but throw it in the river. I saw that it wouldn't be a thing to have about the house, and that you wouldn't want to see it.'

'If that's the way things were,' said the prince, 'you did well to get rid of it.'

'If you had married me the day you married, things wouldn't be this way,' said she. 'I'd have borne proper children.'

The prince had his own opinion about the whole affair, but he said little. The sister kept on at the prince till she came between himself and his wife, and one day he said that he would banish his wife.

'Don't do that,' said the sister. 'Leave her to me, and I'll fix her so that she won't trouble you ever again.'

'Very well,' said the prince.

At that time, some people had a thing called magic, and when they struck somebody with a magic wand, they could turn him into a green stone. That's what the eldest sister did. She struck the prince's wife a blow and made a green stone out of her and left her outside the door where every drop of dirty water from the house would be thrown on top of her. Then she and the prince got married.

It happened that there was a man fishing at the mouth of the river the day the second child was thrown into it, and he saw the box caught in a bush that was growing on the bank. He threw out a hook and hauled in the box to his feet. No sooner did he lift it up than he heard the cry of the poor child. He pulled off the cover, and inside was the nicest little boy that he had ever laid eyes on. He had no children of his own, although he was married, and he thanked God for sending a child to him like this. He took him out carefully and never stopped till he brought him home to his wife. She was seven times as delighted as her husband. She took him in her arms and was as fond of him, or maybe more so, as she would have been if he were her own child.

The boy grew strong, and the news about the fine child the fisherman's wife had went around. Everybody was wondering about it, because she had no children before. The news went from mouth to mouth, and the end of it was that the prince's new wife heard it. She had a suspicion immediately about how the child had been got, and she couldn't close an eye, day or night, until she'd see the child and find out where he had come from. One day while the prince was out hunting, she set out and never stopped till she found out the fisherman's house. She greeted the wife in the manner of those times, and the wife welcomed her in the same way. The child was lying in a cradle near the fire. She hadn't much to say before going over to the cradle, and she immediately saw that he was her sister's son.

'Isn't he a fine child, God bless him?' said she.

'He's a good boy, thank you,' said the fisherman's wife.

'What a pity it is that he isn't your own,' said the other.

'Of course, he's my own. 'Tis unmannerly of you to come into my house and say a thing like that. I don't know who you are or where you're from.'

'I'm not telling any lie,' said the prince's wife. 'And to prove it, you will have to kill that child. You think that he is a normal child of this world, but he isn't. He's a changeling that the hill-folk have left with you, and unless you take my advice, you'll regret it for many a long day.'

The fisherman's poor wife became terrified.

'Well, if that's the way,' said she, 'I won't have any more to do with him. Take him away and do whatever you like with him. I couldn't find it in my heart to lay a finger on him.'

'Yes, 'tis better to give him to me, and he won't give you any more trouble for the rest of your life.'

The prince's wife took away the child and cut his throat immediately. It troubled her no more than if it were a chicken she were killing. Then she took the body out into the garden and buried it in a lonely corner. Her heart was satisfied as she made her way back to the palace.

A tall tree grew up from the child's grave in the corner of the garden, up and up to the sky in the space of a couple of nights, and it bent down to the ground with all the different fruits that ever grew on a tree.

Now, the prince had some cattle grazing on the fisherman's land,

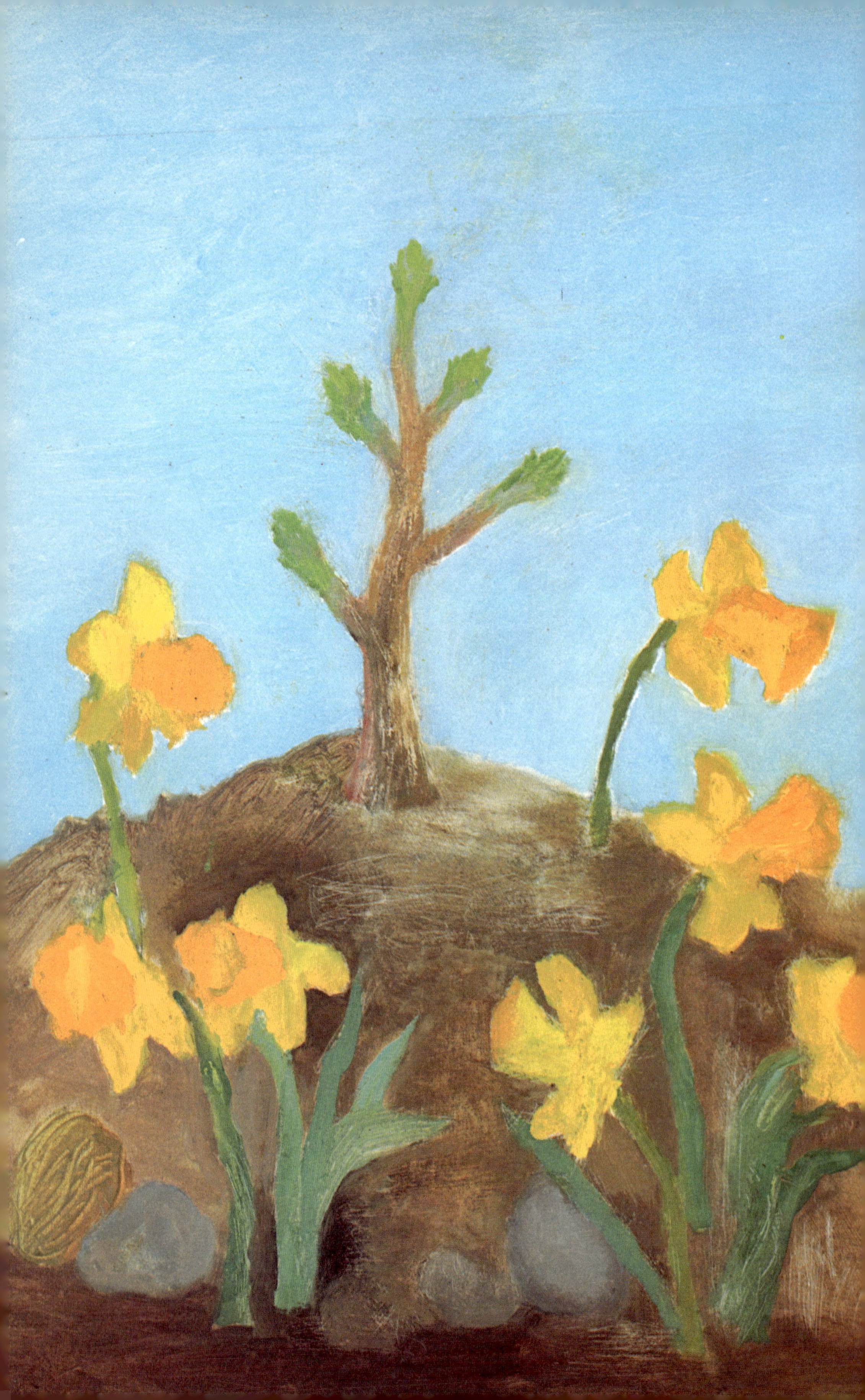

and one day they were driven into the garden where this tree was growing. There was a big speckled cow among the herd, and instead of starting to eat the grass like the others, she started to eat the fruits on the tree. She began to give so much milk that they hadn't enough vessels to hold it. And then, although there was no bull, when her time was up she gave birth to a male speckled calf. Everybody was surprised at this—the prince as well as the rest. He made up his mind to go to see what kind of grazing the cow had, and when he entered the garden he saw the tree of the fruits. He asked the fisherman about it, and he told him the whole story about the child as I have told it to you.

He took his cattle away from the garden and returned home. He said nothing about what he had seen and heard; he wouldn't give his wife that much satisfaction. As soon as he changed the cattle, the speckled cow was just like all the others, not differing in any way. Her speckled calf ran about after her, and in no time at all he was as fine a bull as there was in Ireland. They intended to castrate him, but there weren't enough men in Ireland to catch and hold him. They had to leave him as he was.

The prince's wife heard about the bull, and she had a suspicion that unless he was killed, he would be the cause of her own death some day. She remained awake at night, trying to think of some plan to get rid of him, and at last she hit upon one. She would pretend to be dying and would whisper to a doctor who was in the district that nothing would cure her but the heart and liver of the speckled bull to eat. She was sure that, rather than let her die, the prince would agree to that, and welcome.

One day the prince went out hunting as usual. When she found him gone, she made off to the doctor and told him her plan. She gave him a big fistful of money, and he promised to do what she asked. She went out and brought in a cock and drew its blood. She put the blood into a vessel. Then she went to bed, pretending to be very ill. She put the vessel of blood under the head of the bed. She heard her husband coming in and took a mouthful of the blood and as soon as he darkened the doorway, she bent out over the edge of the bed and spouted the blood from her mouth into the vessel on the floor. He got a terrible start.

'What in God's name is wrong with you?' he cried.

'I don't know what it is,' said she, 'but I have been spouting blood since dinnertime. Get the doctor!'

The doctor was sent for and came immediately. He had been waiting for the call and had even been paid by the woman who was pretending to be sick. He went to her room and examined her pulse.

'She's very ill,' he said. 'I'm afraid she won't last long.'

'Is there anything in the world to cure her?' asked the prince.

'Only one thing to my knowledge,' said the doctor. 'You have a speckled bull. You must kill him and give your wife his heart and liver to eat. If you don't, she will die.'

"'Twould be very hard for me to do that,' said the prince. 'If 'twere anything else, I'd do it gladly. But how can I kill that bull? We tried before to catch him and found that there weren't enough men in Ireland to tie or hold him, let alone kill him.'

'Well, you have two choices,' replied the doctor, 'let your wife die or kill the bull.'

'I can't let her die, and I can't avoid it unless I collect all the men in the country,' said the prince.

He sent word throughout the kingdom, asking every man who could to come immediately to help him in his great trouble. The men began to assemble, and when he thought there were enough to hold the bull, they all entered the field and tried to catch him. One of them threw a rope on top of him. At that, the bull gave a roar and rose up into the sky, dragging along with him the man who held the rope, and he didn't touch the ground again until he was seven miles away. Off went the bull through the air, like the March wind, and never touched earth until he reached a field in the eastern world, where the cattle of the king of the eastern world were grazing.

Next morning, when the milkers went out to milk the king's cows, they saw the huge speckled bull along with them. They were terrified by his size; he was as big as three bulls of the eastern world put together. They threw their milk pails on the ground and ran back to the palace. They told about the bull, and half the people of the kingdom were gathered around the field before dinner time, gazing with awe and wonder at the huge animal.

The king of the eastern world had a very beautiful daughter, who was under a spell never to leave the palace unless her eyes were covered. If she removed the veil from her eyes, she had to marry the first man she saw, even though he were only a beggar. Needless to say, the king was afraid that she might have to marry somebody of lowly birth; so he always put the veil over her eyes when she went outside the palace.

News of the wonderful speckled bull reached the king and of the half of the kingdom who were watching him. So he made up his mind to go to see the animal for himself. It was his custom to take his daughter with him when he was going anywhere, and he couldn't take her where large crowds were assembled. So he sent a messenger out to the field to order the people to go away, because he and his daughter were going to see the bull. The people had to do as they were told, of course, and as soon as they got the order, they scattered east and west. Then the king was told that all was ready.

He and his daughter, who was wearing her veil, walked toward the field. There was the speckled bull. The king had never seen an animal like him. He was as big as twenty of his own bulls. He was so filled with wonder that he thought it fit that his daughter should see the bull also. He looked around him, and as there was no man in sight at any point, he decided to take off the daughter's veil. As soon as she laid eyes on the bull, she fell in a faint at her father's feet. He couldn't understand what in the world had come over her. She lay in the faint for a while, and he thought that she might die on his hands. But she soon recovered, and her father asked her what had happened.

'O, you ought to have had more sense than to bring me to a place like this!' she cried.

'Why is that?' he asked.

'You knew well,' said she, 'that I was under a spell not to gaze on any man's face, except your own, without having my veil on.'

'But you don't need any veil in this place,' said the king. 'There's no man here only the cattle and this speckled bull that everybody is wondering at. I thought that you should see the bull as well as anybody else.'

'But I don't see any bull,' said she.

'What do you see, then?' asked her father.

'I see a king's son,' said she.

'A king's son,' said her father. 'I fear you must have lost your senses, or your eyes are affected since you fainted. Stand still for a while until you recover.'

'Standing still won't do me any good,' said she. 'I see a king's son out there in front of me, and he's the finest man that a young girl, or an old woman either, ever laid eyes on.'

'That's nonsense!' said the king. 'How could a man be there?'

'Place your hand on my left shoulder,' said she; 'and I'll guarantee that you'll see something that will open your eyes for you.'

He placed his hand on her shoulder and saw before him the finest and most handsome man he had ever seen. The moment he laid eyes on him, the king decided that here was the one man in the world whom he would like his daughter to marry. He was wondering how he could get a chance of speaking to him. Then, no sooner had he removed his hand from his daughter's shoulder, than he saw the huge wild speckled bull once more. The daughter said that she would go to speak to him herself; so the pair of them walked over to the middle of the field. The bull did not move until they were within speaking distance of him. Then the king put his hand on his daughter's shoulder again, and they both began to chat with the king's son. They conversed for a long time, and the upshot of it was that the king asked him would he marry his daughter.

'I will, and welcome!' said he. 'But the way I am, I won't be of much use to her or to any other woman.'

'Well,' replied the king, 'it may not be long more until you are free from your spell. My daughter here was also under a spell and now she is free from them. She has met a king's son who has promised to marry her.'

The marriage day was fixed. The people's wonder about the speckled bull grew less. And so the marriage took place. Whatever kind the spell on the king's son were, they allowed him to be a bull by day and a man by night, or a man by day and a bull by night. On the day that they were married, the king's son asked his wife which would

(overleaf) He was a bull day and a man by night.

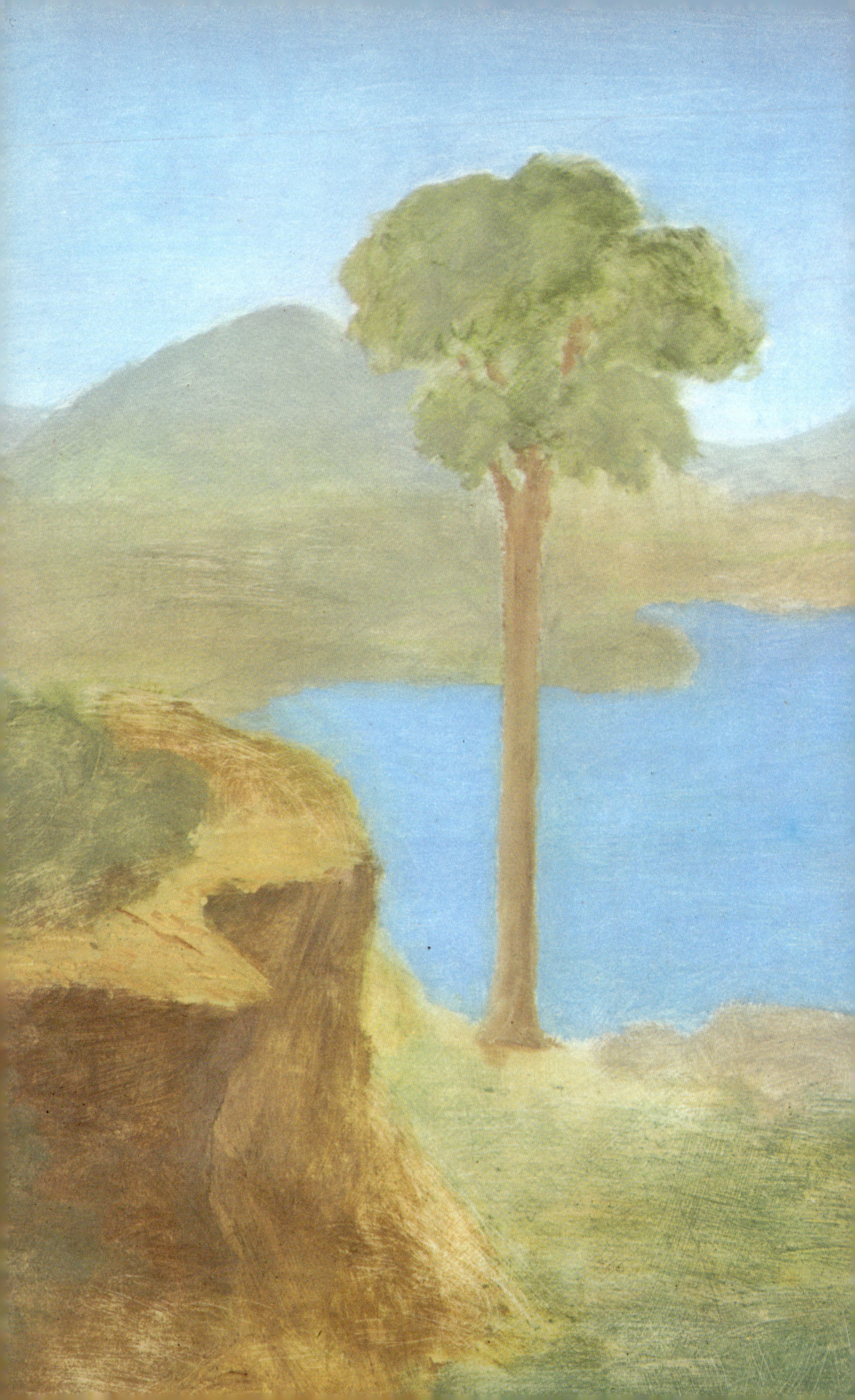

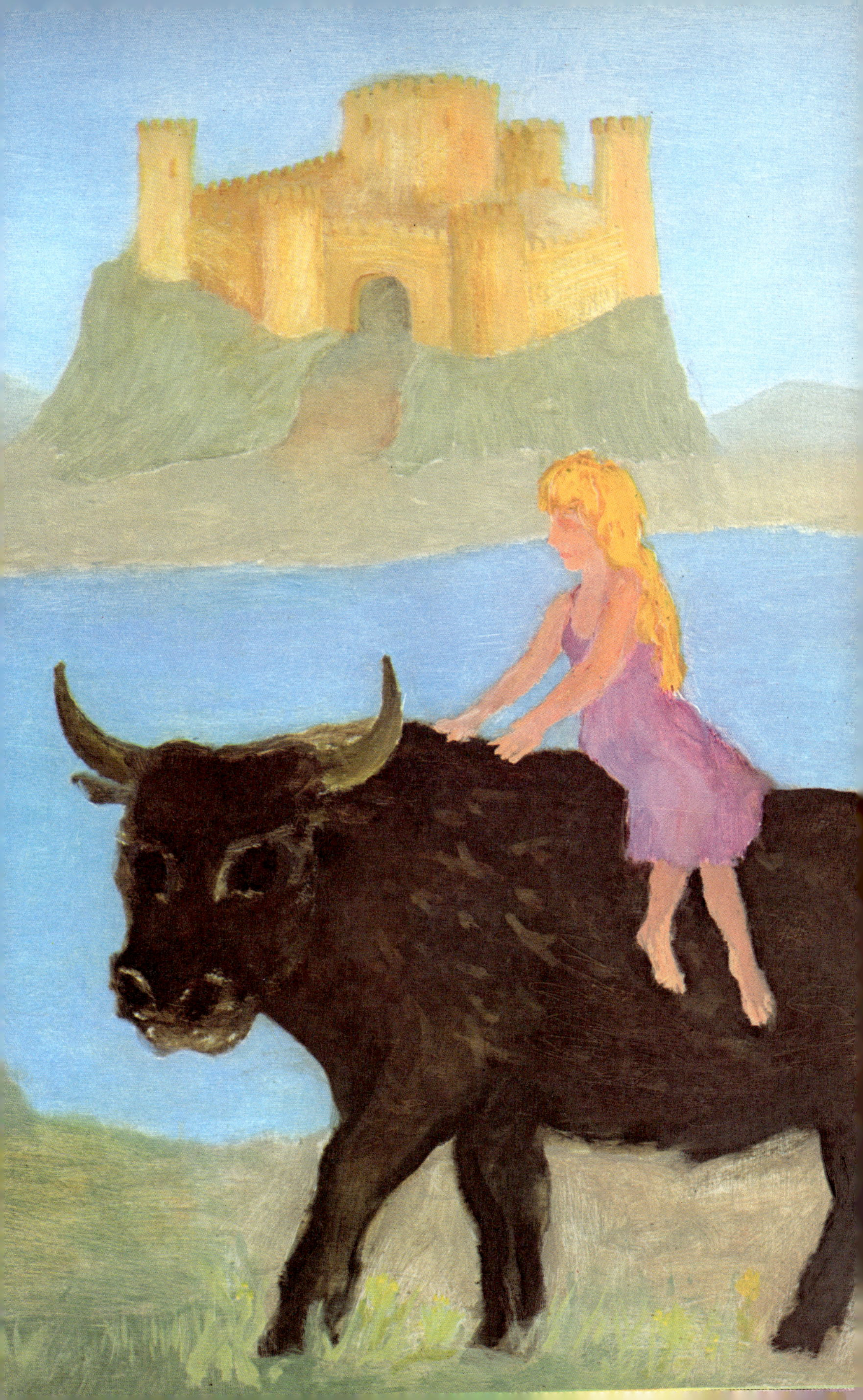

she prefer, and she said she would like best if he were a man by night.

'Very well,' said he. 'I'll be a man by night.'

When night fell, he came to the palace, where his wife was, looking the finest man in the world, well dressed from head to feet. Nobody in the world would believe that he was a bull by day. The king and his wife had the greatest welcome for him; they got ready a great feast, and all ate and drank their fill. He went to bed with his wife and slept his fill until morning—what he hadn't done for a long time. He was up as soon as the sun rose and as soon as he had eaten, out he went and joined the cattle in the field as a bull. He grazed among them until sunset; then he made a man of himself and went back to his wife. She was overjoyed to see him. To make a long story short, he kept coming and going in that manner for some years. His wife loved him more and more, and she used to be heartbroken when he left her each morning.

Now at that time, every king had a wise man, who knew everything in the world, and when the seven years were almost up, the king thought it a suitable time to ask the wise man if there was any remedy in the world which would remove the spell from his daughter's husband. He told the druid the whole story.

'I understand,' said the druid. 'Both your daughter and her husband are in a difficult position, but if you and he do as I tell you, his spell will be over, and he will be a man for ever more. Tell him to start fighting with the other cattle the next day he is grazing; they will all gather about him and half-kill him. His left horn will be broken and the fighting will stop. You must act quickly! As soon as you see the broken horn hanging from him, you must run to him and catch hold of the horn. Inside the horn will be a small drop that looks like water. You must place the little drop in a vessel. Then turn away from the bull and go to the other side of the field. Have a small red cloth in your pocket. You must take this out and hold it toward the bull. He will be so mad when he sees the cloth that he will rush toward you immediately. 'Tis then you must be wide-awake! When he comes near you, you must throw the drop at him, between his two eyes. If you succeed in that, his spell will be over. If you don't, he will kill you.'

'Upon my soul!' said the king. 'All that is more easily said than done. But I'll try it. 'Twould be better to be dead than to see how my poor daughter is suffering, seeing her husband go off as a brute beast every morning.'

'If you succeed in doing what I have told you,' said the druid, 'you and your daughter will live happily for the rest of your lives.'

The next day the fight started between the bull and the cattle. They made hard places of the soft places and soft places of the hard places. They drew wells of water from the green stones, and there wasn't a young or an old person in the kingdom that wasn't running into holes and caves with the dint of terror. Every blow that the bull gave to the cattle knocked an echo out of them as if the two sides of the world were being struck together. But the king stood his ground and did his part. He took the drop and threw it against the bull's forehead. No sooner did the drop touch his forehead than there stood before the king the finest young man he had ever laid eyes on. The spell had gone. The young man shook hands with the king and thanked him for his bravery. They both went to the palace. The king was so overjoyed that he completely forgot about his cattle that had been killed. There was great rejoicing in the palace that night.

The young husband rested for some days, and then he decided that it was time for him to return to his old home to look after his mother and to get rid of his stepmother. He knew well all that had happened, and he would not rest until the evildoer had been punished.

As soon as the day dawned the next morning, he was up and ready

bull gave a roar and up into the sky.

for the journey. But his wife refused to let him out of the palace unless he allowed her to accompany him. He had to yield. They took with them to the shore plenty of food and drink and a magic wand. They put their baggage in a small boat that was there and bade farewell to the king. They hoisted their bulging swelling sails to the tops of the straight masts, turned the prow of the boat toward the sea and her stern toward the land and never stopped or stayed on their course until they sailed in near the palace of the king of Ireland.

There was drinking and music and storytelling; there was no shortage of storytellers there. At last the stranger was asked to tell a story. He began, and what did he start telling but what had happened to himself from the day he was born up to that time. The stepmother, who was guilty of all that, was sitting listening to him, and as he told his story, she quickly guessed who he was.

When he had finished his story, 'Now, people,' said he to the company, 'I'll leave the decision to ye as to what punishment the woman who did that should get.'

Some suggested this and others suggested that. The question was then put to the stepmother. She said that she should be put up on the highest chimney top of the palace, faced towards the wind, and given no food but whatever small grain the wind might blow to her and no drink but whatever drop of rain she could catch on her tongue.

'You have passed judgment on yourself,' said he.

He gave order that what she had suggested should be done to her immediately, and so it was. He then went out into the yard with his magic wand and struck the stone which was his mother. The next moment she rose up as well as she had ever been. He wet her with tears and dried her with kisses and silks and satins. He took her to the shore, where his own wife was waiting for him in the boat. He put her aboard and hoisted his sails as he had done when coming, and left goodbye and his blessing to Ireland, and returned in joy, with wife and mother, to the palace of the king of the eastern world.

THE MAN WHO WENT FISHING ON SUNDAY

There was once a man they called Jack the Fool. Oh, he had all his wits about him and a good few more, but he just couldn't be happy unless he was up to some game to make the neighbours stare and cause a lot of talk and set him grinning. One Sunday when the church bells began to ring he came down the stairs in his work clothes.

''Tis Sunday,' said his old mother.

'I know that,' says Jack the Fool with a grin.

'And the church bells are ringing,' said his old mother.

'I can hear 'em,' says he with another grin.

'You'll be late for church today,' says his old mother.

'I'm not going,' says he, 'I'm going fishing!'

'Fishing on *Sunday*!' says his old mother, all taken aback at this

He caught Old Ni[

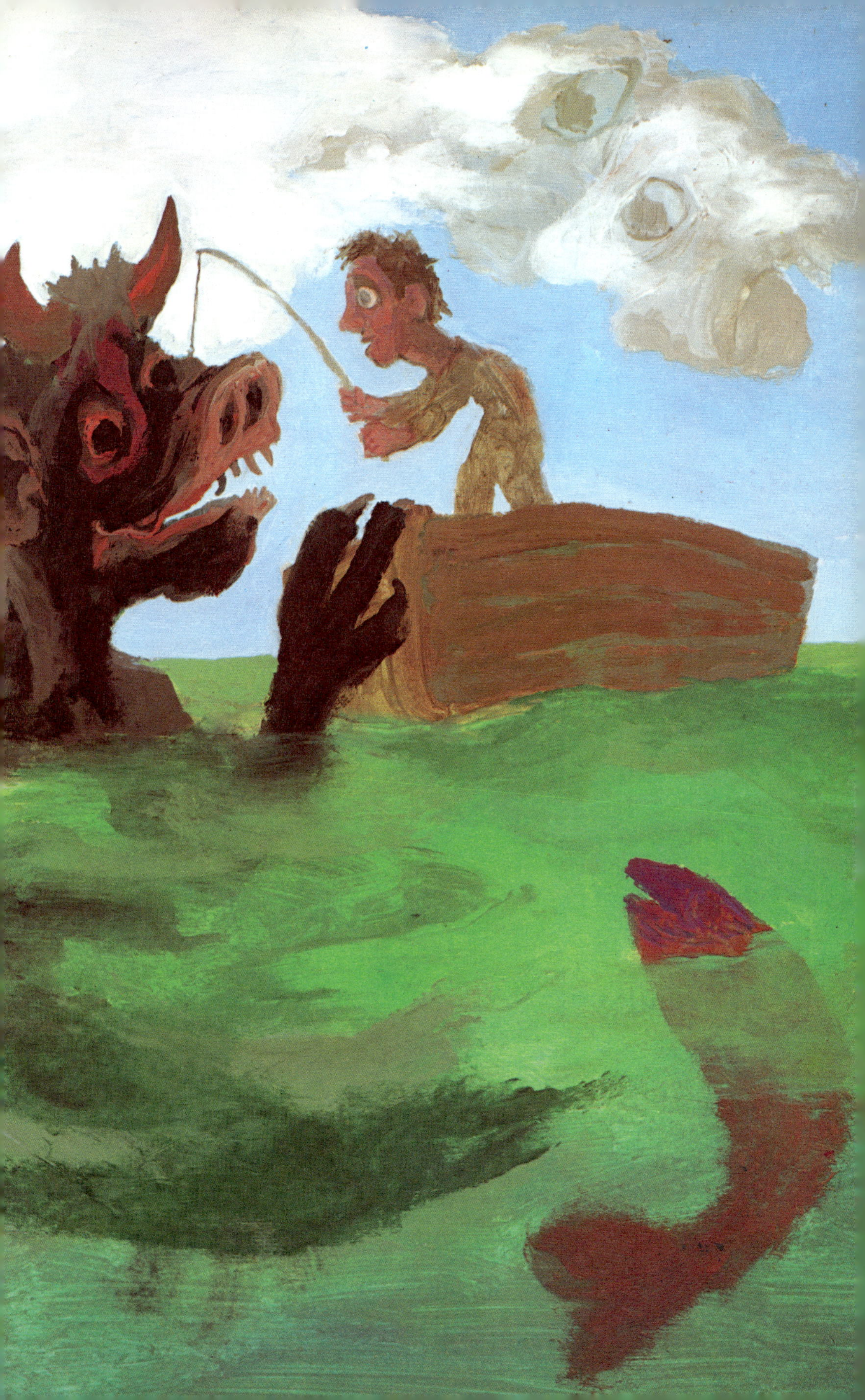

dangerous folly of his. 'You've had all the week to fish.'

'Fish weren't biting,' says he.

''Tis a mortal sin,' said she.

'Then I'll have the Devil's own luck,' said he, and he took his tackle and went out grinning from ear to ear. And she was that frightened she was in too much dread to say one word more in case the church bells stopped ringing and then such words would be terribly dangerous, but she did call after him in warning:

> You will go
> Down Below!

Jack the Fool didn't listen but went and sat on the bank of the mere and sorted his tackle, and the church bells went on ringing and all the neighbours passed by to church.

'Fishing on Sunday!' said they in horror. ''Tis a mortal sin!'

'Then I'll have the Devil's own luck,' says Jack the Fool, grinning all the more.

But at that they all backed away and cried:

> You will go
> Down Below!

And they hurried away to church in case the bells stopped ringing.

'It's a bit warmish Down There,' Jack the Fool shouted after them, 'I'm happy as I am,' and he launched his boat out on the mere.

The sun shone and the church bells rang, and Jack the Fool caught a fine fish. 'I said my luck was in,' he thought, 'and so it is.'

And it *was*. He fished and he fished and he quite forgot it was Sunday, or where he was; he just went on baiting his hook again and again, and soon his boat was loaded with fish and his grin grew so wide it almost met at the back.

Then the church bells stopped and the sun went in and he caught Old Nick! All ready and waiting for him, wet and shiny and scaly with smoke coming out of his nostrils.

'Oh dear! Oh dear!' moaned Jack the Fool. 'You can't come near. 'Tis a Sunday.'

'The bells have stopped ringing,' said Old Nick.

'But I'm a Christian soul,' said Jack the Fool and his teeth chattered like pebbles in a bucket.

'And chose to go fishing instead of going to church to pray,' said Old Nick and he put one wet hand on the boat side.

Well, at that, Jack the Fool was so terrified he couldn't remember a single prayer, all he could say was, 'Oh dear! Oh dear! I'm cold with fear.' 'You won't be cold long,' says Old Nick and he tipped the boat right over.

> And they did go
> Down Below!

So there isn't any more to tell you.

SPIRIT OF THE DOG

There is a boy I knew, one Curtin near Ballinderreen, told me that he was going along the road one night and he saw a dog. It had claws like a cur, and a body like a person, and he couldn't see what its head was like. But it was moaning like a soul in pain, and presently it vanished, and there came most beautiful music, and a woman came out and he thought at first it was the Banshee, and she wearing a red petticoat. And a striped jacket she had on, and a white band about her waist. And to hear more beautiful singing and music he never did, but to know or to understand what she was expressing, he couldn't do it. And at last they came to a place by the roadside where there was some bushes. And she went in there and disappeared under them, and the most beautiful lights came shining where she went in. And when he got home, he himself fainted, and his mother put her beads over him, and blessed him and said prayers. So he got quiet at last.

I would easily believe about the dog having a fight with something his owner couldn't see. That often happens in this island, and that's why every man likes to have a black dog with him at night—a black one is the best for fighting such things.

And a black cock everyone likes to have in their house—a March cock it should be.

We don't give in to such things here as they do in the middle island; but I wouldn't doubt that about the dog. For they can see what we can't see. And there was a man here was out one night and the dog ran on and attacked something that was in front of him—a faery it was—but he could see nothing. And every now and again it would do the same thing, and seemed to be fighting something before him, and when they got home the man got safe into the house, but at the threshold the dog was killed.

Sure a man the other day coming back from your own place, Inchy, when he came to the big tree, heard a squealing, and there he saw a sort of a dog, and it white, and it followed as if holding on to him all the way home. And when he got to the house he near fainted, and asked for a glass of water.

One night I saw the dog myself, in the lane near my house. And that was a bad bit of road, two or three were killed there.

And one night I was between Kiltartan Chapel and Nolan's gate where I had some sheep to look after for the priest. And the dog I had with me ran out into the middle of the road, and there he began to yelp and to fight. I stood and watched him for a while, and surely he was fighting with another dog, but there was nothing to be seen.

And in the same part of the road one night I heard horses galloping, galloping past me. I could hear their hoofs, and they shod, on the stones of the road. But though I stood aside and looked—and it was bright moonlight—there were no horses to be seen. But they were there, and believe me they were not without riders.

That dog I met in the lane at Ballinamantane, he was the size of a

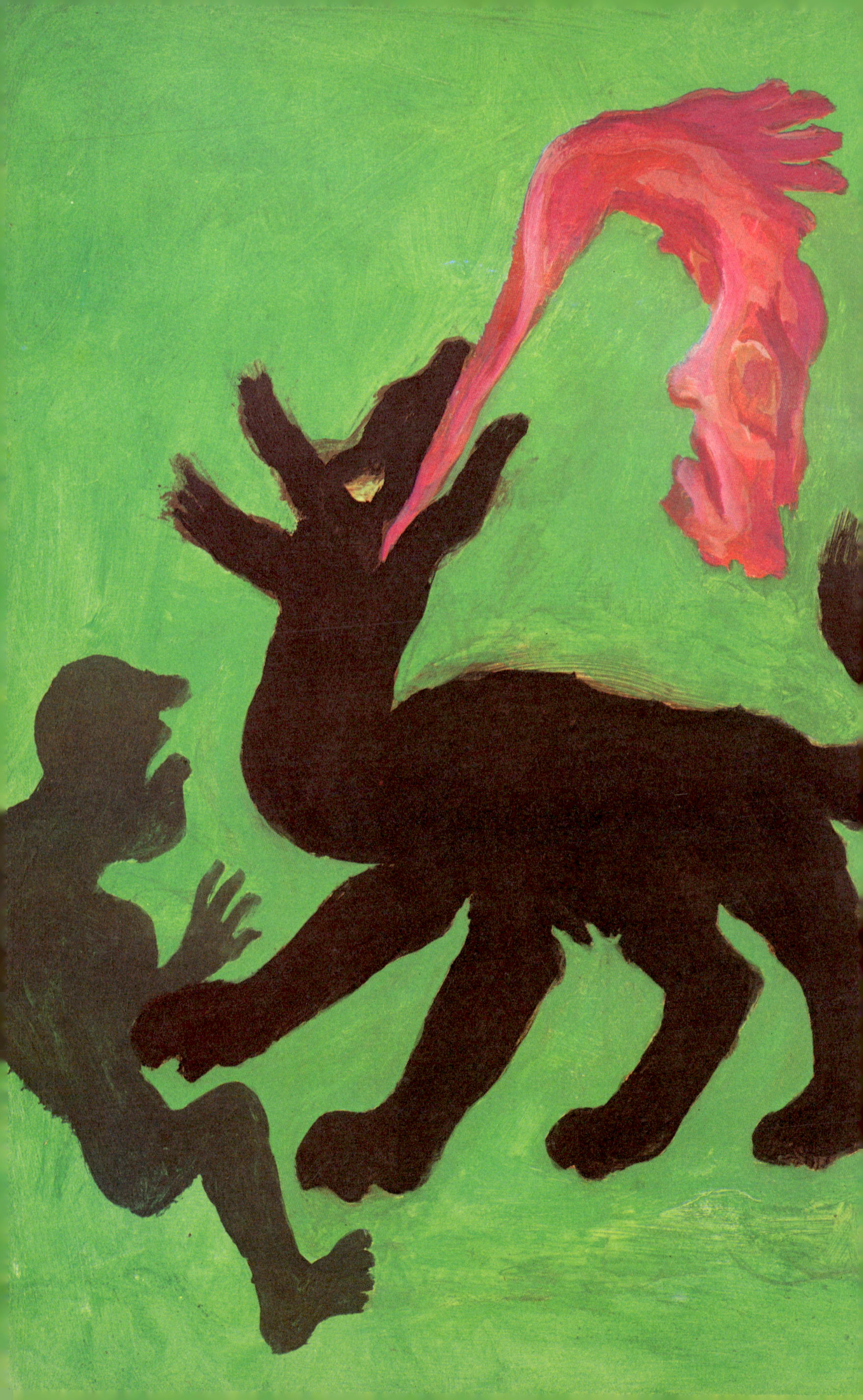

calf, and black, and his paws the size of I don't know what. I was sitting in the house one day, and he came in and sat down by the dresser and looked at me. And I didn't like the look of him when I saw the big eyes of him, and the size of his legs. And just then a man came in that used to make his living by making mats, and he used to lodge with me for a night now and again. And he went out to bring his cart away where he was afraid it'd be knocked about by the people going to the big bonfire at Kiltartan cross-roads. And when he went out I looked out the door, and there was the dog sitting under the cart. So he made a hit at it with a stick, and it was in the stones the stick stuck, and there was the dog sitting at the other side of him. So he came in and gave me abuse and said I must be a strange woman to have such things about me. And he never would come to lodge with me again. But didn't the dog behave well not to do him an injury after he hitting it? It was surely some man that was in that dog, some soul in trouble.

THE QUEEN OF THE PLANETS

There was a man and his wife long ago. The husband had the blessing of everybody, but his wife had the blessing of nobody. She was so hardhearted. The husband was the first to die, and only that the neighbors were so grateful to him, he couldn't be buried at all, the day of the funeral was so wet and stormy. His wife died some time afterward, and she got the two finest days that ever came out of heaven for her wake and funeral. The people were greatly surprised at this, seeing that she had nobody's blessing. Their son then said that he would not sleep a second night on the same bed or eat a second meal at any table until he found out why it was that his father, who had everybody's blessing, got a bad funeral day, while his mother, who had nobody's blessing, got a fine day.

Off he set on his travels. He was a good distance from home when he came to a house, and he got lodgings there for the night. It was the house of a widow who had three daughters. After a meal, the widow asked him where he was going and he told her the whole story.

'Well,' said she, 'if you get the answer to your questions, would you find out why no man wants to marry my eldest daughter? They all want to marry the other two, but they won't even look at the eldest one. I don't know why it is.'

'I have enough troubles of my own,' said the young man, 'without taking more on my shoulders, but if I get any word for you, I'll bring it back.'

He left the house next morning and traveled on until the night came on him. He came to the house of a smith and got lodgings for the night. The smith asked him where he was going, as the widow had, and he told him about his father and mother.

'If you can at all, will you try to bring me some account of what's causing my troubles?' said the smith.

'What troubles have you?' asked the young man.

'Well,' said the smith, 'I'm working here in my forge from morning till night, from Monday to Saturday, and I can't save a penny. I'm as poor as ever at the end.'

'I'll do my best,' said the young man, 'but I don't suppose I'll ever return again.'

He took to the road again the following morning and walked on during the day. He got lodgings in a farmer's house for the night. As they were sitting near the fire, the farmer asked him where he was going, as the other two had done. He told him his story about his father and mother.

'If you can bring me any word, I hope you will,' said the farmer. 'There's a part of the roof down there at the door, and the rain is always coming through. I have called in the best thatchers, but they can't dry it.'

'I have plenty of troubles now to find out about,' said the young man. 'I'm getting no answer to my own questions, but everyone inquires about his own. I'll do my best, and if I get any news for you, I'll bring it back and welcome.'

He set out again the next morning and traveled on during the day with no house meeting him. Night was coming on when at last he saw a light in a house some distance from the road. He made for the house and found the door wide open before him. The kitchen was large and clean and warm; a fine fire was on the hearth, and a big chair in front of it. But there wasn't a sign of a person anywhere. He sat down on the chair, and after a while, in the door came a beautiful woman. She saluted him courteously and kindly, and he answered her in like manner. She prepared a meal for him, and 'twas no trouble to her. He sat down and ate his fill. She then gave him water to bathe his feet in, after his walk. He sat near the fire again, chatting with her. She was as affable a woman as he had ever met.

When they had talked for a long time, she said that it was time for him to go to bed, that he was tired after the day. His room was at the end of the kitchen with a door through which he could see the kitchen from his bed. There was a large pot of water, almost boiling, on the fire. He stretched himself in bed, but tired and all though he was, he didn't fall asleep. It wasn't long till he could see that the pot was boiling over the kitchen fire, but the woman left it there. Then he could see her putting her head down into the boiling pot. She went down, down, down, until all he could see was her two feet sticking up over the rim of the pot. Finally, they too disappeared as well, and not a bit of the woman could be seen. He could see all this clearly through the room door as he lay in the bed. I need hardly tell you, 'twasn't of sleep he was thinking. He was wondering at, and terrified by, what he was seeing. When he thought she was long enough in the boiling pot to be melted away, up she rose out of it again, bit by bit, as she had sunk into it, as much alive as she had been before. The man was frightened out of his wits. He thought he'd be next for the pot.

She then got a rope, made a noose at one end, and threw it over one of the rafters of the kitchen. She stood on a stool, put her head into the noose, and hanged herself. There she was, kicking as she hung, until she finally made no move. When he thought that she must be quite dead with her tongue protruding from her mouth, out from the noose she came as live and energetic as she had ever been.

She next fetched a razor and cut her throat. The blood ran as it would from an ox, until she dropped on the floor and lay there kicking her heels and complaining and moaning. At last she lay quite still.

'She's finished now or never,' said the man below in the bed to himself.

After she had lain on the floor for a while, she stood up again as sound and live as she had been before. The man's thoughts were in a whirl, wondering what was best for him to do. Everything that he had seen was so strange.

It wasn't long till she started another trick. She went and fetched a bag and put it on the table. She pulled the table out on to the center of the floor and started to count the gold and silver coins that were in the bag. She kept at this for a long time, until she had a lot of it counted; then she collected it all together and put it back into the bag.

She next got a silken dress, put it on, picked up a book, and spent a long time reading it. Just as long as she had spent in the pot, in the noose, on the floor with her throat cut, and counting the coins. After reading the book for a time, she came down to the room to the man.

'Are you asleep?' she asked.

He gave no reply.

'I know that you're not asleep,' said she. 'Far from sleeping you are. You saw,' she asked, 'everything I did tonight?'

'I did.'

'Did you ever hear mention of the queen of the planets?'

'I did,' said he.

'I am she,' she said. 'You saw how long I spent in the boiling pot?'

'I did.'

'That's the death which is in store for any child who came into the world during that time. And you saw how long I was hanging?'

'I did,' said he.

'That's the death which is in store for any child born during that time. You saw the time I spent lying on the floor, my throat cut and bleeding?'

'I did.'

'That's the death which is in store for any child born during that time. You saw how long I spent counting the money?'

'I did.'

'That's the way of life which is in store for any child born while I was counting. And you saw how long I spent reading the book?'

'I did.'

'That's the way of life which is in store for any child born during

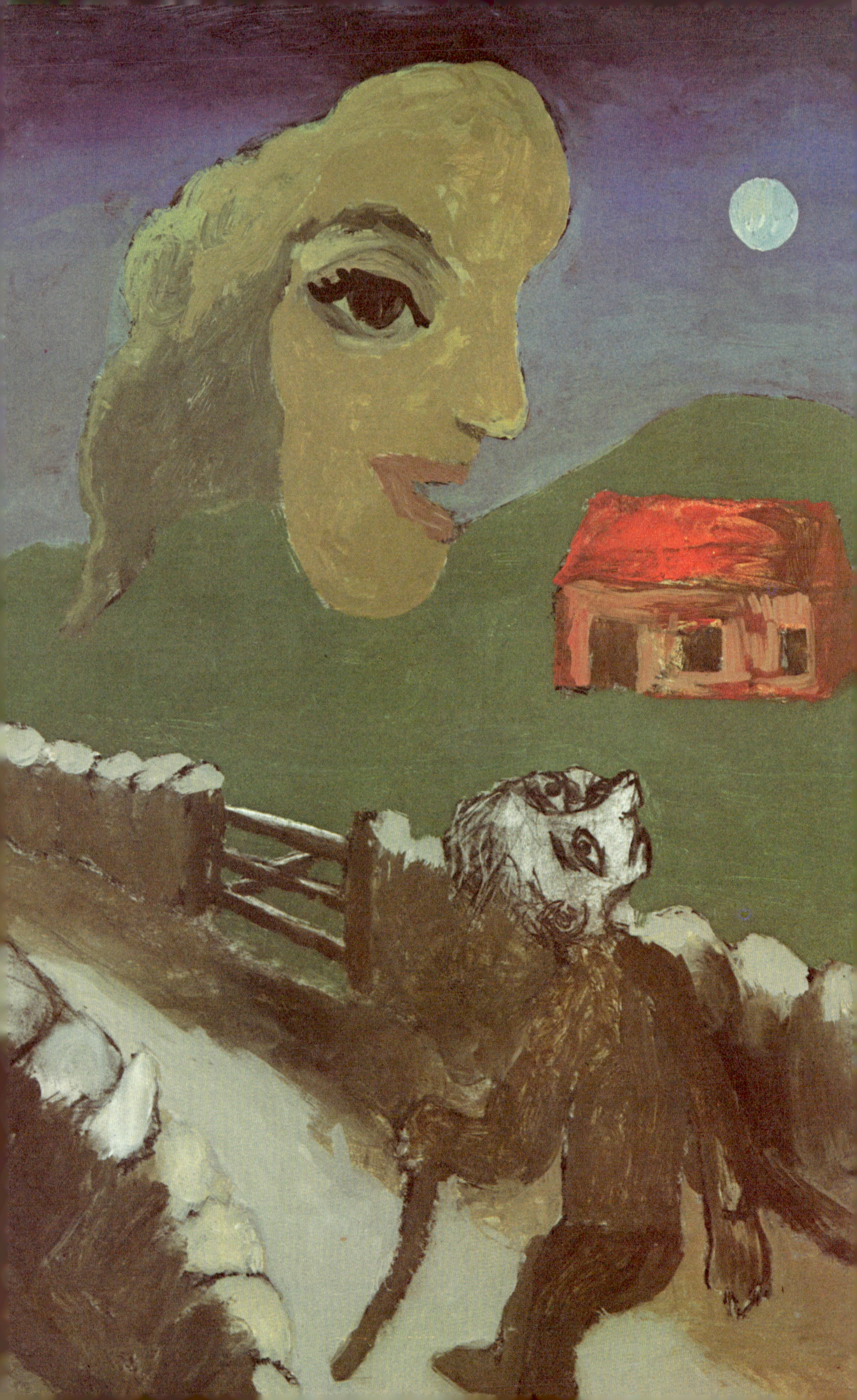

that time. I know what brought you here—to find out about your father and mother. Nobody was ever unthankful to your father. He had the blessing of everybody. His purgatory lasted only during those two wet, stormy days of his funeral. Your mother never got a blessing from a poor person, and all that was in store for her was the two fine days of her funeral. Now, tomorrow you will meet your mother with her mouth open, while two mastiffs pursue her. Here is a brazen apple. You must throw it toward her, and unless it goes straight into her mouth, she will devour you to prevent you from bringing home news of her plight. Tell the widow who is worried about her eldest daughter that if the daughter takes her to Mass two Sundays on her back, everybody will have a high opinion of her. Tell the smith that no luck ever followed those who toil from early on Monday morning until late on Saturday night. As for the farmer, tell him to give back the straw thatch that he stole for his roof, and his house will be dry.'

The young man spent that night in the woman's house and set out for home next morning. He had not traveled far when he saw his mother coming toward him open-mouthed and pursued by two mastiffs. He threw the brazen apple toward her, and it went into her mouth. Down she fell on the road, in the form of a lump of jelly, and the two mastiffs ran off. He traveled home, giving the queen's advice to the farmer, the smith, and the widow on his way. They all followed it and prospered ever after.

THE SHEPHERD OF MYDDVAI

Up in the Black Mountains in Caermarthenshire lies the lake known as Lyn y Van Vach. To the margin of this lake the shepherd of Myddvai once led his lambs, and lay there whilst they sought pasture. Suddenly, from the dark waters of the lake, he saw three maidens rise. Shaking the bright drops from their hair and gliding to the shore, they wandered about amongst his flock. They had more than mortal beauty, and he was filled with love for her that came nearest to him. He offered her the bread he had with him, and she took it and tried it, but then sang to him:

> Hard-baked is thy bread,
> 'Tis not easy to catch me.

and then ran off laughing to the lake.

Next day he took with him bread not so well done, and watched for the maidens. When they came ashore he offered his bread as before, and the maiden tasted it and sang:

> Unbaked is thy bread,
> I will not have thee

and again disappeared in the waves.

A third time did the shepherd of Myddvai try to attract the maiden, and this time he offered her bread that he had found floating about near the shore. This pleased her, and she promised to become his wife if he were able to pick her out from among her sisters on the following day. When the time came the shepherd knew his love by the strap of her sandal. Then she told him she would be as good a wife to him as any earthly maiden could be unless he should strike her three times without cause. Of course he thought that this

*The maidens in t[he]
had more than m[ortal]
beauty.*

could never be; and she, summoning from the lake three cows, two oxen, and a bull, as her marriage portion, was led homeward by him as his bride.

The years passed happily, and three children were born to the shepherd and the lake-maiden. But one day they were going to a christening, and she said to her husband it was far to walk, so he told her to go for the horses.

'I will,' said she, 'if you bring me my gloves which I've left in the house.'

But when he came back with the gloves, he found she had not gone for the horses; so he tapped her lightly on the shoulder with the gloves, and said 'Go, go.'

'That's one,' said she.

Another time they were at a wedding, when suddenly the lake-maiden fell a-sobbing and a-weeping, amid the joy and mirth of all around her.

Her husband tapped her on the shoulder, and asked her, 'Why do you weep?'

'Because they are entering into trouble; and trouble is upon you; for that is the second causeless blow you have given me. Be careful; the third is the last.'

The husband was careful never to strike her again. But one day at a funeral she suddenly burst out into fits of laughter. Her husband forgot, and touched her rather roughly on the shoulder, saying, 'Is this a time for laughter?'

'I laugh,' she said, 'because those that die go out of trouble, but your trouble has come. The last blow has been struck; our marriage is at an end, and so farewell.' And with that she rose up and left the house and went to their home.

Then she, looking round upon her home, called to the cattle she had brought with her:
>Brindle cow, white speckled,
>Spotted cow, bold freckled,
>Old white face, and gray Geringer,
>And the white bull from the king's coast,
>Grey ox, and black calf,
>All, all, follow me home.

Now the black calf had just been slaughtered, and was hanging on the hook; but it got off the hook alive and well and followed her; and the oxen, though they were ploughing, trailed the plough with them and did her bidding. So she fled to the lake again, they following her, and with them plunged into the dark waters. And to this day is the furrow seen which the plough left as it was dragged across the mountains to the tarn.

Only once did she come again, when her sons were grown to manhood, and then she gave them gifts of healing by which they won the name of the Physicians of Myddvai.

THE GREEN LADIES OF ONE TREE HILL

There were once three tall trees on a hill and on moonlight nights singing could be heard and three Green Ladies danced there. No one dared go near except the farmer and he only climbed the hill once a year on Midsummer Eve to lay a posy of late primroses on the root of each tree. The leaves rustled and the sun shone out, and he made quite sure he was safe indoors before sunset. It was a rich farm and he often said to his three sons, 'My father always said our luck lies up there; when I'm dead don't forget to do as I did, and my father before me, and all our forbears through the years.'

And they listened, but did not take much heed, except the youngest.

When the old man died the big farm was divided into three. The eldest brother took a huge slice, and the next brother he took another, and that left the youngest with a strip of poor rough ground at the foot of the hill, but he didn't say much but set to work about it and sang as he worked and was indoors before sunset.

One day his brothers came to see him. Their big farms were not doing very well and when they saw his rich little barley fields and the few loaded fruit trees, and his roots and herbs growing so green and smelling so sweet, and his three cows giving rich milk, they were angry and jealous.

'Who helps you in your work?' they asked. 'They say down in the village there's singing and dancing at night. A hard-working farmer should be abed.'

But the youngest never answered.

'Did we see you up the hill by the trees as we came? What were you about?'

'I was doing as Father told us years ago. 'Tis Midsummer Eve,' he said quietly enough then. But they were too angry to even laugh at him.

'The hill is mine,' cried the eldest. 'Don't let me see you up there again. As for the trees, I need timber for my new great barn, so I'm cutting one down. And you two can help me.' But the second brother found he had to go to market, and the youngest never answered. The next day, Midsummer Day too, the eldest came with carts and men and axes, and called to his youngest brother, who was busy in the herb garden but he only said, 'Remember what day it is.' But the eldest and his team went on up the hill to the three trees. When he laid his axe to the first tree it screamed like a woman, the horses ran away and the men after them, but the eldest went on hacking. The wind howled and the two other trees lashed their branches in anger. Then the murdered tree fell down, down on top of him and killed him. By and by his servants came and took the dead man and the dead tree away and then there were only two Green Ladies on moonlit nights.

The second brother came back from market and took both the farms for himself, and the youngest he still worked his little strip of

No one dared go r hill.

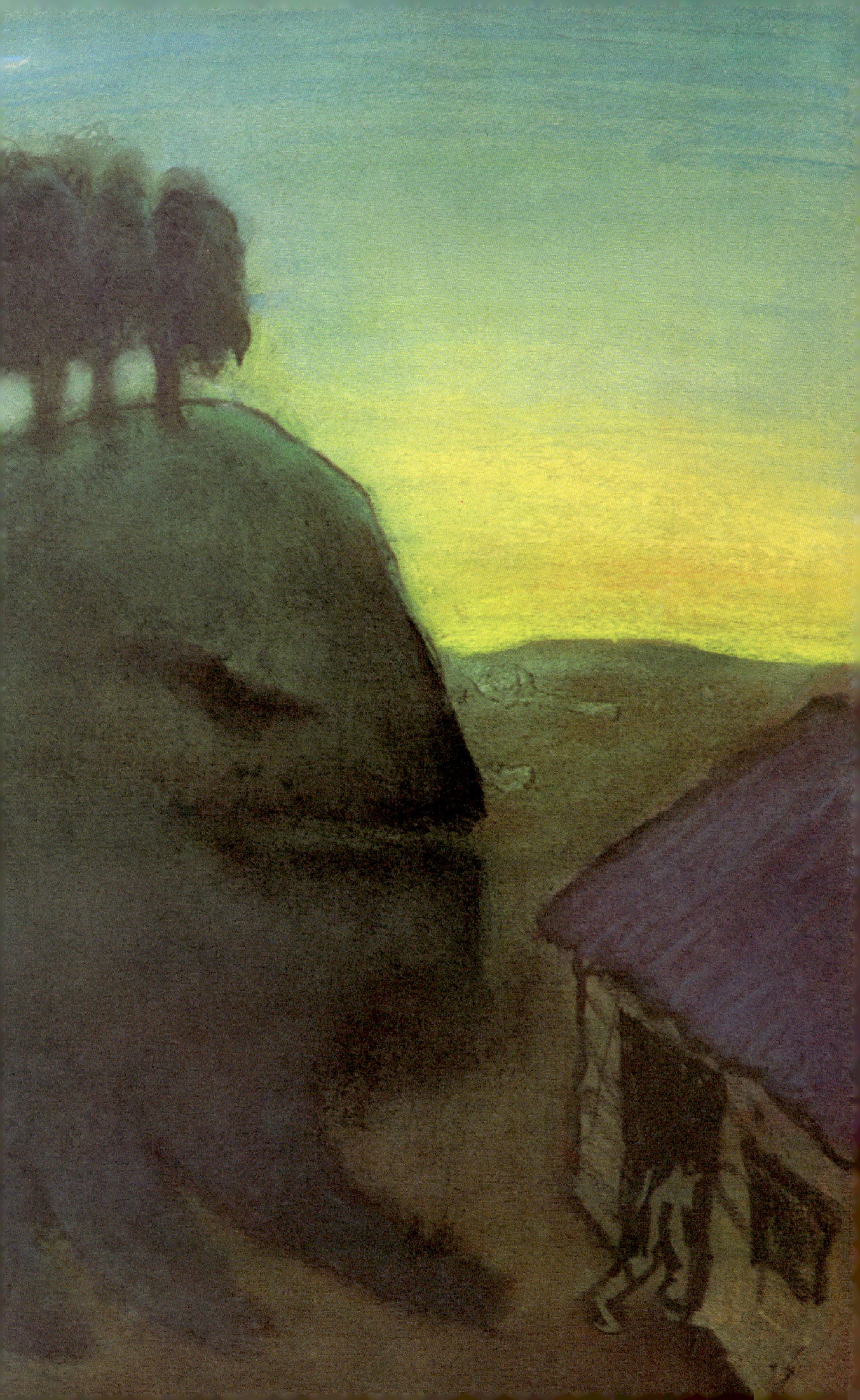

land and took primroses up the hill on Midsummer Eve. But the big farms didn't prosper at all and one Midsummer Eve the second brother saw the youngest brother up by the two trees. He was afraid to go up there, so he yelled, 'Come off my land and take your cows away breaking my hedges down. I'll build a stout timber fence round my hill and I'll cut down one of the trees to make it with.' That night there was no dancing together, there was no music but the crying of many leaves, and the youngest brother was very sad. The next morning the second brother came with an axe and the two trees shuddered but he only made sure there was no wind to drop the tree his way. The tree screamed like a woman as it fell and the youngest brother watching from the lane below with his cows saw the last tree lift a great branch and bring it down on his brother's head and kill him.

People came and took the second dead tree and man away, and the youngest brother now had all three farms, but he still lived in his little farm near the hill and the lonely Green Lady. And sometimes she would dance alone to a sad little tune on moonlit nights, and he always left a bunch of late primroses at the roots of the one tree every Midsummer Eve and his farms prospered from that day.

There are many people nowadays who won't climb One Tree Hill, especially on Midsummer Eve, and one or two very old people remember being told when they were little children that it must never be fenced because it belonged to a Green Lady.

>The hill and the tree are standing there alone.
>It is a sad and dangerous place.

HEROES AND WARRIORS

ASSIPATTLE

Assipattle was the youngest of seven sons. He lived with his father and mother and brothers on a fine farm beside a burn. They all worked hard except Assipattle, who could be persuaded to do little. He lay beside the big open fire in the farm kitchen, caring nothing that he became covered with ashes. His father and mother shook their heads over him; his brothers cursed him for a fool and kicked him. Everyone hooted with mirth when Assipattle told, of an evening, stories of incredible battles in which he was the hero.

One day awful news reached the farm. It was said that the muckle mester Stoor Worm was coming close to land. The Stoor Worm was the most dreaded creature in all the world. People grew pale and crossed themselves when they heard his name, for he was the worst of 'the nine fearful curses that plague mankind'.

If the earth shook and the sea swept over the fields, it was Stoor Worm yawning. He was so long that there was no place for his body until he coiled it around the earth. His breath was so venomous that when he was angry and blew out a great blast of it every living thing within reach was destroyed and all the crops were withered. With his forked tongue he would sweep hills and villages into the sea, or seize and crush a house or ship so that he could devour the people inside.

When he came close to the country where Assipattle lived, and began to yawn, the people knew that he must be fed, otherwise he would get into a rage and destroy the whole land. The news was that the king had consulted a wise man, a spaeman, about what must be done. After thinking a while, the spaeman said that the only way to keep the Stoor Worm happy was to feed him on young virgins, seven of them each week. The people were horrified by this, but the danger was so appalling that they consented.

Every Saturday morning seven terrified girls were bound hand and foot and laid on a rock beside the shore. Then the monster raised his head from the sea and seized them in the fork of his tongue and they were seen no more.

As they listened to what the king's messenger, who had brought the news, had to tell, the faces of Assipattle's father and brothers grew grey and they trembled, but Assipattle declared he was ready to fight the monster. All through the years, he bragged, he had been saving his strength just for this. His brothers were furious and pelted him with stones, but his father said sadly, 'It's likely you'll fight the Stoor Worm when I make spoons from the horns of the moon.'

There were even more dreadful things for the messenger to relate. He said that the people of the country were so horrified by the deaths of the loveliest and most innocent girls that they demanded some other remedy. Once again the king consulted the spaeman, who declared at long last, with terror in his eyes, that the only way to persuade the monster to depart was to offer him the most beautiful girl in the land, the Princess Gem-de-lovely, the king's only child.

Gem-de-lovely was the king's heir and he loved her more than anyone else. But the people were so frantic with grief at the loss of their own children, that the king said with tears rolling down his cheeks, 'It is surely a wonderful thing that the last of the oldest race in the land, who is descended from the great god Odin, should die for her folk.'

There was only one possible way of saving the princess, so the king asked for sufficient time to send messengers to every part of his realm. They were to announce that the princess would become the wife of any man who was strong enough and brave enough to fight the monster and overcome him. The wedding gift to the champion would be the kingdom itself and the famous sword Sikkersnapper that the king had inherited from Odin.

Thirty champions had come to the palace, but only twelve of them remained after they had seen the Stoor Worm. Even they were sick with fear. It was certain that the king had no faith in them. Old and feeble as he was, he had taken the sword Sikkersnapper out of the chest behind the high table, and had sworn that he would fight the monster himself rather than let his daughter be destroyed. His boat was pulled down from its mooring and was anchored near the shore, so as to be ready when he needed it.

Assipattle listened eagerly to all this, but no one heeded him. The messenger mounted his horse and slowly rode away. Soon the father and mother went to bed. From where he lay in the ashes beside the flickering fire, Assipattle heard them saying that they would go next day to see the fight between the king and the monster. They would ride Teetgong, who was the swiftest horse in the land.

How was it that Teetgong could be made to gallop faster than any other horse? asked the mother. It was a long time before Assipattle's father would tell her, but at last, worn out by her questions, he said, 'When I want Teetgong to stand I give him a clap on the left shoulder; when I want him to run quickly I give him two claps on the right shoulder; and when I want him to gallop as fast as he can go I blow through the wind-pipe of a goose that I always keep in my pocket. He has only to hear that and he goes like the wind.'

After a while there was silence and Assipattle knew that they were asleep. Very quietly he pulled the goose pipe out of his father's pocket. He found his way to the stable, where he tried to bridle Teetgong. At first the horse kicked and reared, but when Assipattle patted him on his left shoulder he was as still as a mouse. When Assipattle got on his back and patted his right shoulder he started off with a loud neigh. The noise wakened the father, who sprang up and called his sons. All of them mounted the best horses they could find and set off in pursuit of the thief, little knowing that it was Assipattle.

The father, who rode fastest, almost overtook Teetgong, and he shouted to him,

> 'Hi, hi, ho!
> Teetgong wo.'

At that, Teetgong came at once to a halt. Assipattle put the goose pipe to his mouth and blew as hard as he could. When Teetgong heard the sound he galloped away like the wind, leaving his master and the six sons far behind. The speed was such that Assipattle could hardly breathe.

It was almost dawn when Assipattle reached the coast where the Stoor Worm was lying. There was a dale between the hills. In the dale was a small croft house. Assipattle tethered his horse and slipped into the croft. An old woman lay in bed, snoring loudly. The fire had been banked, and an iron pot stood beside it. Assipattle seized the pot. In it he placed a glowing peat from the fire. The woman did not waken as he crept quietly out of the house, but the grey cat which lay at the bottom of her bed yawned and stretched itself.

Down to the shore Assipattle hurried. Far out from the land there was a dark high island, which was really the top of the Stoor Worm's head. But close to the shore a boat was rocking at anchor. A man stood up in the boat beating his sides, for it was a cold morning. Assipattle shouted to the man, 'Why don't you come on shore to warm yourself?'

'I would if I could', replied the man, 'but the king's steward would thrash me black and blue if I left the boat.'

'You had better stay then,' said Assipattle, 'a whole skin is better than a shirtful of sore bones. As for myself, I am going to light a fire to cook limpets for my breakfast.' And he began to dig a hollow in the ground for a fireplace.

He dug for a minute or two, then he jumped up crying, 'Gold! It must be gold! It's yellower than the corn and brighter than the sun!'

When the man in the boat heard this he jumped into the water and waded ashore. He almost knocked Assipattle down, so anxious was he to see the gold. With his bare hands he scratched the earth where Assipattle had been digging.

Meanwhile, Assipattle untied the painter and sprang into the boat with the pot in his hand. He was well out to sea when the man looked up from his digging and began to roar with rage. The sun appeared like a red ball over the end of the valley as Assipattle hoisted his sail and steered towards the head of the monster. When he looked behind, he could see that the king and all his men had gathered on the shore. Some of them were dancing with fury, bawling at him to come back. He paid no heed, knowing that he must reach the Stoor Worm before the creature gave his seventh yawn.

The Stoor Worm's head was like a mountain and his eyes like round lochs, very deep and dark. When the sun shone in his eyes the monster wakened and began to yawn. He always gave seven long yawns, then his dreadful forked tongue shot out and seized any living thing that happened to be near. Assipattle steered close to the monster's mouth as he yawned a second time. With each yawn a vast tide of water was swept down the Stoor Worm's gullet. Assipattle and his boat were carried with it into the mighty cavern of a mouth, then down the throat, then along twisting passages, like tremendous tunnels. Mile after mile he was whirled, with the water gurgling around him. At last the force of the current grew less, the water got shallower, and the boat grounded.

Assipattle knew that he had only a short while before the next yawn, so he ran, as he had never run in his life, around one corner after another until he came to the Stoor Worm's liver.

He pulled out a large knife and cut a hole in the liver. Then he took the peat out of the pail and pushed it into the hole, blowing for all he

The monster seized them with the fork of his tongue.

137

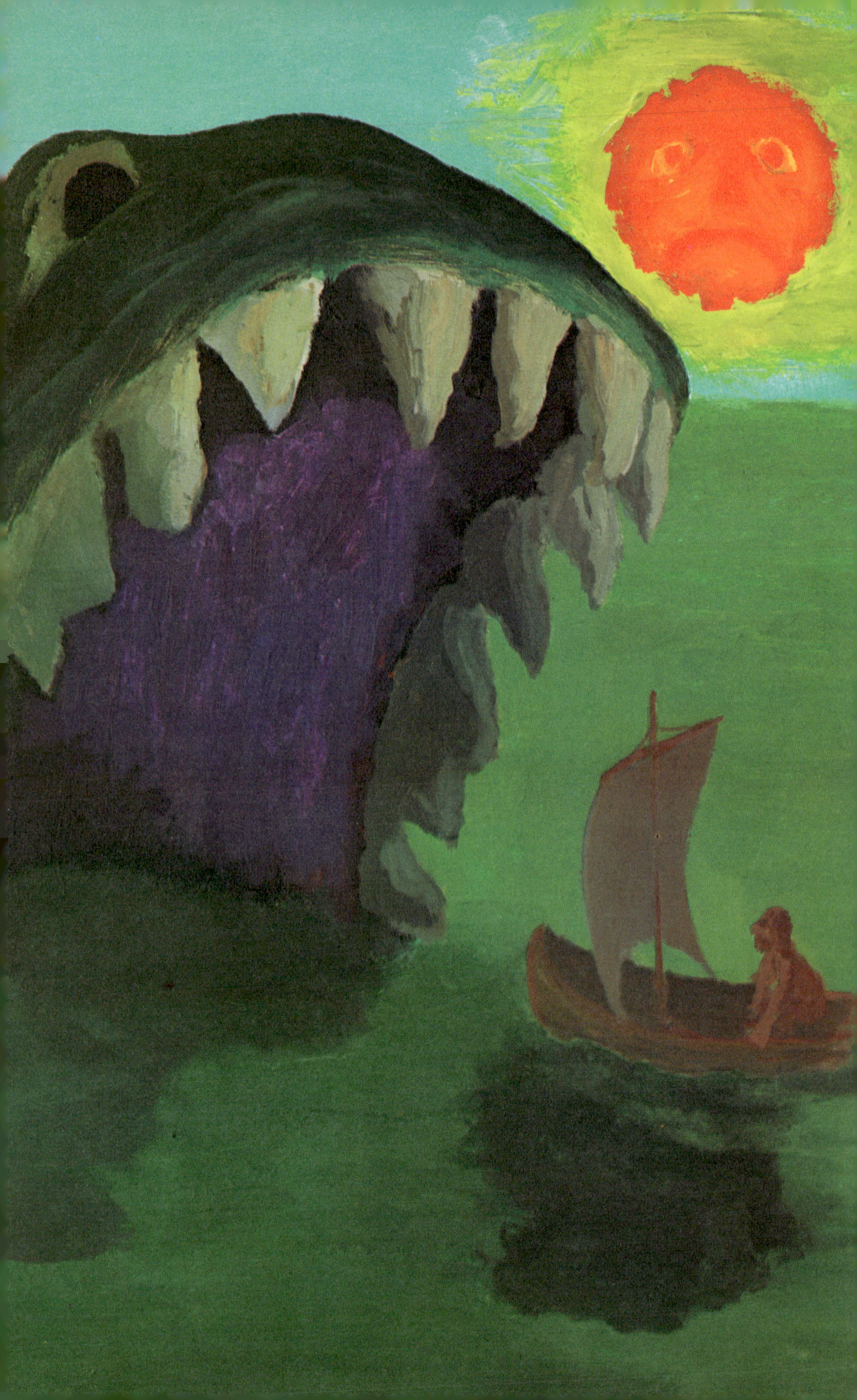

was worth to make it burst into flame. He thought the fire would never take, and had almost given up hope, when there was a tremendous blaze and the liver began to burn and sputter like a Johnsmas bonfire. When he was sure that the whole liver would soon be burning, Assipattle ran back to his boat. He ran even faster than he had done before, and he reached it just in time, for the burning liver made the Stoor Worm so ill that he retched and retched. A flood of water from the stomach caught the boat and carried it up to the monster's throat, and out of his mouth, and right to the shore, where it landed high and dry.

Although Assipattle was safe and sound, no one had any thought for him, for it seemed that the end of the world had come. The king and his men, and Assipattle, and the man who had been in the boat, and the old woman, who had been wakened by the noise, and her cat, all scrambled up the hill to escape from the floods that rushed from the Stoor Worm's mouth.

Bigger and bigger grew the fire. Black clouds of smoke swirled from the monster's nostrils, so that the sky was filled with darkness. In his agony he shot out his forked tongue until it laid hold of a horn of the moon. But it slipped off and fell with such a shock that it made a deep rift in the earth. The tide rushed into the rift between the Dane's land and Norrowa. The place where the end of the tongue fell is the Baltic Sea. The Stoor Worm twisted and turned in torment. He flung his head up to the sky, and every time it fell the whole world shook and groaned. With each fall, teeth dropped out of the vile spewing mouth. The first lot became the Orkney Islands; the next lot became the Shetland Islands; and last of all, when the Stoor Worm was nearly dead, the Faroe Islands fell with an almighty splash into the sea. In the end the monster coiled himself tightly together into a huge mass. Old folk say that the far country of Iceland is the dead body of the Stoor Worm, with the liver still blazing beneath its burning mountains.

After a long while the sky cleared and the sun shone, and the people came to themselves again. On the top of the hill the king took Assipattle into his arms and called him his son. He dressed Assipattle in a crimson robe, and put the fair white hand of Gem-de-lovely into the hand of Assipattle. Then he girded the sword Sikkersnapper on Assipattle. And he said that as far as his kingdom stretched, north, south, east and west, everything belonged to the hero who had saved the land and people.

A week later, Assipattle and Gem-de-lovely were married in the royal palace. Never was there such a wedding, for everyone in the kingdom was happy that the Stoor Worm would never trouble them again. All over the country there was singing and dancing. King Assipattle and Queen Gem-de-lovely were full of joy, for they loved each other so much. They had ever so many fine bairns; and if they are not dead, they are living yet.

ssipattle and his boat ere carried into the ıping mouth.

FINN IN SEARCH OF HIS YOUTH

One fine day, Finn mac Cool and fourteen of his men were hunting on the top of Muisire Mountain. They had spent the whole day since sunrise there but met no game.

Late in the evening, Finn spoke,"Tis as well for us to face for home, men. We're catching nothing, and it will be late when we, hungry and thirsty, reach home.'

'Upon my soul. We're hungry and thirsty as it is,' said Conán.

They turned on their heels and went down the mountainside, but if they did, they weren't far down when a dark black fog fell on them. They lost their way and didn't know whether to go east or west. Finally they had to sit down where they were.

'I'm afraid, men, that we're astray for the evening,' said Finn. 'I never yet liked a fog of this kind.'

After they had sat for a while talking and arguing, whatever look Diarmaid gave around, he saw a beautiful nice lime-white house behind them.

'Come along, men, to this house over there,' said he. 'Maybe we'll get something to eat and drink there.'

They all agreed and made their way to the house. When they entered, there was nobody before them but a wizened old man who was lying in a bent position at the edge of the hearth and a sheep which was tied along by the wall. They sat down. The old man raised his head and welcomed Finn and his men heartily.

'By my soul,' said Diarmaid to himself. "Tisn't very likely that our thirst or hunger will be eased in this hovel.'

After awhile, the old man called loudly to a young woman who was below in a room telling her to come up and get food ready for Finn and his men. Then there walked up the floor from below, a fine strapping handsome young woman, and it didn't take her long to get food and drink ready for them. She pulled a long ample table out into the middle of the floor, spread a tablecloth on it, and laid out the dinner for the Fianna. She seated Finn at the head of the table and set every man's meal in front of him. No sooner had each of them put the first bite of food into his mouth than the sheep which was tied along the wall stretched and broke the hard hempen tying that was holding her and rushed towards the table. She upset it by lifting one end of it and not a scrap of food was left that wasn't thrown to the floor in front of the Fianna.

'The devil take you,' cried Conan. 'Look at the mess you have made of our dinner, and we badly in need of it.'

'Get up, Conán, and tie the sheep,' said Finn.

Conan, looking very angry at the loss of his dinner, got up against his will and walked to the sheep. He caught her by the top of the head and tried to drag her toward the wall. But if he broke his heart in the attempt, he couldn't tie her up. He stood there looking at her.

'By heavens,' said he. 'As great a warrior and hero as I am, here's this sheep today, and I can't tie her. Maybe someone else can?'

'Get up, Diarmaid, and tie the sheep,' said Finn.

Diarmaid stood up and tried, but if he did, he failed to tie her. Each of the fourteen men made an attempt, but it was no use.

'My shame on ye,' said the old man. 'To say that as great as your valor has ever been, ye can't tie an animal as small as a sheep to the side of the wall with a bit of rope.'

He got up from the edge of the hearth and hobbled down the floor. As he went, six pintsful of ashes fell from the backside of his trousers, because he had been so long lying on the hearth. He took hold of the sheep by the scruff of the head, pulled her easily in to the wall, and tied her up. When the Fianna saw him tie the sheep, they were seized with fear and trembling, seeing that he could do it after themselves had failed, brave and all though they were. The old man returned to his place by the fire.

'Come up here and get some food ready for Finn and his men,' he called to the young woman.

She came up from the room again, and whatever knack or magic she had, she wasn't long preparing new food to set before them.

'Start eating now, men; ye'll have no more trouble,' said the old man. 'This dinner will quench your thirst and hunger.'

When they had eaten and were feeling happy with their stomachs full, they drew their chairs back from the table. Whatever peering around Finn had—he was always restless—he looked toward the room and saw the young woman sitting on a chair there. He got a great desire to talk to her for a while. He went down to the room to her.

'Finn mac Cool,' said she; 'you had me once and you won't have me again.'

He had to turn on his heel and go back to his chair. Diarmaid then went down to her, but he got the same answer; so did each of the rest of the Fianna. Oisin was the last to try, but she said the same thing to him. She took him by the hand and led him up the floor till she stood in front of the Fianna.

'Finn mac Cool,' said she; 'ye were ever famous for strength and agility and prowess, and still each of you failed to tie the sheep. This sheep is not of the usual kind. She is Strength. And that old man over there is Death. As strong as the sheep was, the old man was able to overcome her. Death will overcome ye in the same way, strong and all as ye are. I myself am a planet sent by God, and it is God who has placed this hovel here for ye. I am Youth. Each of you had me once but never will again. And now, I will give each of you whatever gift he asks me for.'

Finn was the first to speak, and he asked that he might lose the smell of clay, which he had had ever since he sinned with a woman who was dead.

Diarmaid said that what he wanted was a love spot on his body, so that every young woman who saw it would fall in love with him.

Oscar asked for a thong which would never break for his flail.

Conán asked for the power of killing hundreds in battle, while he himself would be invulnerable.

On hearing this, Diarmaid spoke.

'Alas!' said he. 'If Conán is given the power of killing hundreds, for heaven's sake, don't let him know how to use it. He's a very strong, but a very vicious man, and if he loses his temper, he won't leave one of the Fianna alive.'

And that left Conán as he was ever afterward. He never knew how to use this power that he had, except once at the Battle of Ventry, when he looked at the enemy through his fingers and slew every one of them.

THE EVERLASTING FIGHT

It was long ago, and a long time ago it was. If I were alive then, I wouldn't be alive now. If I were, I would have a new story or an old one, or I mightn't have any story!

There was a warrior in Ireland long ago, and his occupation was hunting and fowling on the hillside, listening to the baying of hounds and the clanging of chains, to the whistle of the man from the east and the call of the man from the west, and no sweeter to him would be the storm from the west across the lake than the coming of Conán Maol as he threw stones! One day when the warrior was hunting and fowling with his pack of hounds, he saw three men bearing a box like a coffin on their shoulders. He went towards them and stood in front of them to find out what they had in the box, but they weren't willing to tell him that or where they were taking it to. So he decided to take the box from them, if he were strong enough, and see what was in it. They attacked one another, and it wasn't long until he had beaten them badly and taken the box from them. He then opened it to see what was inside. It was a woman whose like he had never seen, so beautiful was she.

'I'm taking this woman with me,' said he, 'whether ye like it or not!'

'You're not!' said one of the men. 'We'll lose our heads rather than let you take her!'

'I'm taking her and cutting the heads off the three of you as well!' said the warrior.

One of the three was bolder than the other two, so the warrior drew a blow of his sword at him and severed one of his arms.

'Go off home now and take your arm with you!' said the warrior.

He took the woman home that evening and put her into a room until next day, when he intended to take her to a monk or a priest—whichever sort was there at that time—to get married. As soon as he got up next morning, he went to the room where he had left the woman, but she wasn't there. He didn't know where she had gone to, so he said to himself that he would never stop or stay until he found

He kept walking u
the day was drawi
a close.

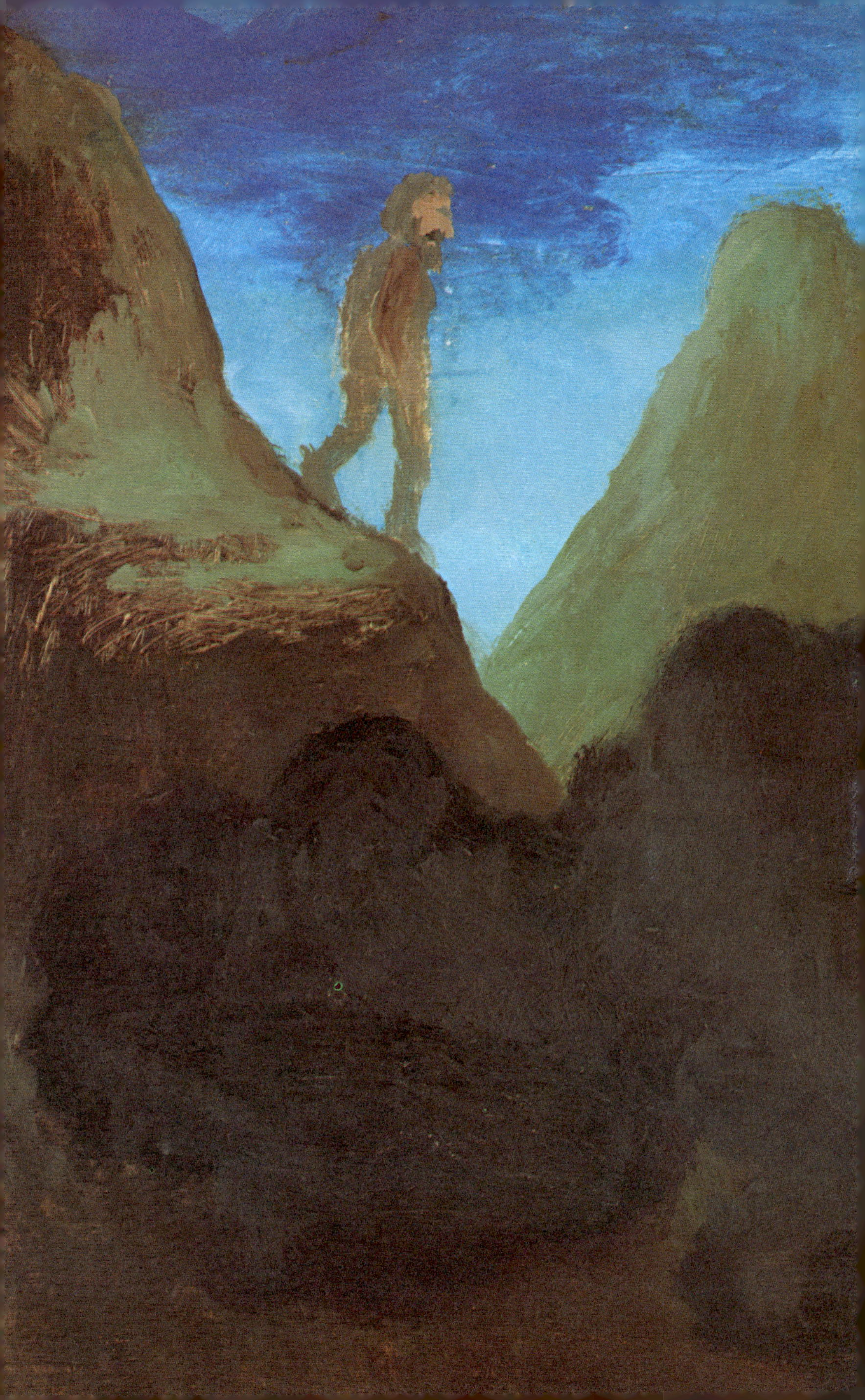

her, wherever in Ireland she might be. He set forth and kept on walking and travelling until the day was drawing to a close; until the white gelding was seeking the shade of the dock-leaf, though the dock-leaf wouldn't stand still for him; and until the sun had sunk into the earth and night was falling. He saw a light far away, and not near him, so he went towards it and entered a house. No sooner had he come in than the young woman for whom he was searching came down from a room. She smothered him with kisses and drowned him with tears, and then dried him with fine, silken towels and with her own hair. There wasn't a man anywhere she thought more of! The arm which he had severed from one of the three men the previous day was lying on a table at the other side of the room. It rose up from the table suddenly and struck him a painful blow on the jaw-bone.

'You wouldn't do that again, arm,' said the warrior, 'if I thought it worth my while to strike you back!'

'Well,' said the young woman, 'the three men who were carrying me yesterday when you took me from them are my three brothers, and when they come home here tonight, they'll kill me and they'll kill you, unless they promise me that they won't harm you. But I must hide you until I get that promise from them.'

She left him, and when he had eaten his supper, she hid him and told him about her brothers. They had to spend every day of their lives, she said, fighting against three waves of enemies, who wanted to take their land from them and banish them.

'My brothers kill them all every day,' said she, 'but they are alive next morning, ready to fight again! And since you cut the arm off one of them, it will take them longer each day to kill the enemy, and they will come home later in the evening.'

That was that! The three brothers came into the house later in the night and sat down to eat their supper. Each one of them said that all he asked for was to have revenge on the man who had cut off the arm of one of them. When they were seated at the table, eating, their sister didn't sit down with them. They asked her why she wasn't eating.

'I won't ever eat anything again,' said she, 'unless ye promise me something.'

'We'll promise you anything in the world that we can,' they said, 'except to spare the man who cut the arm off your brother!'

'Ye must promise me whatever I ask for,' said she.

Well, rather than keep her from eating, they promised to do what she wanted, if she ate her food. When they had eaten their supper, she told them what she wanted and uncovered the warrior. Each of the three brothers rushed to attack him, but when they remembered their promise to their sister, not to kill or harm him, they sat down again. Next morning, as soon as they had eaten their breakfast, they got ready to leave the house. He asked them where they were going, and they told him about the three waves of enemies they had to fight each day of their lives.

'They are alive again next morning,' they told him, 'although we have been killing them for many years. If we didn't kill them every day, we would soon have to leave this place altogether.'

'I'll go with ye today to see what I can do,' said the warrior, 'I should be able to do at least as well as the one of you that has lost his arm!'

'Stay at home today! Tomorrow will be soon enough for you,' they said.

twisted the King of Bridge around and k his body up to the ist in the earth.

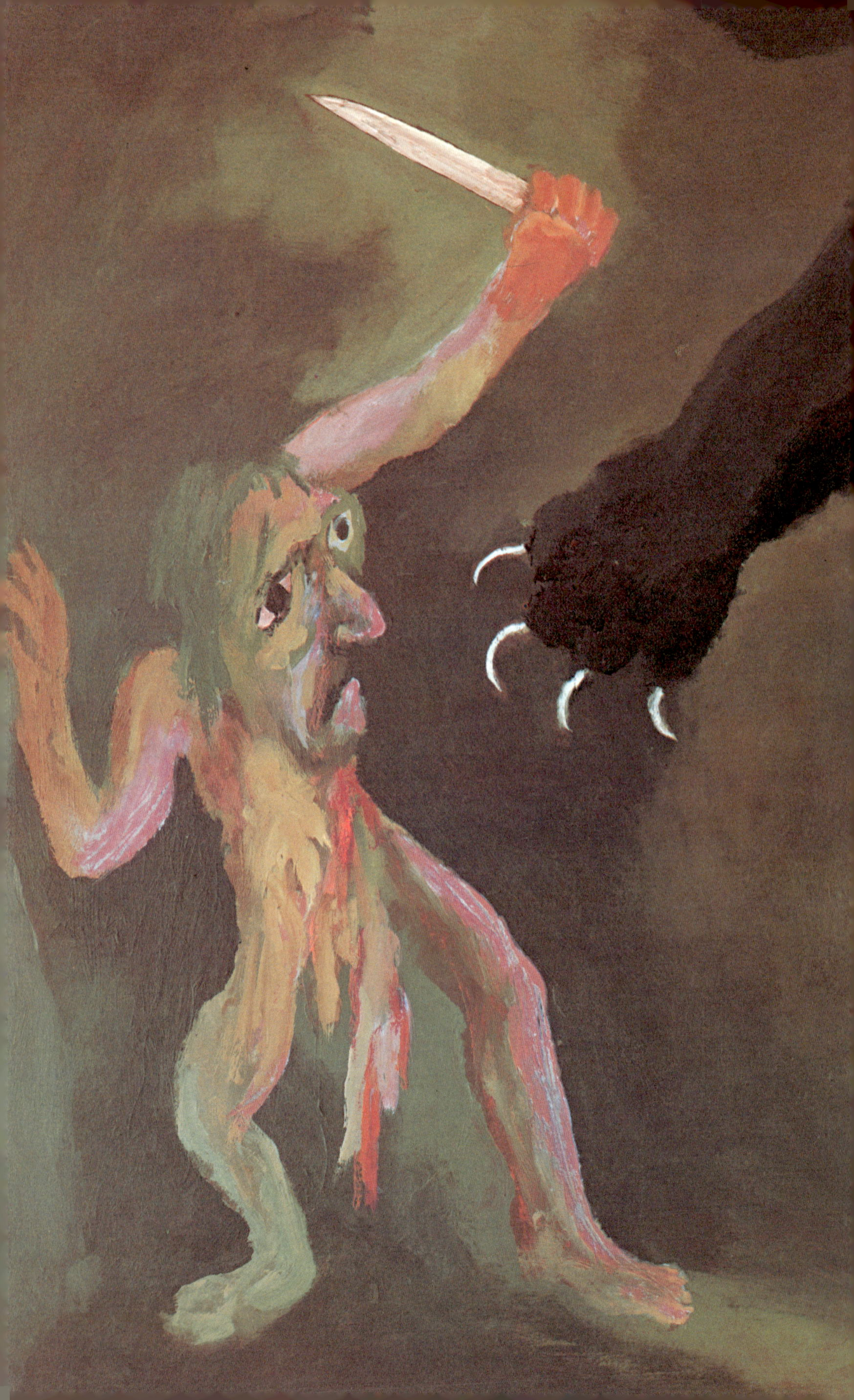

'I won't,' said he. 'I'll go with ye today to see how these men that ye are killing every day can be alive again next morning.'

He went along with them, although they didn't want him to leave the house that day. They were very friendly towards him, in spite of the blame they had on him the previous day. They reached the place where the three waves of enemies were waiting for them, armed with swords and every kind of weapon they could get for the fight.

'Ye must sit down now,' said the warrior to the three brothers, 'until I see what I'm able to do against these.'

He made the three sit down. Then he seized his sword and started to cut off the heads of the enemies, and by the end of two hours, not one of them was alive! It used to take the three brothers the whole day and part of the night to do as much!

'Ye are to go home now,' he told the brothers, 'but I won't leave this place until I find out what is making them alive again every night.'

'You mustn't stay,' said the brothers. 'If you stay here and we go home, our sister will say that we killed you, and she will lose her mind.'

'I don't care,' said the warrior. 'I won't ever leave here until I find out what is making these dead alive again. Go home, and ye can come again tomorrow, if I don't return to the house.'

The three brothers went home, and the warrior remained watching the dead bodies. When night came, he threw heaps of them here and there and lay down between them. It was just midnight when he saw a hag approaching with a small pot in which there was a quill in her hand. She started to throw a dash with the quill of whatever was in the pot on the bodies, and hundreds of them rose up as well and strong and healthy as they had ever been. He kept watching her until she had sprinkled them a few times, and said to himself that, unless he stopped her in time, he would have plenty to do against her and the enemy, if they all came back to life! He attacked them, and it didn't take him long to kill all the men she had revived. Himself and the hag then attacked each other, and he found it harder to overcome her than the three waves of enemies he had killed the previous day. He knocked her down at last and was ready to cut off her head.

'I put a spell on you,' said the hag, 'never to stop or rest until you go to the King of the Bridge and tell him that you killed the Sow and her Litter!'

He cut off her head and set out to find the King of the Bridge. When he came to where he lived, he struck the challenge-pole. He didn't leave a foal in a mare, a calf in a cow, a kid in a she-goat, or a piglet in a sow that he didn't turn around nine times in their skins, with the dint of the blow. The King of the Bridge came out to him.

'I killed the Sow and her Litter tonight,' said the warrior.

'If you did,' said the King of the Bridge, 'you won't ever again kill anybody, after I have finished with you—or else, you're a great warrior.'

They attacked each other, wrestling an arm above and an arm below. They made the hard places soft and the soft places hard; they drew springs of fresh water up through the middle of the grey stones by the dint of hatred and anger and strife. They threw out from themselves four showers of battle: a shower of blood from their waists, a shower of frenzy from their swords, a shower of sweat from their brows and a shower of anger from their teeth. So it went on until the day was drawing to a close and a robin alighted on the warrior's shoulder and said:

'O son of the Irish king, you have come to a bad place to die! It will take me many days to cover your dead body with the leaves of the trees.'

A spasm of anger passed through the warrior. He twisted the King of the Bridge around and sank his body to the waist in the earth; with a second twist, he sank him to the apple of his throat; and with the third twist, he shouted:

'Clay over your body, churl!'

'Let it be so!' said the King of the Bridge. 'But I place you under a spell never to halt or rest until you go to the King of the Churchyard and tell him that you have killed the Sow and her Litter and the King of the Bridge.'

The warrior went off and kept travelling until he came to where the King of the Churchyard was. He struck the challenge-pole and didn't leave a calf in a cow, a foal in a mare, a lamb in a ewe, a kid in a she-goat or a piglet in a sow that he didn't turn about nine times in their skins with the sound of the blow! The King of the Churchyard came out to him.

'I killed the Sow and her Litter and the King of the Bridge,' said the warrior.

'You will never again kill anyone, unless you are a better man than I am!' said the King of the Churchyard.

They attacked each other like mad lions, like two bulls in a field, like two excited rams or two proud enemies that hated each other. They used to throw out from themselves four showers of battle: a shower of blood from their waists, a shower of frenzy from their swords, a shower of sweat from their brows and a shower of anger from their teeth. So it went on until the day was drawing to a close. They didn't know which of them was the better. Then a robin alighted on the warrior's shoulder and said:

'You have come a long way to die here, and it will take me many days to cover your dead body with the leaves of the trees!'

A spasm of anger passed through the warrior's mind, and he pulled himself together. He gave a twist to the King of the Churchyard and sank him to his waist in the earth; with a second twist, he sank him to the apple of his throat, and with the third twist, he shouted:

'That's clay over your body, churl!'

'It is so, best warrior whom I have ever seen,' said the King of the

Churchyard. 'But before you cut off my head, I place you under a spell never to halt or rest until you go to the Great Cat of the Cave and tell him that you have killed the Sow and her Litter, the King of the Bridge and the King of the Churchyard!'

The warrior went off and kept travelling until he reached the place where the Cat of the Cave had made his cave. He entered the mouth of the cave; it was three miles long from mouth to end. So bright was the light that came from the cat's eyes that the warrior could see a small pin that might have fallen on the floor on the darkest night that ever came, even though the cat was a long distance away from him. He kept walking in through the cave, his sword in his hand, ready for the cat, until he reached the very end where the cat was. He looked around everywhere, and then upwards towards a ledge high up in the cave. He caught sight of a small, little cat, sitting on an arch-way and looking down. From the cat's eyes there shone the brightest and finest light that he had ever seen, and it blinded him when it fell on his own face. He stood in front of the cat and said:

'I have killed the Sow and her Litter, the King of the Bridge and the King of the Churchyard!'

The cat swelled in size until his back reached the roof of the cave. Then he stretched down one of his paws and tore the warrior's body from the waist upwards, and dragged his heart and lungs out on to the floor of the cave. The cat then stretched down his other paw to tear the other side of the warrior's body. As he did so, the warrior caught sight of a black spot under the cat's armpit. He thrust his sword upwards through the spot and pierced his heart. The cat fell down, dead, on to the floor on top of the warrior, who was also dead. So large was the cat's body that it completely covered that of the dead warrior!

That was that! On the following day, the woman and her three brothers went to where the battle used to be fought every day. They found all the enemy lying dead, and so too was the hag who used to bring them back to life. The little pot and the quill lay on the ground beside her. The young woman picked them up and put them in her pocket. They walked on towards where the King of the Bridge lived, as they thought that the warrior might have been killed by him, for they knew that he had always been helping their enemies. They made up their minds to search for the warrior, alive or dead. When they came on the body of the King of the Bridge, they went on to where the King of the Churchyard lived. They found him dead also, and knew that it was the warrior who had killed them all so far. Then they thought that the King of the Churchyard might have sent him to the Great Cat of the Cave, and that he was dead, as the cat had never let anybody escape alive.

They reached the cave of the Great Cat. There was no light within when they entered. They made their way slowly to the end of the cave, and there they found the dead body of the cat. They couldn't see any sign of the warrior, alive or dead. So they turned back again, not knowing where the warrior might be found. The young woman was behind the others and, as she walked along in the dark, her foot struck against the shoe of the warrior, who was lying dead under the cat's body. She shouted to her brothers that he was lying under the body of the cat, and that they should try to release him and bring him back to life with the contents of the pot of the old hag. The four of them tried to lift the cat's body off the warrior, but it was no use—they couldn't even move it. They had to cut the cat's body into pieces with their swords, and lay bare what was underneath it. When they dragged the pieces of the cat aside, they put the heart and lungs back into the warrior's body as they had been when he was alive. When they had that done, they rubbed the contents of the pot to his wounds and to his heart and lungs, and he rose to his feet as well as he had ever been.

There weren't in the whole world three men or a young woman more happy than they, at having found him, and at all their enemies whom they had fought for so long being dead. The warrior and the young woman got married, and they spent seven nights and seven days celebrating. They didn't know whether the first night or the last was the better. Every bite had the taste of honey, and no bite was tasteless!

YOUNG CONALL OF HOWTH

One time, Conall, son of the king of Howth, decided to marry, and if he did, it wasn't to his counselors that he went for any advice about it. He went off to his father's wise man and asked him could he find out where the most beautiful young woman in the whole country lived.

'I'll search my books,' said the wise man.

A few days later, he went to Conall.

'I can't find any young woman in the country who is more beautiful than the daughter of the king of Ulster,' said he.

Conall got ready and set out for the castle of the high king of Ulster. The daughter was upstairs in the highest storey of the castle, with twelve women minding her. Conall walked around the lawn in front of the castle, as he didn't wish to announce himself until somebody would come to speak to him. It wasn't long until one of the women happened to look out the window, and she saw the young man walking on the lawn. She went and told the princess that the finest young man she had ever laid eyes on was outside on the lawn.

'But he's very small,' added the woman.

'That's no great fault,' said the princess.

She went to the window and spent a while looking at Conall, and the more she looked at him, the better he appeared in her eyes. She knocked sharply on the window. Conall looked up to see what made the noise. She spoke to him, and he replied.

'Wait there a while, young man,' she shouted. 'We won't delay you long. We have plenty of quilts and blankets here to tie together, and we'll pull you up.'

*He sprang on his
through the windo*

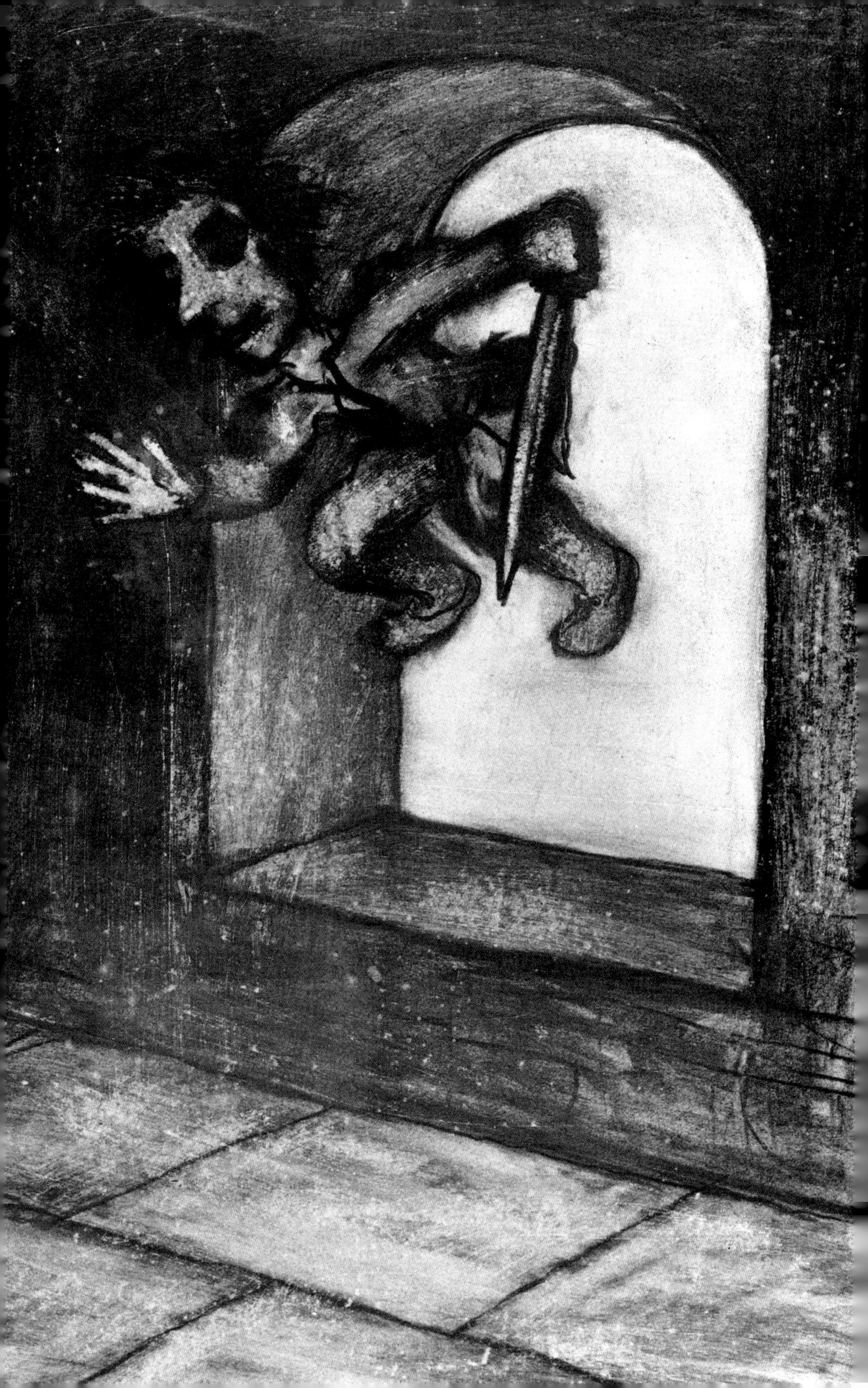

'Is it how you want me to go up to you?' asked Conall.

'I'd like to talk to you for a while,' said she, 'if we can pull you up.'

''Tis a cold outlook I have in the world if I must have blankets and quilts to reach your room,' said Conall. 'Open the window, please.'

When she opened it, Conall stepped back a few feet, not many, and rose up by the activity of his limbs and the pressure of his toes; he put the tip of his sword under him, and the first thing the princess knew he was standing in the room in front of her! She took him into the fine quarters she had there and seated him on a chair. She sat on another chair near him, and they started to talk. Conall got plenty of care and attention from the women.

'Well, I must leave ye for the night,' said Conall when it was growing dark.

'Will you come again tomorrow?'

'I will, indeed, to keep ye company,' said Conall.

He went back to the house where his horse was kept and spent the night there. Next morning, he didn't ask for a quilt or blanket to reach the princess's room. The king didn't know that he was in the castle at all, although he spent two or three days there.

'Do you know the best way to fix things, Conall?' said the princess.

'No, I don't,' said Conall.

'Tonight, when you think everybody in the castle is asleep, bring your horse with you, and before day dawns tomorrow, we'll be a long distance away. My father won't know where I'll be when he gets up tomorrow and he can't find me.'

'Not a bad plan at all,' said Conall.

He went to the castle when all were asleep—as he thought—and she came downstairs and got on the horse behind him. They rode away, but they hadn't gone far when a thought struck Conall. He pulled up the horse.

'Why are you delaying, Conall?' asked the princess.

'A thought has struck me, and I'm going to put it into effect.'

'What is it?'

'I'll tell you, and it won't be any lie,' said Conall. 'I won't let it be said of me in the province of Ulster that I came to steal you from your father and mother. If I can't get you in a fair fight, I'll let you stay with them.'

He turned his horse about and put the princess back into her room again. Next morning after breakfast, he made off for the king's castle and struck the challenge pole. The king sent out a messenger to ask what he wanted. Conall said he wanted the princess or a fight. The messenger was sent out again to find out how many men he wanted against him. Conall named the number, and if he did, he had the last man of them killed before it was very late in the day and no more were sent against him.

Next day he went to the castle again, as the king himself was getting ready to fight him that day. They started to fight. Conall didn't want to harm the king, if he could avoid it by any means. The king was attacking him as hard as he could, but the blows all went wide of the mark. Early in the day Conall saw his chance to grapple with the king, and he knocked him under him on the ground.

'Will I get her now?' he asked.

'You will, and welcome. You well deserve her,' said the king.

All the castle folk gathered around them. The king gave a great feast, which lasted for seven days and nights before the marriage. When the seven days and nights were up, those invited all returned to their own homes and castles, and Conall was married. Soon afterward, he told the king that he would have to return home as there was nobody there except the wise man to look after things.

''Tis your duty to return,' said the king. 'A house without a head is no house.'

Conall and his wife set out with good provisions for the journey, and had reached the border of the province when Conall suggested that they would take a little rest.

'We have been in the saddle a long time now,' said he.

'Do you know what you'll do now, Conall?' said his wife. 'Stay on the saddle until you reach your own castle. If you dismount, you will fall into a warrior's sleep for seven days and seven nights; and before the seventh day is up, I may find myself in the eastern world. That would cause you more trouble than to remain in the saddle now.'

'I never heard any tune by a woman but to hurry home,' said Conall.

It was useless for her to be talking to him. He got off the horse and had barely sat on the ground when he started to fall asleep.

'Get up, Conall!' said the princess. 'You're nodding to sleep and you'll be off in a minute.'

'What I said to you already, I say again,' said Conall. 'If anybody comes after you, all you need do is pull me by the ear.'

'Little good that will do,' said his wife.

He was sound asleep in a moment, and it wasn't long before she saw, wading in through the sea, a huge warrior with a basket on his back. Whenever he spied a fish that he liked, he flicked it over his shoulder into the basket with his toes. She tried to hide herself from him as well as she could, but it was no use. He was so tall that even a bird on the ground couldn't escape his eye. He saw her easily and never stopped or stayed till he stood in front of her.

'There you are,' said he.

'Here I am.'

''Tis funny that I should leave home this morning to seize the daughter of the king of Ulster. If she were behind my back now, I wouldn't take my eyes off you to look at her.'

'That shows that you have never seen her. If you did, you'd turn your back on me. 'Tisn't me you'd have eyes for!'

'Stop your chatter! Get into the basket,' said the warrior.

'How can I go into your basket, and I married to this young fellow?' she asked.

'That makes no difference to me, whether you're married or not,' said he. 'Get into the basket.'

'If this fellow were awake, I'd say you'd have to fight hard before I'd go into it,' said she.

'Is it that child you're talking about?'

'Whatever way he looks in your eyes,' said she, 'if he were awake, I don't think I'd go into your basket.'

'Give over your arguing, and hop in,' said he.

'Well, if you're going to force me to,' said she, 'make a mark on the ground to tell who you are, where you came from, and where you are bound for.'

He did as she asked. When Conall awoke at the end of the seventh day, he thought that he had slept only an hour or two at the most. He also thought that as a joke his wife had gone somewhere so that he would have to search for her. He looked around and searched but failed to find her. There were seven or eight boys herding cows and dry cattle nearby, and he went to talk to them. Some of them were small, others taller.

'Have ye seen any woman around here since morning?' he asked one of the big lads.

'We haven't seen any woman since seven days ago,' he replied.

'Seven days ago!'

'Yes.'

'Where did she go?' asked Conall.

The boy described the warrior who had taken her away.

'Have ye seen my horse anywhere?' asked Conall.

'Your horse is at the other side of that hillock over there, and each day she comes and stands over you, licking and washing you from the top of your head to the soles of your feet. When she has that done, she goes back to graze again.'

Conall went back to where he had been asleep and saw the marks the warrior had left on the ground.

'You were quite right in what you told me, boy,' said Conall. 'Do you know if there is any old boat or ship around here?'

'I know of only one old vessel that's below there on the shore. The cows are rubbing themselves against it every day.'

They went down to it, and at last got it on the tide.

'Now, boys, I'll have to kill your cattle,' said Conall.

The boys started to cry.

'Don't be crying at all. Laughing ye should be, for I'll pay ye double the value of every animal I'll kill. Wait till ye see how glad your father and mother will be when they see all the money. I'll start on the cows.'

He killed some of the animals and skinned them and nailed the skins to the old vessel until he had fixed her for the sea journey.

'Now, boys,' said he, 'keep an eye to my horse until I return. I don't know whether I will return or not. If I don't, ye can sell her and divide the money between ye. Take good care of her.'

Conall defeated t
and they sailed o

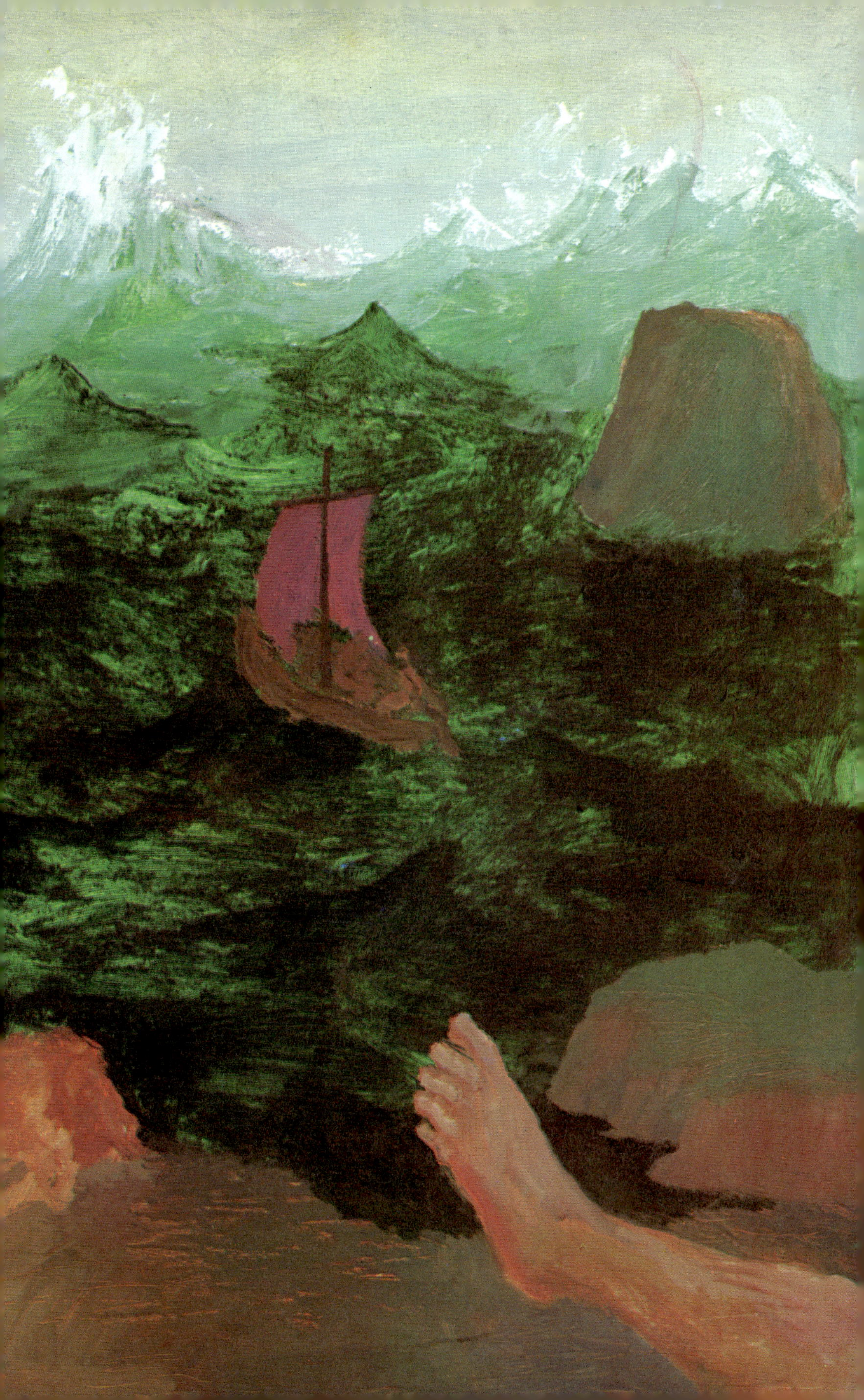

He set out. He hoisted his soft bulging sails on his delightful, beautiful, one-legged vessel, which was smooth and slippery from stem to stern. He sailed over the sea swiftly and as he did he thought that he saw a harbor some distance off. He turned the prow of the vessel toward the harbor and sailed in as far as left him suitably deep water for his return when the tide ebbed. He moored her for a year and a day, even though he might be gone from her only for an hour: one rope landward and two ropes toward the sea—where wind would not toss her about or sun split her or birds of the air befoul her. On shore he soon met an old man who was poorly dressed. They started to chat, and Conall offered him some money.

'May God reward you!' said the old man. 'I have been here for many years, and you are the first to give me anything.'

Now there happened to be in the king's castle in this country an old man from Ireland who had been carried off by a griffin in her talons and had been dropped by the bird on the king's land. He had arrived at the king's castle, and the king, the queen, the sons, and the women of the house had been very kind to him. They all loved one another very much. When the king's sons came home, having met young Conall on the shore and played a hurling game with him, they went into a room by themselves without looking at mother or sister or anybody else. They sat down in the room and not a word out of them. After a while, the king came home and asked had the sons returned yet.

'They have,' said the queen.

'How did the game go today?' asked the king.

'That we can't tell you,' said the queen. 'They never spoke to us when they returned, and we didn't ask them. They're sitting in there in the room with not a word out of them.'

'They must have been beaten today,' said the king, 'to say that they're taking it so badly. 'Tis no great loss to me to send a pig or a beef to every house in the country. They are well used to winning themselves. Why shouldn't they lose now and again?'

'I know nothing about their affairs,' said the queen. 'I can't give you any information.'

The king went to the door of the room and called out the eldest son to the fireplace. 'Were ye beaten today?' he asked.

'We were.'

'Why are ye taking it so badly that ye wouldn't even speak when ye came home? 'Tis no trouble to me to send a pig or a beef to every house in the country.'

''Tisn't a pig or a beef we lost,' said the son. 'We're going to lose our heads.'

'Is that the way it is?' said the king.

'That's the way. And I wouldn't mind if it was a man that beat us.'

'And who beat ye, if it wasn't a man?'

'Well it was a man, but he wasn't the height of my chest.'

'As sure as I'm alive this day,' said the old Irishman, 'it must be young Conall. He could never get enough hurling. He doesn't want your heads. If he did, would he have let ye come home? 'Tis a great shame for ye that ye didn't invite him to the castle. Maybe he's in need of a bite to eat or a drink. Let someone go and ask him in. 'Tis nobody but young Conall. Small and all as he is, no one ever got the upper hand of him.' The queen and her daughter went down to the strand to invite Conall to the castle.

'I'll go with you and welcome,' said Conall. 'But, if I do, it isn't to get the heads of your sons. I don't want their heads at all. If I did, I wouldn't have allowed them to go home.'

They walked back to the castle, and the king and his sons had the greatest welcome and handshakes in the world for Conall. The old Irishman jumped up when he saw him, threw his arms around him, and asked him would he take his bones back to Ireland.

'How sure you are that I'll take even my own bones back!' said Conall.

'That's true enough, Conall,' said the old man. 'But, if you do go back there, will you take me with you?'

'I will and welcome,' said Conall.

A feast was got ready. Only the first of the food had been laid on the table when a man strode in the door, snatched up the dish of meat, or whatever it was, and went off out the door with it.

'Is this some kind of tribute ye have to give him?' asked Conall.

'No,' said the king. 'That man is the greatest warrior in this country and everybody is afraid to stop him.'

'Well, if I knew that,' said Conall, 'he'd have left the food on the table.'

He stood up. The warrior had gone only a short distance from the door when Conall overtook him. He caught him by the collar and turned him about.

'Put that back where you got it,' said Conall.

The warrior obeyed.

'Get up,' said Conall to the old Irishman, 'and tie up this fellow tightly.'

The old man got up and bound every limb of the warrior with hard hempen rope, and left him, lying on his back outside the door under the dripping of the royal candle.

'Were you ever in a worse plight than you are now?' he asked.

'Indeed I was,' said the warrior. 'Give me a bite of food first, and I'll tell you about it.'

The old man loosened his bonds, and he was taken indoors and seated at the table. Nobody interfered with him while he was eating, although he ate almost everything they had for the feast. While the table was being got ready for the others, Conall asked the warrior to tell his story.

''Tis I that will tell it,' said he. 'There wasn't a day that I didn't go out a bit into the sea in a small pleasure boat that I had. One day when I was out, I saw a man coming toward me and his head seemed

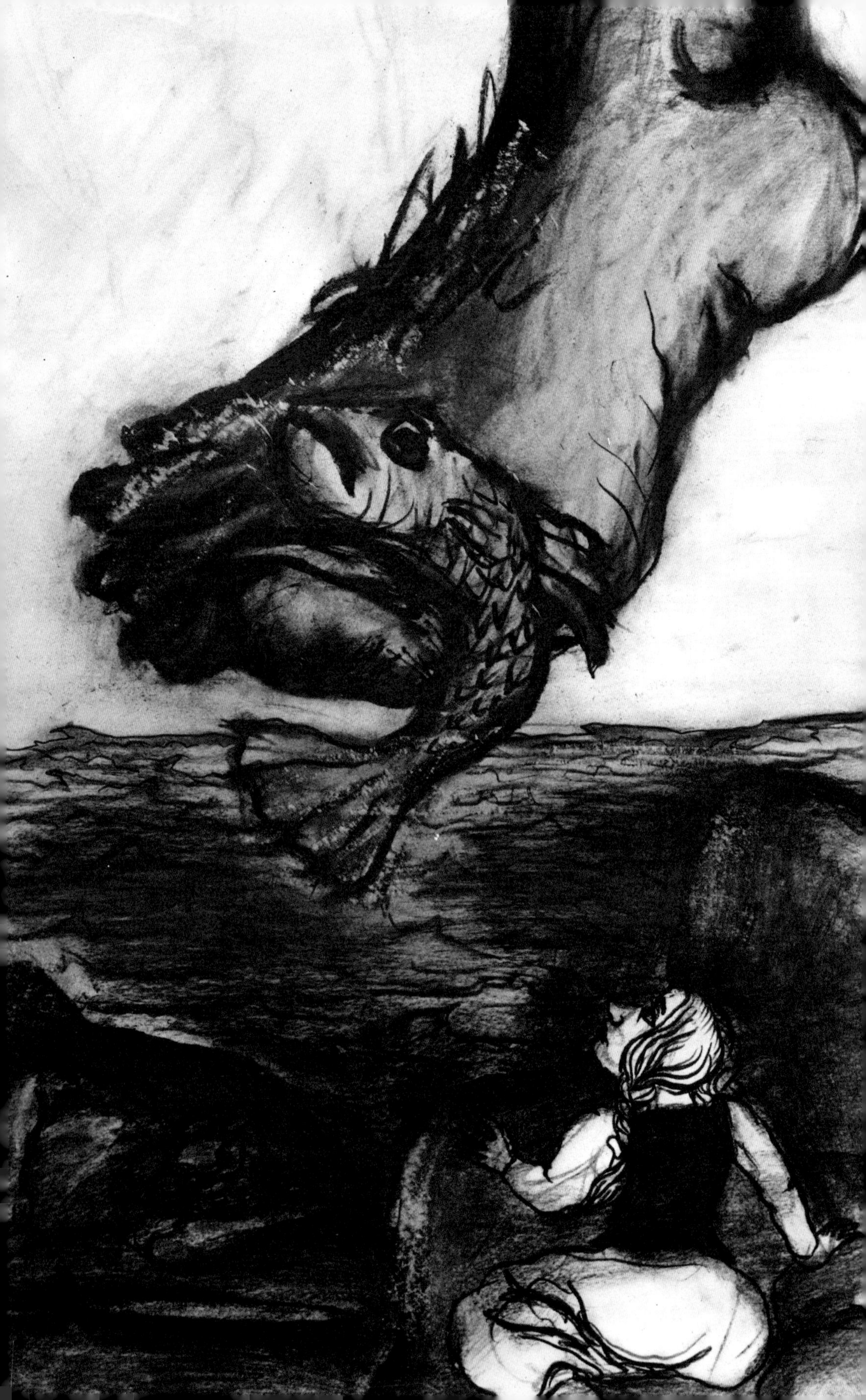

to be touching the sky. In a basket on his back was the most beautiful woman I had ever seen. Well, the notion struck me that if I could give her one kiss, it would ease my mind greatly; so I brought the little boat in close to him. What did the fellow do but let myself and the little boat pass back between his two legs. I brought the boat close again, raised the mast, and climbed to the top. I put my two arms around the woman's neck and kissed her. The man put back his hand and caught me and bound every bone in my body with hard hempen rope. Then he threw me into the sea. Now, I had the gift that no water could ever drown me; so I drifted on the water in and out as the tide flowed and ebbed. I had no food except any small fish I could catch in my mouth and swallow. I was like that for several days. At last one of the knots in the rope became loose, and they all softened, one after another, till the last knot came free. I was ashore then and decided to go up to a grassy patch at the foot of a cliff to rest myself. I was exhausted. When I got there, I found a griffin's nest with three young fledglings in it. I went into the nest. No sooner did I close my eyes to sleep than they started to pick at me, until at last I got up, twisted the neck of each of them, and threw them out into the sea.

When the mother griffin came home and saw her young ones floating on the water with their necks twisted, she flew to the nest, took me in her talons and flew so high with me that I thought there couldn't be any more sky or clouds above us. Then she let me go. I fell down on to the strand and thought that every bone in my body was in bits. She came at me again and did the same thing to me. I let on to be dead, as she stood over me planning how to kill me. I suddenly pulled out my sword and, with one blow, swept off her head. I decided then that the one house where I could get food was the king's castle. That's what brought me here.'

'What's your name?' asked Conall.

'Short Grey Warrior.'

'Well, you're not hungry now?' said Conall.

'No,' said the warrior. 'Wasn't I in a worse plight with the griffin than tied up out there by you?'

'You were,' said Conall. 'And now you'll make a good guide for us.'

'I'll go, if you promise to hide me under the ballast of your ship when we land,' said the warrior. 'The big man might catch sight of me again.'

'We'll hide you all right,' said Conall.

Next morning when they had eaten, Conall set out in the ship with the king's three sons, the queen, her daughter, Short Grey Warrior, and the old Irishman, and they never stopped till they reached the eastern world. They went ashore and made for the big man's castle.

Conall's wife was in a room upstairs. She had placed a spell and judgment on the big man not to interfere with her for a year and a day; she would marry him at the end of that time. So he had confined her to an upstairs room, and when he went off each day, she got her own meals ready. Conall walked around the castle, looking about

enever he spied a fish ked he flicked it into basket with his toes.

him, but he could see nobody. At last, whatever look he gave, he spied her at the window.

'You have fine fresh air up there,' he shouted.

'I have,' said she. 'If you take my advice, Conall, you'll go back home again. It would be a pity that you'd leave your bones here when the big man killed you.'

'Here my bones will stay or else you'll come home with me,' said Conall. 'Come down quickly, or I'll go up for you.'

She came down, and he put her on board his ship.

'Sail away as quickly as ye can now,' said she.

'No,' said Conall.

He gave orders to the king's three sons to go ashore with him, after they had hidden away Short Grey Warrior on board. The big man came down from the castle toward them.

'Now,' said Conall, to the king's three sons, 'see if I can beat him in fair fight. But, if ye see that I'm getting the worst of it, ye can help me.'

'We will and welcome,' said they. 'We'll give any help we can.'

'I suppose it is you who has taken my wife from me, you blackguard,' said the big man.

'Not to make you a short answer,' said Conall, 'you had no wife that I could take. You took *my* wife from *me*. You call me a blackguard. 'Tis you the name fits and not me. I'm not going home until I get satisfaction from you for all the trouble you have caused me.'

They attacked each other. For two days and nights they fought, and Conall's fury was increasing all the time. No matter how he tried, the big man could not strike any blow on Conall, who was too expert and swift for him. On the evening of the third day, Conall delivered a warrior's blow so weighty and fierce that it twisted the big man around, and he fell on his back.

'I have you now,' said Conall.

'You have. If you spare my head now, you will never need for anything.'

'I never wanted for anything before I ever met you,' said Conall. 'And I won't want for anything after meeting you either.'

He sent the king's three sons for the old Irishman to tie up the big man. When this was done, Short Grey Warrior was sent for to get satisfaction for all he had suffered from him. He had to be stopped at last, for, not being satisfied with cutting the big man into pieces, he wanted to mince him altogether.

They sailed away finally and, as they were passing by a harbor, Conall said, 'We'll go in here now, to see what kind of country it is.'

They hadn't gone very far toward the shore when they saw three castles all facing one another.

''Tis very strange that these castles should be built that way,' said Conall.

They moored their ship.

Conall went ashore and made off to a man at the top of the strand.

'Tell me, my good man, why those three castles are built facing one another?' said he.

'Take hold of the tips of my fingers, and I'll tell you,' said the man.

'I will and of your whole palm,' said Conall. 'And maybe, of other parts of you too before we part company.'

Conall took hold of the tips of his fingers, but the other man couldn't shift him off the ground. They gripped hold of each other and spent the whole day wrestling until the tide mark was dug up by them. At last the man got Conall down. The next moment, Conall was on top of him.

'I never yet met a man I couldn't keep down,' said the other, 'except my young brother, Conall. We often wrestled each other, and although I always knocked him down, I was never able to keep him under. He would always come out on top.'

'That's he on top of you now,' said Conall. 'Are you my eldest brother?'

'That's who I am, indeed!'

'How is my father?' asked Conall.

'Getting heavy and old. Many's the blow he has warded off since he came here, and many's the blow he has struck.'

'How are ye getting on?' asked Conall.

'The enemies of this country were advancing all the time until we arrived, and the soldiers, making no fight, were being driven before them like animals. But since we came, they haven't advanced a foot; neither have we driven them back.'

Conall's father got a great surprise when he saw him.

'How are you, Father?' asked Conall.

'I'm getting plenty to do. Still, I'm not doing too badly.'

'Take a rest for yourself now,' said Conall next morning after breakfast. 'I'll take your place today.'

Conall and his two brothers, the king's three sons, the Short Grey Warrior, and any other who joined them went into battle that day. They killed so many of the enemy that the rest fled in terror, and those they couldn't overtake drowned themselves. There wasn't a single one of the enemy to be found that evening except the dead ones.

They came home that evening and had a great night together. Next day, Conall took his father, his two brothers, the king's three sons, and the Short Grey Warrior on board his ship. He took the king's wife and her sons and daughter back home, and returned to Howth with his own relatives. I hear that he is alive and strong there still.

THE VOWS OF CRONICERT

There were five hundred blind men, and five hundred deaf men, and five hundred limping men, and five hundred dumb men, and five hundred cripple men. The five hundred deaf men had five hundred wives, and the five hundred limping men had five hundred wives, and the five hundred dumb men had five hundred wives, and the five hundred cripple men had five hundred wives. Each five hundred of these had five hundred children and five hundred dogs. They were in the habit of going about in one band, and were called the Sturdy Strolling Beggarly Brotherhood. There was a knight in Erin called O'Cronicert, with whom they spent a day and a year; and they ate up all that he had, and made a poor man of him, till he had nothing left but an old tumble-down black house, and an old lame white horse. There was a king in Erin called Brian Boru; and O'Cronicert went to him for help. He cut a cudgel of grey oak on the outskirts of the wood, mounted the old lame white horse, and set off at speed through wood and over moss and rugged ground, till he reached the king's house. When he arrived he went on his knees to the king; and the king said to him, 'What is your news, O'Cronicert?'

'I have but poor news for you, king.'

'What poor news have you,' said the king.

'That I have had the Sturdy Strolling Beggarly Brotherhood for a day and a year, and they have eaten all that I had, and made a poor man of me,' said he.

'Well!' said the king, 'I am sorry for you; what do you want?'

'I want help,' said O'Cronicert; 'anything that you may be willing to give me.'

The king promised him a hundred cows. He went to the queen, and made his complaint to her, and she gave him another hundred. He went to the king's son, Murdoch Mac Brian, and he got another hundred from him. He got food and drink at the king's; and when he was going away he said, 'Now I am very much obliged to you. This will set me very well on my feet. After all that I have got there is another thing that I want.'

'What is it?' said the king.

'It is the lapdog that is in and out after the queen that I wish for.'

'Ha!' said the king, 'it is your mightiness and pride that has caused the loss of your means; but if you become a good man you shall get this along with the rest.'

O'Cronicert bade the king goodbye, took the lapdog, leapt on the back of the old lame white horse, and went off at speed through wood, and over moss and rugged ground. After he had gone some distance through the wood a roebuck leapt up and the lapdog went after it. In a moment the deer started up as a woman behind O'Cronicert, the handsomest that eye had ever seen from the beginning of the universe till the end of eternity. She said to him, 'Call your dog off me.'

He went through wood on an old l[ame] white horse.

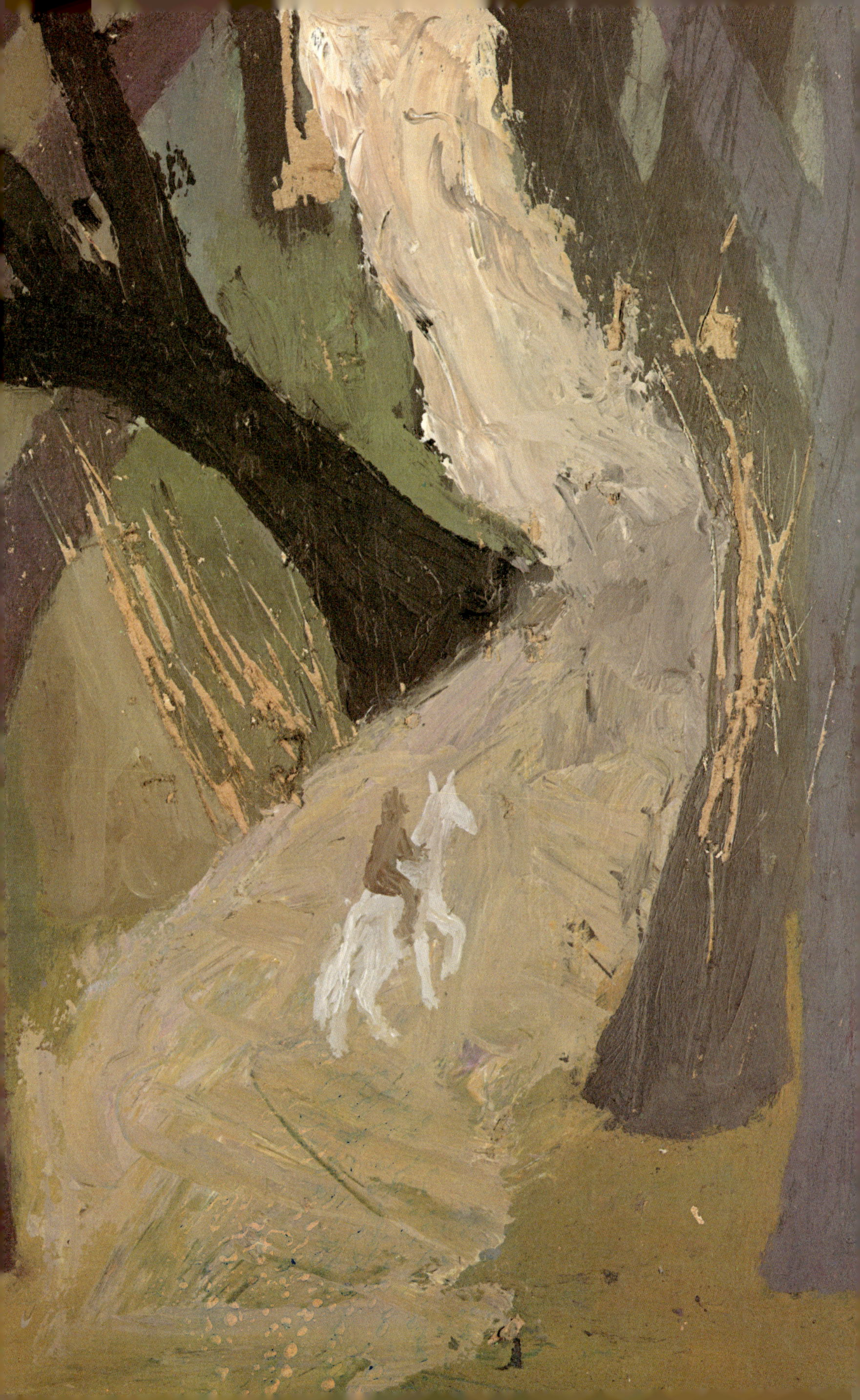

'I will do so if you promise to marry me,' said O'Cronicert.

'If you keep three vows that I shall lay upon you I will marry you,' said she.

'What vows are they?' said he.

'The first is that you do not go to ask your worldly king to a feast or a dinner without first letting me know,' said she.

'Hoch!' said O'Cronicert, 'do you think that I cannot keep that vow? I would never go to invite my worldly king without informing you that I was going to do so. It is easy to keep that vow.'

'You are likely to keep it!' said she.

'The second vow is,' said she, 'that you do not cast up to me in any company or meeting in which we shall be together, that you found me in the form of a deer.'

'Hoo!' said O'Cronicert, 'you need not to lay that vow upon me. I should keep it at any rate.'

'You are likely to keep it!' said she.

'The third vow is,' said she, 'that you do not leave me in the company of only one man while you go out.' It was agreed between them that she should marry him.

They reached the old tumble-down black house. Grass they cut in the clefts and ledges of the rocks; a bed they made and laid down. O'Cronicert's wakening from sleep was the lowing of cattle and the bleating of sheep and the neighing of mares, while he himself was in a bed of gold on wheels of silver, going from end to end of the Tower of Castle Town.

'I am sure that you are surprised,' said she.

'I am indeed,' said he.

'You are in your own room,' said she.

'In my own room,' said he. 'I never had such a room.'

'I know well that you never had,' said she; 'but you have it now. So long as you keep me you shall keep the room.'

He then rose, and put on his clothes, and went out. He took a look at the house when he went out; and it was a palace, the like of which he had never seen, and the king himself did not possess. He then took a walk round the farm; and he never saw so many cattle, sheep, and horses as were on it. He returned to the house, and said to his wife that the farm was being ruined by other people's cattle and sheep. 'It is not,' said she: 'your own cattle and sheep are on it.'

'I never had so many cattle and sheep,' said he.

'I know that,' said she; 'but so long as you keep me you shall keep them. There is no good wife whose tocher does not follow her.'

He was now in good circumstances, indeed wealthy. He had gold and silver, as well as cattle and sheep. He went about with his gun and dogs hunting every day, and was a great man. It occurred to him one day that he would go to invite the king of Erin to dinner, but he did not tell his wife that he was going. His first vow was now broken. He sped away to the king of Erin, and invited him and his great court to dinner. The king of Erin said to him, 'Do you intend to take away the cattle that I promised you?'

'Oh! no, king of Erin,' said O'Cronicert; 'I could give you as many today.'

'Ah!' said the king, 'how well you have got on since I saw you last!'

'I have indeed!' said O'Cronicert. 'I have fallen in with a rich wife who has plenty of gold and silver, and of cattle and sheep.'

'I am glad of that,' said the king of Erin.

O'Cronicert said, 'I shall feel much obliged if you will go with me to

y were playing away
ancing and music.

dinner, yourself and your great court.'

'We will do so willingly,' said the king.

They went with him on that same day. It did not occur to O'Cronicert how a dinner could be prepared for the king without his wife knowing that he was coming. When they were going on, and had reached the place where O'Cronicert had met the deer, he remembered that his vow was broken, and he said to the king, 'Excuse me; I am going on before to tell that you are coming.'

The king said, 'We will send off one of the lads.'

'You will not,' said O'Cronicert; 'no lad will serve the purpose so well as myself.'

He set off to the house; and when he arrived his wife was diligently preparing dinner. He told her what he had done, and asked her pardon. 'I pardon you this time,' said she: 'I know what you have done as well as you do yourself. The first of your vows is broken.'

The king and his great court came to O'Cronicert's house; and the wife had everything ready for them as befitted a king and great people; every kind of drink and food. They spent two or three days and nights at dinner, eating and drinking. They were praising the dinner highly, and O'Cronicert himself was praising it; but his wife was not. O'Cronicert was angry that she was not praising it and he went and struck her in the mouth with his fist and knocked out two of her teeth. 'Why are you not praising the dinner like the others, you contemptible deer?' said he.

'I am not,' said she: 'I have seen my father's big dogs having a better dinner than you are giving tonight to the king of Erin and his court.'

O'Cronicert got into such a rage that he went outside of the door. He was not long standing there when a man came riding on a black horse, who in passing caught O'Cronicert by the collar of his coat, and took him up behind him: and they set off. The rider did not say a word to O'Cronicert. The horse was going so swiftly that O'Cronicert thought the wind would drive his head off. They arrived at a big, big palace, and came off the black horse. A stableman came out, and caught the horse, and took it in. It was with wine that he was cleaning the horse's feet. The rider of the black horse said to O'Cronicert, 'Taste the wine to see if it is better than the wine that you are giving to Brian Boru and his court tonight.'

O'Cronicert tasted the wine, and said, 'This is better wine.'

The rider of the black horse said, 'How unjust was the fist a little ago! The wind from your fist carried the two teeth to me.'

He then took him into that big, handsome, and noble house, and into a room that was full of gentlemen eating and drinking, and he seated him at the head of the table, and gave him wine to drink, and said to him, 'Taste that wine to see if it is better than the wine that you are giving to the king of Erin and his court tonight.'

'This is better wine,' said O'Cronicert.

'How unjust was the fist a little ago!' said the rider of the black horse.

When all was over the rider of the black horse said, 'Are you willing to return home now?'

'Yes,' said O'Cronicert, 'very willing.'

They then rose, and went to the stable: and the black horse was taken out; and they leaped on its back, and went away. The rider of the black horse said to O'Cronicert, after they had set off, 'Do you know who I am?'

'I do not,' said O'Cronicert.

'I am a brother-in-law of yours,' said the rider of the black horse; 'and though my sister is married to you there is not a king or knight in Erin who is a match for her. Two of your vows are now broken; and if you break the other vow you shall lose your wife and all that you possess.'

They arrived at O'Cronicert's house; and O'Cronicert said, 'I am ashamed to go in, as they do not know where I have been since night came.'

'Hoo!' said the rider, 'they have not missed you at all. There is so much conviviality among them, that they have not suspected that you have been anywhere. Here are the two teeth that you knocked out of the front of your wife's mouth. Put them in their place, and they will be as strong as ever.'

'Come in with me,' said O'Cronicert to the rider of the black horse.

'I will not: I disdain to go in,' said the rider of the black horse.

The rider of the black horse bade O'Cronicert goodbye, and went away.

O'Cronicert went in; and his wife met him as she was busy waiting on the gentlemen. He asked her pardon, and put the two teeth in the front of her mouth, and they were as strong as ever. She said, 'Two of your vows are now broken.' No one took notice of him when he went in, or said, 'Where have you been?' They spent the night in eating and drinking, and the whole of the next day.

In the evening the king said, 'I think that it is time for us to be going'; and all said that it was. O'Cronicert said, 'You will not go tonight. I am going to get up a dance. You will go tomorrow.'

'Let them go,' said his wife.

'I will not,' said he.

The dance was set a-going that night. They were playing away at dancing and music till they became warm and hot with perspiration. They were going out one after another to cool themselves at the side of the house. They all went out except O'Cronicert and his wife, and a man called Kayn Mac Loy. O'Cronicert himself went out, and left his wife and Kayn Mac Loy in the house, and when she saw that he had broken his third vow she gave a spring through a room, and became a big filly, and gave Kayn Mac Loy a kick with her foot, and broke his thigh in two. She gave another spring, and smashed the door and went away, and was seen no more. She took with her the Tower of Castle Town as an armful on her shoulder and a light burden on her back, and she left Kayn Mac Loy in the old tumble-down black house in a pool of rain-drip on the floor.

At daybreak next day poor O'Cronicert could only see the old house that he had before. Neither cattle nor sheep, nor any of the fine things that he had was to be seen. One awoke in the morning beside a bush, another beside a dyke, and another beside a ditch.

CONALL THE YELLOW-HAND

It fell out once that the children of the king of Erin and the children of Conall came to blows. The children of Conall got the upper hand, and they killed the king's big son. The king sent a message for Conall, and he said to him—'Oh, Conall! what made thy sons go to spring on my sons till my big son was killed by thy children? but I see that though I follow thee revengefully, I shall not be much the better for it, and I will now set a thing before thee, and if thou wilt do it, I will not follow thee with revenge. If thou thyself, and thy sons will get for me the brown horse of the king of Lochlann, thou shalt get the souls of thy sons.' 'Why,' said Conall, 'should not I do the pleasure of the king, though there should be no souls of my sons in dread at all. Hard is the matter thou requirest of me, but I will lose my own life, and the life of my sons, or else I will do the pleasure of the king.'

After these words Conall left the king, and he went home. When he rose on the morrow, he set himself and his four sons in order, and they took their journey towards Lochlann, and they made no stop but were tearing ocean till they reached it. When they reached Lochlann they went into the house of the king's miller. Conall told the miller that his own children and the children of the king had fallen out, and there was nothing that would please the king but that he should get the brown horse of the king of Lochlann. 'If thou wilt do me a kindness, and wilt put me in a way to get him, for certain I will pay thee for it.' 'The thing is silly that thou art come to seek,' said the miller; 'for the king has laid his mind on him so greatly that thou wilt not get him in any way unless thou steal him; but if thou thyself canst make out a way, I will hide thy secret.' 'This, I am thinking,' said Conall, 'since thou art working every day for the king, that thou and thy gillies should put myself and my sons into five sacks of bran.' 'The plan that came into thy head is not bad,' said the miller. The king's gillies came to seek the bran, and they took the five sacks with them, and they emptied them before the horses. The servants locked the door, and they went away.

When they rose to lay hand on the brown horse, Conall said, 'You shall not do that. It is hard to get out of this; let us make for ourselves five hiding holes, so that if they perceive us we may go in hiding.' They made the holes, then they laid hands on the horse. The horse was pretty well unbroken, and he set to making such a terrible noise through the stable, that the king heard the noise. 'It must be my brown horse,' said he to his gillies; 'try what is wrong with him.'

The servants went out, and Conall and his sons went into the hiding holes. The servants looked amongst the horses, and they did not find anything wrong. When the gillies had time to be gone, Conall and his sons laid the next hand on the horse. If the noise was great that he made before, the noise he made now was seven times greater. The king sent a message for his gillies again, and said for certain there was something troubling the brown horse. 'Go and look well about him.' The servants went out and rummaged well, and did not find a thing. They returned and they told this. 'That is marvellous for me,' said the king: 'go you to lie down again, and if I perceive it again I will go out myself.' When Conall and his sons perceived that the gillies were gone, they laid hands again on the horse, and one of them caught him, and if the noise that the horse made on the two former times was great, he made more this time.

'Be this from me,' said the king; 'it must be that someone is troubling my brown horse.' The king was a wary man, and he saw where the horses were making a noise. 'Be clever,' said the king, 'there are men within the stable, and let us get them somehow.' The king followed the tracks of the men, and he found them. Every man was acquainted with Conall, for he was a valued tenant by the king of Erin, and when the king brought them up out of the holes he said, 'Oh, Conall, art thou here?' 'I am, O king, without question, and necessity made me come. I am under thy pardon, and under thine honour, and under thy grace.' He told how it happened to him, and that he had to get the brown horse for the king of Erin, or that his son was to be put to death. 'I knew that I should not get him by asking, and I was going to steal him.' 'Yes, Conall, it is well enough, but come in,' said the king. 'Now, O Conall,' said the king, 'wert thou ever in a harder place than to be seeing thy lot of sons hanged to-morrow? But thou didst set it to my goodness and to my grace, and that it was necessity brought it on thee, and I must not hang thee. Tell me any case in which thou wert as hard as this, and if thou tellest that, thou shalt get the soul of thy youngest son with thee.' 'I will tell a case as hard in which I was,' said Conall.

'I was a young lad, and my father had much land, and he had parks of year-old cows, and one of them had just calved, and my father told me to bring her home. I took with me a laddie, and we found the cow, and we took her with us. There fell a shower of snow. We went into the cowherd's cottage, and we took the cow and the calf in with us, and we were letting the shower pass from us. What came in but one cat and ten, and one great one-eyed fox-coloured cat as chief over them. When they came in, in very deed I myself had no liking for their company. "Strike up with you," said the head cat, "why should we be still? and sing a refrain to Conall the Yellow-hand." I was amazed that my name was known to the cats themselves. When they had sung the refrain, said the head cat, "Now, O Conall, pay the reward of the refrain that the cats have sung to thee." "Well, then," said I myself, "I have no reward whatsoever for you, unless you

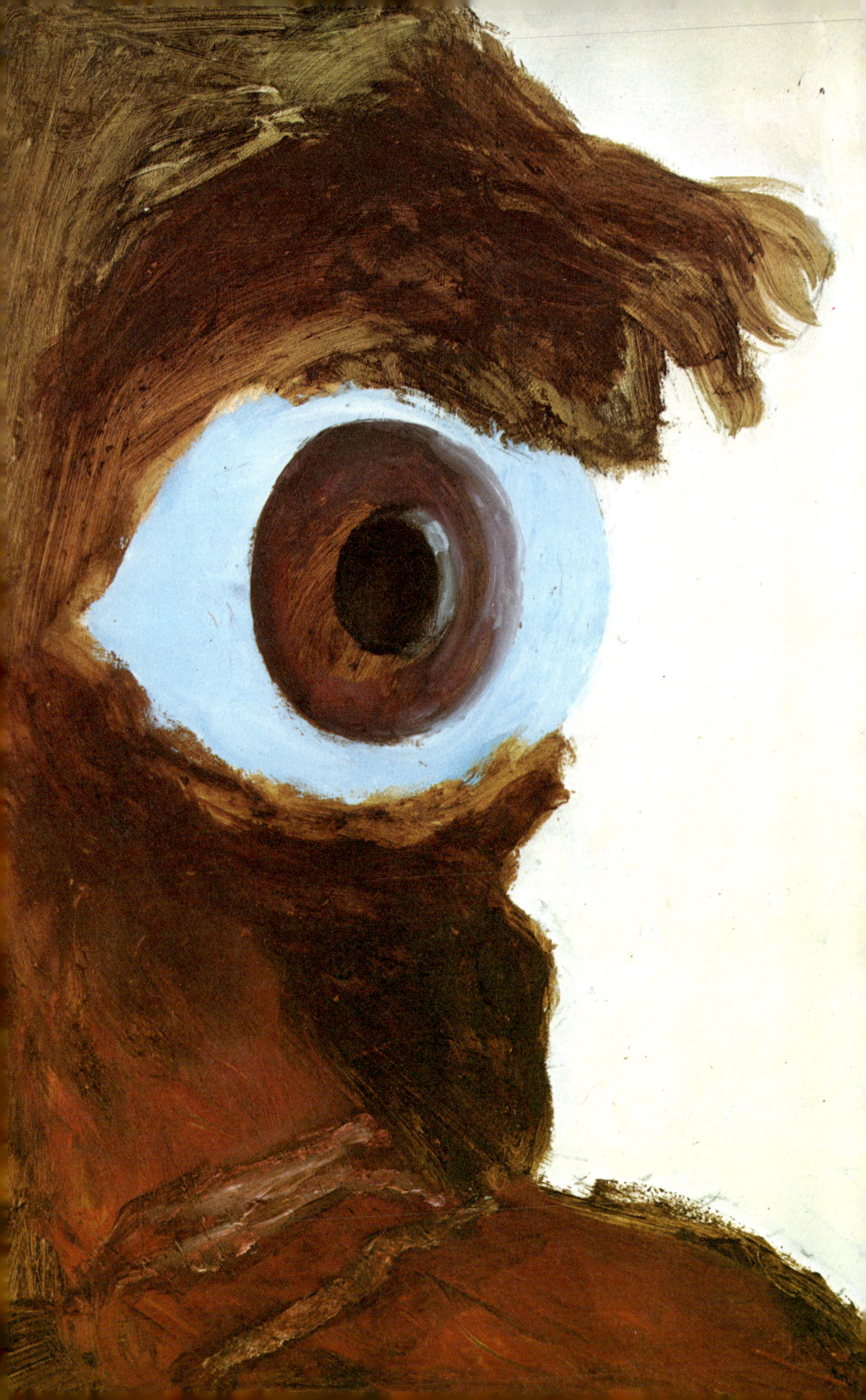

should go down and take that calf." No sooner said I the word than the two cats and ten went down to attack the calf, and, in very deed, he did not last them long.

'"Why will you be silent? Go up and sing a refrain to Conall the Yellow-hand," said the head cat. And surely, oh, king, I had no care for them or for their cronan, for I began to see that they were not good comrades. When they had sung me the refrain they betook themselves down where the head cat was. "Pay now their reward," said the head cat; and for sure, oh, king, I had no reward for them; and I said to them, "I have no reward for you, unless you will take that laddie with you and make use of him." When the boy heard this he took himself out, and the cats after him. And surely, oh, king, there was yowling and catterwauling between them. When they took themselves out, I took myself off as hard as I might into the wood. I was swift enough and strong at that time; and when I felt the rustling of the cats after me I climbed into as high a tree as I saw in the place; and I hid myself as well as I might. The cats began to search for me through the wood, and they were not finding me; and when they were tired, each one said to the other that they would turn back. "But," said the one-eyed fox-coloured cat that was commander-in-chief over them, "you saw him not with your two eyes, and though I have but one eye, there's the rascal up in the top of the tree." When he had said that, one of them went up in the tree, and as he was coming where I was, I drew a weapon that I had and I killed him. "Be this from me!" said the one-eyed one—"I must not be losing my company thus; gather round the root of the tree and dig about it, and let down that extortioner to earth." On this they gathered about the tree, and they dug about her root, and the first branching root that they cut, she gave a shiver to fall, and I myself gave a shout. There was in the neighbourhood of the wood a priest, and he had ten men with him delving, and he said, "There is a shout of extremity and I must not be without replying to it." And the wisest of the men said, "Let it alone till we hear it again." The cats began, and they began wildly, and they broke the next root; and I myself gave the next shout, and in very deed it was not weak. "Certainly," said the priest, "it is a man in extremity—let us move." And the cats arose on the tree, and they broke the third root, and the tree fell on her elbow. I gave the third shout. The stalwart men hasted, and when they saw how the cats served the tree, they began at them with the spades; and they themselves and the cats began at each other, till they were killed altogether—the men and the cats. And surely, oh king, I did not move till I saw the last one of them falling. I came home. And there's for thee the hardest case in which I ever was; and it seems to me that tearing by the cats were harder than hanging to-morrow by the king of Lochlann.

'Od! Conall,' said the king, 'thou art full of words. Thou hast freed the soul of thy son with thy tale; and if thou tellest me a harder case than thy three sons to be hanged to-morrow, thou wilt get thy second youngest son with thee, and then thou wilt have two sons.' 'I was,' said Conall, 'a young lad, and I went out hunting, and my father's land was beside the sea, and it was rough with rocks, caves, and gullies. When I was going on the top of the shore, I saw as if there were a smoke coming up between two rocks, and I began to look what might be the meaning. When I was looking, what should I do but fall; and the place was so full of manure, that neither bone nor skin was broken. I knew not how I should get out of this. It was terrible for me to be there till I should die. I heard a great clattering commotion coming, and what was there but a great giant and two dozen of goats with him, and a buck at their head. And when the giant had tied the goats, he came up and he said to me, "Hao O! Conall, it's long since my knife is rusting in my pouch waiting for thy tender flesh." "Och!" said I, "it's not much thou wilt be bettered by me, though thou should'st tear me asunder; I will make but one meal for thee. But I see that thou art one-eyed. I am a good doctor, and I will give thee the sight of the other eye." The giant went and he drew the great cauldron on the site of the fire. I myself was telling him how he should heat the water, so that I should give its sight to the other eye. I got heather and I made a brush of it, and I set him upright in the cauldron. I began at the eye that was well, pretending to him that I would give its sight to the other one, till I left them as bad as each other; and surely it was easier to spoil the one that was well than to give sight to the other.

'When he knew that he could not see a glimpse, and when I myself said to him that I would get out in spite of him, he gave a spring out of the water, and he stood in the mouth of the cave, and he said that he would have revenge for the sight of his eye. I had but to stay there crouched the length of the night, holding in my breath in such a way that he might not feel where I was.

'When he felt the birds calling in the morning, and knew that the day was, he said—"Art thou sleeping? Awake and let out my lot of goats." I killed the buck. He cried, "I will not believe that thou art not killing my buck." "I am not," said I, "but the ropes are so tight that I take long to loose them." I let out one of the goats, and he was caressing her, and he said to her, "There thou art thou shaggy, hairy white goat, and thou seest me, but I see thee not." I was letting them out by the way of one and one, as I flayed the buck, and before the last one was out I had him flayed bag wise. Then I went and I put my legs in place of his legs, and my hands in place of his fore legs, and my head in place of his head, and the horns on top of my head, so that the brute might think that it was the buck. I went out. When I was going out the giant laid his hand on me, and he said, "There thou art thou pretty buck; thou seest me, but I see thee not." When I myself got out, and I saw the world about me, surely, oh, king! joy was on me. When I was out and had shaken the skin off me, I said to the brute, "I am out now in spite of thee." "Aha!" said he, "hast thou done this to me. Since thou wert so stalwart that thou hast got out, I will give thee a ring, and keep the ring, and it will do thee good." "I will not take the

Conall was thrown in the cauldron.

ring from thee," said I, "but throw it, and I will take it with me." He threw the ring and I put it on my finger. When he said me then. "Is the ring fitting thee?" I said to him, "It is." He said, "Where art thou ring?" And the ring said, "I am here." The brute betook himself towards where the ring was speaking, and now I saw that I was in a harder case than ever I was. I drew a dirk. I cut the finger off from me, and I threw it from me as far as I could out on the loch, and there was a great depth in the place. He shouted "Where art thou, ring?" And the ring said, "I am here," though it was on the ground of ocean. He gave a spring after the ring, and out he went in the sea.

'When the giant was drowned I went in, and I took with me all he had of gold and silver, and I went home, and surely great joy was on my people when I arrived. And as a sign for thee, look thou, the finger is off me.'

'Yes, indeed, Conall, thou art wordy and wise,' said the king. 'I see thy finger is off. Thou hast freed thy two sons, but tell me a case in which thou ever wert that is harder than to be looking on thy two sons being hanged to-morrow, and thou wilt get the souls of thy other sons with thee.'

'Then went my father,' said Conall, 'and he got me a wife, and I was married. I went to hunt. I was going beside the sea, and I saw an island over in the midst of the loch, and I came there where a boat was, and many precious things within her. I put in the one foot, and the other foot was on the ground, and when I raised my head what was it but the boat was over in the middle of the loch, and she never stopped till she reached the island. When I went out of the boat the boat returned where she was before. I came to a glen; I saw in it, at the bottom of a chasm, a woman who had got a child, and the child was naked on her knee, and a knife in her hand. She would attempt to put the knife in the throat of the babe, and the babe would begin to laugh in her face, and she would begin to cry, and she would throw the knife behind her. I called to the woman, "What art thou doing here?" And she said to me, "What brought thee here?" I told her myself word upon word how I came. "Well then," said she, "it was so I came also." I went in, and I said to her, "What was in fault that thou wert putting the knife on the neck of the child?" "It is that he must be cooked for the giant who is here, or else no more of my world will be before me." I went up steps of stairs, and I saw a chamber full of stripped corpses. I cast the child into a basket of down, and I asked her to cook a corpse for the giant in place of the child. "How can I do that?" said she, "when he has count of the corpses." "Do thou as I ask thee, and I will strip myself, and I will go amongst the corpses, and then he will have the same count," said I. She did as I asked her. We put the corpse in the great cauldron, but we could not put on the lid. When he was coming home I stripped myself, and I went amongst the corpses. He came home, and she served up the corpse on a great platter, and when he ate it he was complaining that he found it too tough for a child.

'"I did as thou asked me," said she. "Thou hadst count of the corpses thyself, and go up now and count them." He counted them and he had them. "I see one of a white body there," said he. "I will lie down a while and I will have him when I wake." When he rose he went up and gripped me, and I never was in such a case as when he was hauling me down the stair with my head after me. He threw me into the cauldron. And now I was sure I would scald before I could get out of that. As fortune favoured me, the brute slept beside the cauldron. There I was scalded by the bottom of the pot. When she perceived that he was asleep, she set her mouth quietly to the hole that was in the lid, and she said to me was I alive. I said I was. I put up my head, and the brute's forefinger was so large, that my head went through easily. Everything was coming easily with me till I began to bring up my hips. I left the skin of my hips about the mouth of the hole, and I came out. When I got out of the cauldron I knew not what to do; and she said to me that there was no weapon that would kill him but his own weapon. I began to draw from him his spear, and every breath that he would take I would think I would be down his throat, and when his breath came out I was back again just as far. But with every ill that befell me I got the spear loosed from him. I drew the dart as best I could, and I set it in his eye. When he felt this he gave his head a lift, and he struck the other end of the dart on the top of the cave, and it went through to the back of his head. And he fell cold dead where he was: and thou mayest be sure, oh king, that joy was on me. I myself and the woman went out on clear ground, and we passed the night there. I went and got the boat with which I came, and took the woman and the child over on dry land; and I returned home.'

The king's mother was putting on a fire at this time, and listening to Conall telling the tale about the child. 'Is it thou,' said she, 'that wert there?' 'Well then,' said he, 'twas I.' 'Och! och!' said she, ''twas I that was there, and the king is the child whose life thou didst save; and it is to thee that life thanks might be given.' Then they took great joy.

The king said 'Oh Conall, thou camest through great hardships. And now the brown horse is thine, and his sack full of the most precious things that are in my treasury.'

They lay down that night, and if it was early that Conall rose, it was earlier than that that the queen was on foot making ready. He got the brown horse and his sack full of gold and silver and stones of great price, and then Conall and his four sons went away, and they returned home to the Erin realm of gladness. He left the gold and silver in the house, and he went with the horse to the king. They were good friends evermore. He returned home to his wife, and they set in order a feast; and that was the feast, oh son and brother!

ACKNOWLEDGEMENTS

Thanks are due to the following for permission to use stories:—

The Giant of Grabbist, Tom Tit Tot, The Hunted Soul, Goblin Combe, The Old Man at the White House, The Fairy Follower, The Apple Tree Man, Summat Queer on Batch from *Folktales of England* by Katharine M. Briggs and R. L. Tongue published by The University of Chicago Press, 1965; the stories *The Red Etin, Three Heads of the Well, Whuppity Stoorie* from *Popular Rhymes of Scotland* by Robert Chambers published by W. & R. Chambers; the stories *That's Enough To Go On With, Chips and the Devil, The Old Woman Who Lived In A Vinegar Bottle* from *Dictionary of British Folk Tales in the English Language* by Katharine Briggs published by Routledge & Kegan Paul Ltd.; the stories *Wild Alasdair of Roy Bridge, 'Kintail Again'* from *Stories from South Uist* by Angus MacLellan by courtesy of John Campbell; the stories *The Fairy Wife, The Queen of the Planets, The Speckled Bull, The Man Who Had No Story, Finn In Search of His Youth, Young Conall of Howth* from *Folktales of Ireland* by Sean O'Sullivan published by The University of Chicago Press, 1966; the stories *Silken Janet or Mucketty Meg, The Green Ladies of One Tree Hill, Rat's Castle, The Man Who Went Fishing on Sunday* from *Forgotten Folk Tales of English Counties* by R. L. Tongue published by Routledge & Kegan Paul Ltd.; the stories *Tattercoats, The Three Cows, Brewery of Eggshells, The Sprightly Tailor, The Shepherd of Myddvai, The Vows of O'Cronicert* reprinted from the complete edition of Joseph Jacobs' *English Fairy Tales* and *Celtic Fairy Tales* published by The Bodley Head; the story of *Sir Gammers Van* reprinted from *Popular Rhymes and Nursery Tales of England* collected by James Orchard Halliwell published by The Bodley Head; the story *Teig O'Kane and the Corpse* from *Fairy and Folk Tales of Irish Peasantry* by W. B. Yeats by courtesy of Colin Smythe Ltd. and the Estate of Dr. Douglas Hyde; the stories *The Little People, Spirit of the Dog* from *Visions and Beliefs in the West of Ireland* by Lady Gregory by courtesy of Colin Smythe Ltd., publishers of the Coole edition of Lady Gregory's writings; the stories *The Cakes of Oatmeal and Blood, The Soul as a Butterfly, The Everlasting Fight* from *The Folklore of Ireland* by Sean O'Sullivan published by B. T. Batsford Ltd.; for the stories *Peerifool* and *Assipattle* from *The Folklore of Orkney and Shetland* by E. Marwick published by B. T. Batsford Ltd.; the stories *Nicht Nought Nothing* and *The Dead Moon* from *Folklore* by Andrew Lang; the story *Orange and Lemon* from *Folklore of the Magyars* by W. H. Jones published by W. W. Norton & Co. Inc.